Dear Reader,

If you've picked [...] love a good wedding [...] Silhouette. Henc [...] which features t [...] new stories about three couples as they make their way to the altar in very different ways.

USA TODAY bestselling author **Sharon Sala** starts us off with a humorous, heart-tugging tale about a Southern beauty who wakes up married to a stranger. Good thing he's a sexy, good-hearted son-of-a-gun. Because this bride is ready to see the marriage through—no matter what her family might say!

Next up is award winner **Dixie Browning**'s tale of a big sister who tries to stop her baby sister's wedding—only to discover she's got the hots for the groom's millionaire uncle! Could it be the millionaire is going to lead this reluctant lady to the altar himself?

Rounding out the collection, beloved author **Stella Bagwell** brings you a bride who escapes her society wedding—only to run smack-dab into the cowboy of her dreams. Of course she does what any wishful bride would do: she marries him! Now she just has to lasso his heart....

We hope you enjoy this celebration of love and marriage.

Happy reading!

The Editors
Silhouette Books

SHARON SALA

Sharon Sala "...knows just how to steep the fires of romance to the gratification of her readers."
—*Romantic Times*

Sharon Sala is a child of the country. As a farmer's daughter, her vivid imagination made solitude a thing to cherish. During her adult life, she learned to survive by taking things one day at a time. An inveterate dreamer, she yearned to share the stories her imagination created. For Sharon, her dreams have come true, and she claims one of her greatest joys is when her stories become tools for healing.

DIXIE BROWNING

"You can always count on Dixie Browning for salt-of-the-earth romance to brighten your day."
—*Romantic Times*

Dixie Browning is an award-winning painter and writer, as well as a mother and grandmother. Her father was a big-league baseball player, her grandfather a sea captain. In addition to nearly eighty contemporary romances, Dixie and her sister, Mary Williams, have written more than a dozen historical romances under the name Bronwyn Williams. Contact Dixie at www.dixiebrowning.com, or at P.O. Box 1389, Buxton, NC 27920.

STELLA BAGWELL

"Stella Bagwell dishes up a dandy love story..."
—*Romantic Times*

Stella Bagwell sold her first book to Silhouette in November 1985. More than forty novels later, she still loves her job and says she isn't completely content unless she's writing. Recently, she and her husband of thirty years moved from the hills of Oklahoma to Seadrift, Texas, a sleepy little fishing town located on the coastal bend. Stella says the water, the tropical climate and the seabirds make it a lovely place to let her imagination soar and to put the stories in her head down on paper. She and her husband have one son, Jason, who lives and teaches high school math in nearby Port Lavaca.

SHARON SALA

DIXIE BROWNING
STELLA BAGWELL

Going to the Chapel

Silhouette Books

Published by Silhouette Books

America's Publisher of Contemporary Romance

SILHOUETTE BOOKS

GOING TO THE CHAPEL

Copyright © 2002 by Harlequin Books S.A.

ISBN 0-373-48464-X

The publisher acknowledges the copyright holders
of the individual works as follows:

IT HAPPENED ONE NIGHT
Copyright © 2002 by Sharon Sala

MARRYING A MILLIONAIRE
Copyright © 2002 by Dixie Browning

THE BRIDE'S BIG ADVENTURE
Copyright © 2002 by Stella Bagwell

CONTENTS

IT HAPPENED ONE NIGHT
Sharon Sala

* * *

Life never lasts long enough
to learn everything we need to know.

Sometimes the biggest mistakes
we make can turn out to be blessings in disguise.
Being able to laugh about our "detours"
makes acceptance far easier than holding the blame
for what we've done so close to our chests.

So, for all my readers who are willing to admit
their lives are not perfect but are happy in spite
of their circumstances, this book is for you.

Live. Laugh. Love often.

Dear Reader,

Traditionally, something always goes wrong at a wedding. Sometimes it's laughable...sometimes it's not. Sometimes it takes years of living and a lot of good humor to be able to look back at what was supposed to be the best day of your life without regrets.

Keeping all of that in mind, you will understand why I chose to write "It Happened One Night" with humor. Of course I made sure there's plenty of romance, but the hitch in my heroine's life came when she drank too much at her best friend's wedding and woke up to the fact that she was not only married to a man she didn't know but had a tattoo of his name on her hip. Of course the only place something this outrageous could happen had to be in Las Vegas—at the Love Me Tender wedding chapel—with the ceremony conducted by a preacher who looked like Elvis.

Hope you enjoy reading my story as much as I enjoyed writing it.

I love to hear from my readers and can be reached online at sharonsala@romanticfiction.com or at P.O. Box 127, Henryetta, OK 74437.

Sharon Sala

Chapter 1

Harley June Beaumont had been awake for at least
five minutes and still didn't have the guts to move,
not even an eyelid. Her head was pounding, her stomach wanted to heave and the taste in her mouth was
disgusting.

The last thing she remembered was being in Las
Vegas, toasting her best friend Susan and her new husband, Mike, as they cut their wedding cake. There
were a few vague images of a champagne glass that
never seemed to empty, throwing streamers and rice,
then dancing on a table and looking down at the bald
spot on a waiter's head. After that, everything else was
a blur.

What she did know was that she needed to go to

the bathroom, which meant getting out of bed, which meant she would have to move. And, because she hadn't wet the bed since the age of three, it also meant she was going to have to get up.

Opening her eyelids in minuscule increments, she took a slow, shallow breath. So far, so good. The room looked vaguely familiar. Oh yes, the Las Vegas Motel.

From where she was lying, she could see a sheer mauve dress that had been tossed casually on the back of a chair. One matching shoe was on the table beside it, the other nowhere in sight.

My maid of honor dress… I think.

With a groan, she began to inch toward the side of the bed, wincing as the movement increased the pounding in her temples. When she felt space, she stopped, convinced she had come to the edge. Now it was sit up or die. Her bladder won out. Unwilling to be found dead in a puddle of pee, she got up, consoling herself with the notion that she could always die later.

There was a large pile of bedclothes on the floor at the foot of the bed. She frowned as she sidestepped them, thinking to herself that was why she'd woken up cold, and was halfway to the bathroom before it dawned on her that she was naked. She glanced around the room, wondering where her nightgown had gone, then saw her bra draped over a lampshade and her panties hanging on the doorknob. She winced again.

At least she could be thankful her mother was not present to give her hell.

Harley June's mother, Marcie Lee Beaumont, was a direct descendant of General Robert E. Lee, and according to Marcie, genteel Southern ladies did not sleep in the altogether. But right now, Harley June was sick and a missing nightgown was the least of her worries.

The bathroom tiles were cold beneath her feet and she shivered as she hurried to the commode. As she lifted the lid to sit down, she gasped. There were flowers growing in the water in her toilet!

She leaned a little bit closer, then snorted lightly and fished Susan's bridal bouquet out of the commode before tossing it in the trash. Talk about a lost weekend. All she wanted was to get cleaned up, pack her things and catch the plane back home to Savannah. Later, when she could think without wanting to throw up, she might be willing to pursue the vagaries of her memory, but for now, survival depended on minimal thought and motion.

A couple of minutes later, she stepped into the shower, relishing the warm jets of water sluicing her face and body. Later, as she began to dry off, she glanced toward the full-length mirror on the back of the door and frowned. What little she could see of herself was just like she felt—wet and foggy. Impulsively, she gave the mirror a swipe with her towel, then as she started to turn, caught a glimpse of something red on the left side of her hip. Frowning even more, she dried a larger spot on the mirror and then turned sideways, angling for a better view of her backside.

What came out of her throat was little more than a squeak and was nothing to describe the shock she was feeling at seeing something red and heart-shaped on the left side of her rear.

She stepped closer, peering intently into the mirror only to realize there were words inside the heart. Unable to believe her eyes, she began scrubbing at the spot and then winced and quickly stopped. It was tender! Dropping the towel, she traced the shape with her fingers as her mind accepted the only obvious conclusion.

"Oh. My. God. A tattoo. I have a tattoo."

She moved closer, squinting at the heart. The words were backward in the mirror and it took her a few moments to spell them out and then reverse the order of letters.

Junie Loves Sam.

"Sam? Who, in the name of all that's holy, is Sam?"

The tone of her voice rose several decibels as reality hit. It didn't matter as much that she didn't know a Sam as it did that the name was on there.

"Sweet Lord… I have a man's name tattooed on my butt."

She moaned and began rubbing harder at the tattoo,

praying that if she scrubbed it enough, it would come off, which of course, it didn't.

"This can't be happening," she moaned, and at that moment, heard the distinct but horrifying sound of someone moving around in her bedroom.

Grabbing the towel she'd discarded, she yanked it up in front of her and started to lock the door when it began to open.

With heart thundering and a scream hovering on her lips, she gasped. Too stunned to cut loose with the scream, she found herself face-to-face with the biggest man she'd ever seen. His shoulders spanned the width of the doorway, his long, muscular legs were firmly planted as he ran a hand through his short, spiky hair. His eyes were a sleepy blue, his smile slightly crooked and apologetic and his hair was black as coal. His features were strong and regular, although his nose looked as if it had been broken at least once. But it was none of the above that brought the impending scream she'd been holding into fruition as quickly as the fact that he was naked.

Harley cut loose with the scream she'd been saving, then started to beg.

"Oh God...oh God...don't hurt me! Please don't hurt me! My purse is in there...somewhere. Take it! Take everything I've got, just please don't hurt me!"

The man smiled and glanced over his shoulder to the bed she'd recently vacated.

"Honey, you already gave me everything you had...and then some...last night."

Harley yanked the towel a little further beneath her chin and glared.

"What are you talking about?"

He looked back at her and grinned.

Unaware that the pupils of her eyes had just doubled in size, she grabbed a hairbrush, aiming it at him like a gun.

"You're lying. You stay away from me, you pervert."

He swooped her up into his arms and planted a slow, sexy kiss in the middle of her mouth. The moment their lips met, Harley knew it had happened before. Her lips had curved to fit his mouth as if they had a mind of their own, and even while her good sense told her to stop, there was a part of her that didn't ever want to let go. To her chagrin, the man was the first to pull back. He set her back down on her feet and then grabbed a fresh towel and began drying her backside as if he'd done it a thousand times before.

Harley spun out of his grasp, taking the towel with her.

"Who are you?" she asked.

His smile faltered, but only slightly as he gently tucked a damp strand of her hair behind her ear.

"I'm not a pervert, honey. I'm your husband...and you're my wife."

"Wife? I'm not your wife! I'm not anyone's wife!" she shrieked, and then winced at the sound of her own shriek. Her headache was getting worse, not better.

He reached for her, gently fingering the gold band on the third finger of her left hand.

"How quickly she forgets," he said softly. He lifted her hand to his lips and kissed the ring, then turned her hand palm-side up and kissed it too.

Something close to electricity coiled deep in her belly before settling between her legs. She took a slow breath, startled by the sudden lethargy of her limbs. But even the sexual tension between them did not blind her to the fact that there *was* a ring on her finger that had not been there the night before.

"Who?" she mumbled.

He looked at her and then shook his head.

"Junie, darlin'…please don't tell me you've already forgotten my name, too?"

Junie? She flashed on the tattoo on her hip. Junie Loves Sam.

"Sam?"

"That's my girl," he said slowly, and took the towel out of her hands and dropped it on the floor between them.

Harley saw the want in his eyes and shuddered. At that moment, she couldn't have moved to save her life.

"No one calls me Junie."

His blue eyes darkened. "I do," he said, and picked her up.

"What are you going to do?"

"Make love to my wife."

"I'm not...I can't—"

He covered her mouth with a kiss, stifling her answer, laid her down in the middle of the bed and then crawled in beside her, levering himself above her still-damp body.

"Yes, you are, and yes, you can," Sam said. "And very nicely, if I say so myself."

If there was a thought in Harley's mind about arguing, the enigmatic Sam's kisses wiped it away. And when she felt the weight of his body settling down on hers, she knew she'd been here before. God help her, but for everything wrong about what they had done, making love with Sam seemed so right.

It was ten minutes after 11:00 a.m. when Harley awoke again, only this time she was under no illusions as to where she was. Her headache was still present, and only a degree or so less intimidating than the man in whose arms she was lying.

Sam. He'd called himself Sam.

Fighting panic, she closed her eyes, refusing to contemplate how much she liked the weight of his arm across her belly, or the fact that for the first time since she'd left the comfort of her parents' home, she felt safe.

And the sex.

Dear Lord, they were combustible. Twice since he'd

taken her back to bed, she thought she would go up in flames. But that had to be lust, and according to her mother, decent Southern girls made their marriage beds based on good bloodlines and money, not lust.

She took a deep breath to steady her nerves and then began to worm her way out from under his arm. She needed to put space between her and this man, however devastating he might be. She wasn't sure how to go about it, but this marriage had to go away. This was Las Vegas. Surely a marriage could end as simply as it had begun.

Carefully, she inched her way out of his grasp and then, holding her breath, got out of bed. Once on her feet, she looked back at the man. Without thinking, she touched her tattoo and at the still-tender sensation, yanked her hand away in embarrassment. The tattoo was another problem altogether, although something told her it was going to be easier to get rid of the marriage than it would that red heart.

She kept staring, her gaze fixed on the sensuousness of his mouth and the shading of dark lashes on his cheeks. She had to admit he was gorgeous. She sighed. So he was handsome. That only meant liquor did not drown her good taste—just her good sense.

But she was awake now and painfully sober. The way she saw it, her only recourse was to disappear. As quietly as she could, she dressed and packed, stuffing her clothing into her bag without snapping or zip-

ping a single compartment. When she moved to the
dresser to retrieve her watch, her gaze fell on a Pola-
roid picture and the paper beneath.

Oh Lord.

It was their wedding picture—and the license. She
picked up the picture, tilting it toward the light for a
closer look. When she saw the expressions on their
faces, she wanted to cry. They looked so happy. She
focused on her own image and had a small moment
of satisfaction that even though she must have been
drunk out of her mind, she looked normal. Another
Marcie teaching was that decent women did not make
spectacles of themselves.

Harley sighed and laid the picture down, only to
find another peeking out from beneath the license. She
picked it up and then stifled a groan. The man standing
between them couldn't possibly be the preacher, but
then who else could he be? There was an altar behind
them and she was holding her friend Susan's bridal
bouquet. She looked closer, trying to find another reason why an Elvis reject would be in a picture with
them. His black pompadour hairstyle, complete with
sideburns all the way to his chin, looked slick and
greasy, and the white, rhinestone-bedecked jumpsuit
he was wearing was nothing like her pastor's somber
black robes. She glanced down at the marriage certif-
icate and then rolled her eyes in disbelief. She hadn't
been married in her mother's Southern Baptist church

as she'd planned to all her life. She'd gone and gotten married in the Love Me Tender wedding chapel by a man who looked like Elvis.

What in hell had she been thinking?

Her shoulders slumped. Therein lay the problem. She hadn't been thinking, and obviously, neither had Sam. She glanced again toward the bed, thankful that he was still asleep, then back at the paper.

Samuel Francis Clay. His name was Samuel Francis Clay.

My mother was a huge Sinatra fan.

She shivered, suddenly remembering the sound of his voice explaining the significance of his middle name as he leaned over her shoulder to write his name.

Harley's chin quivered. My name is now Harley June Clay.

She turned again, this time staring long and hard at the man still in her bed, then slipped the wedding ring off her finger. Seconds passed as her heart grew heavy. Something inside her kept saying this would be a mistake even bigger than the marriage had been, but she could see no other way out of what they'd done. Slowly, she looked away, laid the ring on top of the dresser beside the pictures, then picked up her bag and slipped out of the room. It wasn't until later when her plane finally took off for Savannah that she let herself cry. And even then, she wasn't sure if she was crying for the mess she'd made of her life by getting married,

or the fact that she'd walked out on the best thing
she'd ever done.

Savannah, Georgia—Four days later

The phone on Harley June's desk rang abruptly,
breaking her train of thought.

"Turner Insurance Agency, how may I help you?
Oh…hello, Mrs. Peabody. Yes, I gave Mr. Turner
your message. No, I'm sorry, but he's still not back
from his meeting. Yes, I will certainly tell him you
have called again. No, ma'am, I am not giving you
the runaround. Yes, ma'am, I know you are a busy
woman. No, ma'am, it isn't polite to lie. Yes, Mrs.
Peabody, I will give my mother your regards. Thank
you for calling."

"Mrs. Peabody still got her panties in a twist?"

Harley looked at one of the other insurance agents
and resisted the urge to sigh.

"What do you think?"

Jennifer Brownlee laughed.

"Oh, I almost forgot. Your mother called while you
were out to lunch."

Harley rolled her eyes, wondering what her mother
could possibly want now. Ever since Harley had come
back from Susan's wedding in Las Vegas, her mother
had been grilling her like a sergeant. First on what
everything looked like and then who attended, always
curling her lip just the least little bit as she asked. Even
though Harley loved her mother dearly, she also knew

and accepted the fact that Marcie Lee Beaumont was a bit of a snob.

She picked up the phone and called her parents' number. Her father answered on the second ring and Harley smiled at the familiar sound.

"Hi, Daddy, it's me. Jennifer said Mama called earlier. Is she home?"

"Yes, she's in the kitchen ironing aluminum foil," Dewey Beaumont said. "Want me to get her?"

Harley stifled a giggle. Her mother's penury was well-known among friends and family. Dewey Beaumont had plenty of money. The Beaumont family home and their lifestyle reflected it, and yet Marcie pinched pennies as if they were about to be evicted. The fact that she washed and ironed used aluminum foil over and over until it completely lost the ability to fold was one of her more quirky habits. It was something Harley had long ago accepted about her mother and something her father prayed had not been passed on to his only child.

"It can wait. Do you have any idea what she wanted?" Harley asked. Then she heard her daddy chuckle.

"No, but I know she made the call right after she talked to Susan's mother, Betty Jean."

Harley's heart skipped a beat, then settled back into its normal rhythm. There was no reason to panic. Susan was long gone by the time Harley must have taken off with Sam Clay. Her fingers tightened around the receiver. If only she could remember the details of that night, she would feel a lot safer.

As her daddy droned on, talking about this and that, Harley let her thoughts drift, and as they did, they headed straight for Sam Clay. The last time she'd seen him he'd been bare naked and barely covered, lying on her motel bed like a sleeping Adonis. In weaker moments, she let herself wonder what might have happened if she'd stayed and faced the music, so to speak. But then reason always seemed to return and Harley accepted the fact that she'd done the right thing by leaving. Somewhere down the road when she could face the truth of what she'd done, she would see a lawyer about getting the marriage set aside. Surely she couldn't be held to something she didn't even remember.

Then she sighed. What she did remember was making slow, sweet love to a most magnificent man. That, she told her errant conscience, was something she *needed* to forget.

"...and so I told her it was none of her business, but you know your mother."

Harley blinked, realizing she hadn't been paying any attention to what her daddy had been saying.

"Hmmm...Oh...yes, I think I do," Harley said.

Dewey hesitated. It wasn't like him to broach tender subjects that he considered "woman business" with his own daughter, but he considered her the best thing he'd ever done in his life, and didn't want to see her waste her life. She was twenty-seven years old and had yet to be engaged. In Savannah, an eligible young lady quite often went through a couple of suitors before settling on the proper one. Harley didn't seem interested in the things that most young women her age focused on and it bothered him greatly. He wanted to see her happy and wanted her children playing around his knees before he was too old to enjoy them, so he cleared his throat and said what was on his mind.

"Harley June, did you have a good time in Las Vegas?"

Again, Harley's heart skipped a beat. Guilt settled heavy on her heart. She hated lying, but how could she tell what she'd done without making herself appear a total fool.

"Why, yes, Daddy, I had a good time. Susan and Mike made such a wonderful couple and the wedding was beautiful."

Dewey frowned. "But what about you? Did *you* have a good time?" He chuckled. "If that had been me at your age, I would have at least hit the gaming tables—gone to a few shows—you know...lived it up a bit before I settled back into the same old routine."

Harley thought about telling him, but how do you say, *Oh sure, Daddy, I cut loose like you wouldn't believe. I not only partied all night, I let Elvis marry me to a total stranger.* Instead, she heard herself saying...

"The wedding was marvelous. I had a very nice time dancing. I even had champagne, Daddy, okay?"

Dewey sighed. "Now, honey girl, I just worry about

you, that's all. It's a daddy's job. Don't take this wrong, but I would hate to see you wind up exactly like your mama, God bless her. I love her with all my heart, but I do not want to know that I sired a daughter who saves buttons and aluminum foil.''

Harley burst out laughing. ''I know, Daddy, and I promise, I won't. I've got to get back to work now. Tell Mama I'll call her tonight, all right?''

''Yes, I will. I love you, Harley June.''

''I love you, too, Daddy.''

Harley was still smiling as she hung up the phone. She glanced across the aisle at Jennifer as she started to swivel her chair back to the computer when Jennifer's eyes suddenly widened and then she let out a fake moan.

''Oh my lord! I think I'm in love.''

''What are you talking about?'' Harley asked.

Jennifer pointed.

Harley turned around.

''Oh God.''

The smile died on her face just as Sam Clay leaned across her desk and planted a kiss square in the middle of her lips, then whispered softly.

''Junie, darlin', I'm not God, I'm Sam. How can you keep forgetting when it's tattooed on your butt?''

Harley June jumped to her feet, poised to bolt. Reading her body language, Sam put himself between her and the door.

''What are you doing here?'' Harley asked.

"I came to take you home," Sam said, and then lifted her jacket from the back of her chair. "Where's your purse?"

She began to sputter. "I can't go yet. I'm at work. Besides, you have no business—"

"You are my wife, therefore you are my business," he said calmly, then looked beneath her desk, spied a handbag and picked it up.

But he hadn't counted on the stir his words would cause. Before Harley could argue, the other two insurance agents, their secretaries and the mail clerk all had to have their say. Shouts of surprise were followed by cries of congratulations. Sam suddenly felt like a bug under glass, but he held his ground. He hadn't had two solid hours of consecutive sleep since he woke up in Las Vegas to find Harley gone. Added to that, his stomach had been in knots ever since he'd found her ring on their picture. He knew what they'd done had been crazy and impulsive, and there had been a brief moment when he'd picked up that ring and thought about following her lead—of going home and never looking back. But that notion had lasted all of a minute until he looked at the bed. Remembering the magic they made together when they made love was all the impetus he'd needed. He'd taken the next flight home to Oklahoma City, worked his shift until he'd had his next four-day hiatus, then had taken a plane straight to Savannah.

And the moment he'd walked into the insurance office and seen her sitting behind that desk and laughing into the phone, he knew he'd done the right thing. All he had to do was convince Harley.

Jennifer was the first to reach Harley's side. She winked at Sam and then hugged Harley.

"Harley June! I can't believe you didn't tell us you were married. When did this happen? Aren't you going to introduce us to your new husband?"

Harley's mouth was moving, but nothing was coming out. Sam figured if anyone was talking, it would have to be him.

"We got married four...almost five days ago," Sam said. "In Las Vegas."

Unknowingly, he flashed Jennifer a smile that made her wish she was fifteen years younger and single.

"And my name is Sam Clay," he added, extending his hand.

Jennifer giggled. "Pleased to meet you, Sam Clay. I'm Jennifer."

Before anyone could answer, Waymon Turner, of Turner Insurance, came in the door.

"What's going on here?" he said.

Harley groaned. The boss was back, and it looked like they were having a party.

"Uh... Mr. Turner, Mrs. Peabody has called four times for you. She's very upset and—"

Sam held out his hand. "Mr. Turner, I'm Sam Clay. Pleased to meet you. I know this is a big imposition, but Junie is turning in her resignation."

"Who's Junie?" he asked, then eyed Sam closely. "Am I supposed to know you, son?"

Harley rolled her eyes and elbowed Sam. "I told you no one calls me that." Then she tried to smile, knowing that her explanation was only going to make everything worse, but it had to be said.

"He's talking about me, Mr. Turner, and uh…Sam is my…well, when I was in Las Vegas we…you see I—"

"I'm her husband," Sam said. "I came to take Junie home."

Now Waymon Turner was thoroughly confused. He eyed Harley June, trying to gauge the mood of the moment by the expression on her face and saw nothing but panic and confusion. He knew just how she felt.

"I didn't know you were married, Harley June. When did this event take place?" he asked.

"Almost five days ago at four-fifteen in the morning at the Love Me Tender chapel in Las Vegas, Nevada," Sam said.

Jennifer squealed. For a woman her age, it was hard to pull off, but somehow she made it work.

"Oh my Gawd! How romantic! I can't wait to tell Johnson."

Harley groaned.

Sam smiled. "Hold out your arms, darlin'," Sam said, and held out the jacket that he'd taken from the back of her chair. He slipped it on her while she was trying to argue.

"Here's your purse, too."

Harley snatched it to her chest like a shield.

"You can't just—"

"Here you go," he said, slipping the long strap over her shoulder and then taking her by the elbow and guiding her to the door. "Everyone, it's been nice meeting you," he said. "If you're ever in Oklahoma City, give us a call."

Harley's heart dropped.

"I'm not going to—"

She found herself outside and standing in the street.

"Listen here, Sam Clay, you can't just—"

Sam cupped her face with his hands and kissed her.

Harley's arguments died along with the last of her good sense. There was nothing in the world that seemed to matter but the feel of his hands on her face, the sensual tug of his mouth against her lips and the scent of his cologne. She'd dreamed about the way he smelled.

When he lifted his head, she moaned aloud.

Sam hid a smile. He didn't have a damn thing going for him except the fact that they were good together in bed. He knew she was afraid. Dang it all, so was he. But the moment he'd walked into that hotel bar and seen her dancing on a table in the middle of a pile of poker chips, he'd been lost. She'd been holding a handful of flowers that looked suspiciously like a bridal bouquet, and had done a neat pivot on the tabletop to the beat of the music playing in the background before giving the flowers a toss. He'd caught them in reflex and then caught her as she started to fall. She didn't look like the kind of girl a serious man took home to Mother. She didn't appear to be the home-maker, baby-loving type—and he was. But she'd gasped when he caught her and then looked up at him with those dark brown eyes and laughed. After that, he was lost. Hours later they'd gotten married and he wasn't going to give up—at least not until they'd given the marriage a serious try.

"What are you really doing here?" Harley asked. "If you've come to make trouble, I can assure you that I don't—"

Sam put his finger in the middle of her lips and then shook his head.

"Sssh, darlin'. I don't make trouble. I make love. Don't you remember?"

Harley's knees went weak. She didn't remember a lot of things, but she well remembered the feel of his weight on her body and sweat-slick hammer of his hips between her thighs.

"Have mercy," she mumbled.

He slipped his arm around her shoulders and began leading her toward a waiting cab.

"I'll give you mercy and anything else your little heart desires," he whispered, as he opened the door.

"Where are we going?" she asked.

"Well...for starters, our flight leaves day after to-morrow morning. That doesn't give us much time."

Flight. The word made her stomach turn. Day after tomorrow. Surely she could come up with something between now and then that would get her out of this mess.

"Time for what?" she asked.

He scooted into the cab beside her.

"To meet your parents. Pack your things. You know. Stuff."

Parents! Lord have mercy, no! Harley opened her mouth to object when Sam leaned over the seat and gave the driver the address to her parents' home.

She stared at him in disbelief, thinking that she must have married herself to a handsome but dangerous stalker. How else would he have known her parents' address? She pulled away from him, shrinking into the corner of the cab and eyed him with something close to panic.

"How do you know where they live?" she whispered.

"You told me," he said.

"I didn't!"

Sam grinned. He was starting to enjoy her discomfiture. She'd put him through four days of hell. It was good for her to be a little bit nervous.

"Oh yes, you did. You told me lots of things," he said, as the cab started to move. "Like..." He hesitated, then leaned over and whispered in her ear.

Harley's eyes widened. Her face flushed and her mouth went slack.

"I did no such thing," she whispered, glancing nervously at the driver who, thankfully, was paying them no attention.

Sam grinned. "Oh, but you did."

Harley felt the blood draining from her face. He had to be telling the truth, because she'd never told anyone that fantasy. Ever.

"Oh no."

"Oh yes," Sam said. "And we did it the night we got married. Twice."

Harley closed her eyes and leaned back against the seat. Her life was seriously out of control.

Chapter 2

Harley was trapped—both by Sam's proximity and the stupidity of her actions. She wanted to be mad at him, but in all fairness, it seemed as if he had married her in good faith. If he'd had any other ulterior motive, it would have been evident the "morning after." All he would have had to do was walk away from what they'd done just as she had. Instead, he'd come after her—like some knight in shining armor come to rescue the fair damsel in distress.

However, distress was a mild word for the trouble Harley considered herself in, and he wasn't exactly a knight in shining armor. She kept eyeing his profile as the cab sped through the streets of Savannah, and as she did, it occurred to her that she had no idea where he lived or what he did for a living. Following that revelation came the thought of what kind of man would marry a woman he'd just met? What was wrong with him that he would settle for a drunk-out-of-her-mind female he'd only just laid eyes on a few hours before?

She shivered in spite of the warmth of the day.

"Sam?"

He turned toward her. "Yeah?"

"Do you have a job?"

He laughed. "You could say that."

Harley frowned. "What do you mean?"

"I'm a fireman for the Oklahoma City Fire Department."

"Oh."

"That wasn't a very enthusiastic 'oh,'" Sam said. "What's the matter, don't I look like the kind of man who could put out fires?"

Harley thought of the sexual chemistry between them and resisted the unladylike urge to snort beneath her breath. From the way they made love, she could have more easily believed he started fires, instead of extinguishing them. There had been a time or two back in the motel after they'd made love, if she could have moved, where she would have gotten up to see if she was smoking.

"I don't know. I was just curious, that's all." Then she added, "Why did you marry me?"

He stared at her, letting his gaze linger longer on

the fan of eyelashes partially shading her soft brown eyes and then on the sensuous curve of her lower lip. It was a good question. One he'd asked himself a thousand times since. He sighed.

"Do you remember our first kiss?"

She flushed, looked away briefly, then made herself face him when she answered.

"I'm ashamed to say I do not."

A wry smile turned up one corner of his mouth. "If you did, I don't think you'd be asking the question."

Her eyes widened. She knew they were volatile together in bed, but surely it hadn't been that sudden.

"You mean—"

"I thought the top of my head was going to come off," Sam said softly, and then threaded his fingers through her hand. "Honey, I'm thirty-seven years old and I've seen the dark side of the moon more than once and lived to tell the tale, but I have never…with any woman…felt the earth tilt beneath my feet like it did at that moment."

"What did I do?" Harley asked and then blushed. "I mean, when we kissed."

"You stared at me like you'd seen a ghost and, truth be told, I knew just how you felt. I'd been thinking about settling down for more than five years but had never met the right woman…until you."

Harley pulled her hand away from Sam and curled it around her purse instead. Her voice was shaking, her heartbeat pounding against her eardrums so loudly she could barely hear herself speak.

"But surely you can see my position. How can you say I'm the right woman? You don't know me, and God knows I'm ashamed to say I don't remember that much of what happened."

"I know a lot about you," Sam said.

Again the thought came to Harley that she might be the victim of a handsome stalker.

"How so?" she asked.

He smiled. "You told me. I know your great-great-Granny Devane personally slapped General Sherman's face when his men rode their horses up the steps of her plantation house. I know that when you were little you were afraid of clowns and that every time your mother fixed fried chicken livers for dinner, you fed yours to the family cat. I know you're afraid of spiders but once rescued your younger cousin from a flooded creek without any thought of your own safety. I know—"

"Stop! Stop!" Harley moaned, and then buried her face in her hands. "My God, how could I turn loose so much of myself and not remember it?"

Sam wanted to hold her, but this wasn't the time. He'd come this far to prove to her he was serious about making their sham of a marriage work. But Harley June was going to have to come the rest of the way to him on her own or it would never work.

"I don't know," Sam said. "All I know is that I

want to give this…give us…a chance. I need it, Junie,
and I think deep down you do too, or you would never
have said, I do.''

"Not Junie," she muttered.

"That's not what it says on your butt," Sam countered.

Her eyes narrowed angrily. "A gentleman would
not remind me of such an indiscretion."

Fed up with her constant referral to Southern gen-
tility, Sam's eyes narrowed sharply.

"Gentleman be damned, Harley June. I told you
once before, I never claimed to be anything but your
husband."

The cab came to a sudden stop.

Both Sam and Harley June looked up, slightly surprised that they had reached their destination so
quickly.

"Looks like we're here," Sam said. Tossing a
handful of bills across the seat to the driver, he
grabbed his suitcase as he got out and pulled a reluctant Harley out of the cab.

The cab drove away from the curb, leaving them on
the sidewalk with nowhere to go but up the front steps
of Harley's childhood home.

"You ready?" Sam asked.

"I can't do this," Harley said, and grabbed Sam by
the arm. "Please! Isn't there anything I can say to
make you stop? You don't understand what this news
will do to my family!"

"Damn it, Junie, you're twenty-seven years old. Are you trying to tell me you still let your parents tell you what to do?"

"Of course not, but—"

"Fine then," Sam said, and took her by the hand, pulling her none too gently up the walk toward the house, his suitcase bouncing against his leg as they went.

Harley's feet were moving but her mind had gone numb. She kept thinking at any moment she would wake up only to find this was all a bad dream. But when she heard her father's voice, she knew the nightmare was only beginning.

"Why, Harley! I didn't expect to see you today! Come look at my Sister Ruth!"

Both Sam and Harley turned. Harley felt a muscle jerk in Sam's hand, but it was the only indication she had that he might be dreading this as much as she.

"Who's Sister Ruth?" Sam asked, as they started across the lawn.

"One of Daddy's rosebushes," Harley said. "Roses are his hobby."

"Oh, yeah, I remember you saying he won a blue ribbon at the Savannah Garden Show last year."

Harley shook her head as they started across the lawn, wondering what else she had told this man that she didn't remember.

Dewey Beaumont was on his knees beside a massive rosebush bursting with blossoms in all stages of bloom. The flower's apricot color was almost as stunning as the scent. Dewey pushed himself up with a grunt, brushing off the knees of his pants as he stood. He eyed the tall man beside his daughter, noted the suitcase he was carrying and the strained expression on Harley's face and wondered what was up.

"Your mother will have a fit if she sees what I've done to the knees of these pants," he said, then smiled at Sam and extended his hand. "I don't believe I've had the pleasure."

Harley jumped, quickly remembering her manners.

"Daddy, this is Samuel Clay. Sam, this is my father, Dewey Beaumont."

Sam smiled. "Mr. Beaumont, it's a pleasure to finally meet you. Harley speaks highly of you, sir."

Dewey beamed. "Harley June is my finest achievement in life."

Harley groaned.

Sam gave her fingers a gentle squeeze.

Dewey frowned.

"Harley…is something wrong? You are pale as one of your mama's sheets."

One glance at Harley and Sam knew if any explanations were forthcoming, they would have to come from him.

"Mr. Beaumont, Harley's a little nervous right now."

"Yes, I can see that," Dewey said, not for the first time eyeing the fact that Sam Clay was still holding his only child's hand. "Might you be able to explain that for me?"

"Yes, sir. Junie and I got married while she was in Las Vegas. I've come to meet the family and then take her home."

Dewey was lost. "Who's Junie? And what does that have to do with—"

"Your daughter, sir. It's what I call her."

Dewey's mouth dropped. "My daughter? You married my daughter?" He stared at Harley. "Harley June Beaumont! Have you nothing to say to me?"

Harley's stomach was rolling, but she surprised herself by answering in a rather calm voice.

"It's true, Daddy. I did marry this man in Las Vegas."

"Lord have mercy," Dewey muttered. "What will your mother say?"

Sam already had a notion that Marcie Beaumont was a true steel magnolia, but he was willing to face anything and anyone for Harley June. He tightened his grip on Harley's hand and smiled.

"Well now, honey, let's just go find out for ourselves, what do you say?"

Without giving her a chance to answer, Sam took off for the house. Harley found herself running to keep up with his stride with Dewey not far behind. They were on the second step of the front verandah when the door opened and Marcie Beaumont came out, her round, cherub-shaped face framed in skillfully dyed, auburn curls. Sam had a moment to notice that her pink, flowing dress was almost the shade of her cheeks and then she was coming toward them.

"Why, Harley June! How sweet of you to surprise your daddy and me like this!" Then she batted her eyelashes at Sam as she must have done since her childhood when she realized that conquering the opposite sex was part of the Southern rite of womanhood. "And who is this good-lookin' man you have on your arm?"

Sam glanced at Harley. Her teeth were clenched so tight there was a white line around her lips and Sam figured that today the introductions were all on him.

"I'm Sam Clay, Mrs. Beaumont, and may I say it's a real pleasure to meet you. I can certainly see where Harley gets her good looks."

Marcie beamed as she tilted her head, having to look up to meet Sam's gaze.

"Now aren't you sweet?" she murmured, and cast Harley a flirtatious grin. "Honey, where on earth have you been keepin' this sweet boy?"

"Under wraps," Harley muttered.

Sam heard her and stifled a grin. Poor Junie. This wasn't her day, but he was feeling better by the minute.

"Five days ago Junie and I were married in Las Vegas."

Marcie's expression fell as the possible suitor she'd envisioned for her daughter just faded away.

"I'm sorry, Harley, I don't remember you having a friend named Junie."

Sam laughed. "This is Junie," he said, and slid his arm around Harley, then gave her a quick kiss on the lips.

While Harley's toes were curling from the contact, her mother's breathing had started to sound as if she was strangling.

Marcie grabbed Harley by the arm, all but yanking her out of Sam's arms.

"Harley June, you better tell me this—"

Sam calmly unwound Marcie's grip from Harley's arm and then tucked her hand beneath his elbow.

"It's Clay, Mrs. Beaumont. She's now Harley June Clay. You know, it's hot as blazes out here in the sun. Do you think you might have something tall and cold for us to drink?"

Without waiting for her to answer, he led Marcie into the house, leaving Harley and her father momentarily alone on the verandah.

Harley looked at her father, almost afraid to speak.

"Daddy?"

Dewey was still a little shell-shocked, but he was starting to grin.

"I don't know where you found him, sugar, but damned if he isn't the first man I've ever seen who got the upper hand on your mama and made her like it."

Harley blinked back tears and tried to smile, although she felt like laying her head on her daddy's shoulder and bawling. This was so messed up.

"Do you love him?" Dewey asked.

Harley shrugged. "I'm not sure, Daddy."

He frowned. "What do you mean?"

She swallowed nervously, but wasn't going to lie. Not to her Daddy, and not about something as serious as this.

"I don't remember a thing about the wedding... only waking up the next morning with that man in my bed and a heart-shaped tattoo on my hip."

Dewey's eyes bugged. "Good Lord! Are you saying you were drugged? If so, then—"

Harley sighed. "No, Daddy. I wasn't drugged. I was drunk."

Dewey stared in disbelief, but the longer he looked at his only child, the more his mouth began to twitch. Harley was twenty-seven, almost twenty-eight, and truth be told, he'd been afraid she was going to turn into an old maid like his oldest sister, Mavis. This stunt was the first truly daring thing that Harley had done since her eleventh birthday when she'd announced to her teacher that she was going to be a stripper when she grew up.

He chuckled.

Harley stared.

"You think this is funny?"

"I just didn't think you had it in you," Dewey said. "At least you can sleep easy now, knowing you will never succumb to the ordinary things in life.'' Then he took her by the hand and started inside. ''We'd better hurry. I wouldn't miss the rest of this show for another year added onto my life.''

They walked in just as Sam was taking a long sealed envelope from inside his jacket pocket. Sam turned, smiling at Harley. She shivered. His smile was almost as devastating as his kisses.

''Mr. Beaumont, I realize you must have a thousand questions you'd like to ask and certainly have concerns as to your daughter's safety.'' He handed the envelope to Dewey. ''Inside are the names and phone numbers of my banker, my boss and my pastor. My parents are dead, but I have a brother and two sisters who all live in Oklahoma. Their names and numbers are also listed, although I'd appreciate it if you'd not take everything they say about me to heart. I'm the oldest and growing up, they didn't much like my bossy nature.''

Once again, Dewey was taken aback by the man's ingenuous nature.

''Yes, well…thank you. Of course we have concerns. I will make some calls later.'' Then Dewey looked at his wife, whose face was two shades of pink deeper than normal. ''Marcie, I think we'd like some of your fine lemonade.''

Marcie sputtered then squeaked. ''Lemonade! You want my fine lemonade? Dewey George Beaumont, have you no sense of decorum? Our daughter has gone and married herself to a total stranger and all you want is lemonade?''

"I'd take something stronger, if you have it,'' Sam said.

Marcie's lips went slack. Harley stifled a grin. Dewey headed for the sideboard in the library where he kept a decanter of sippin' whiskey for occasions out of the ordinary. Dewey was of the mind that this was one of those times.

"You'll be stayin' for supper?'' Dewey said, as he poured liberal shots of the amber-colored liquid into glasses for himself and for Sam.

Marcie moaned. "Dewey! I can't believe you are just standing there letting this happen.''

"Oh, it's already happened,'' Sam said, and grinned at Harley. "Several times now. Right, darlin'?''

Harley wanted to throttle him. How dare he even hint about their lovemaking to her own mother and father?

When Harley didn't answer, Sam just winked and grinned. "We'd be happy to stay for supper, wouldn't we, Junie?''

"I do not answer to that name,'' she muttered, and then pointed at the whiskey.

"Aren't you pouring one for me, too, Daddy?''

Dewey hesitated. "Daughter, after what you told me, I don't think you have the head for drink.''

Sam handed Harley his glass and poured himself another, ignoring Dewey's sputter of disapproval.

"On the contrary, Mr. Beaumont. Junie's about as centered a woman as I've ever met. For me, it was love at first sight."

Marcie's shoulders slumped as she glanced at her daughter, her voice just shy of a whine.

"I can't believe you're married."

Harley tossed back the whiskey as if it were water, blinking back tears as she choked. When she could breathe without fearing fire would come out her nose, she answered.

"Well, Mama, neither can I, but I've got a tattoo on my butt and a ring on my finger that says different." She set her glass down with a thump. "Now I am going to peel potatoes, and if I'm real lucky, my knife will slip and slit my wrist and everyone's misery and disappointments will be over."

She stomped out of the library, knowing that her mother wouldn't be far behind.

"Tattoo? You have a tattoo?" Marcie yelped, and put a hand to her throat in disbelief. "Dewey, did you hear her? Harley June has gone and gotten herself tattooed."

Dewey was feeling pretty good about things so far and chose to pour himself another shot of liquor.

"Marcie, you go help Harley finish up supper now, you hear? I don't know about Sam, but I'm feeling mighty peckish."

Marcie threw up her hands and bolted after her

daughter, muttering beneath her breath about morals and traditions.

Sam felt sorry for what Harley was having to face, but there was nothing he was willing to do to change it. He wasn't giving her up for anything or anyone, and the sooner that became evident to all parties concerned, the better off they would be.

"Mrs. Beaumont, this fried chicken is delicious. You soaked it in buttermilk before you battered it, didn't you?"

To say Marcie was surprised by his question would have been putting it mildly. She had alternated between the certainty that her social standing in the community was forever ruined and the knowledge that her daughter was tattooed. Now, to hear this man—the man who had so smilingly announced himself as her son-in-law—ask if she used buttermilk to soak her chicken was almost ludicrous.

"Why, yes, I did," she muttered.

Sam nodded. "I thought so. My Grannie did the very same thing. Said chicken wasn't worth frying without it."

Marcie was interested in spite of herself. The mention of ancestry in any form was of grave importance to her.

"My grandmother didn't cook," Marcie said.

Sam frowned. "Wow. I'll bet her husband had a

fine time with that. How on earth did her family get fed?''

Marcie's nose tilted upward to snooty and Harley winced. She knew what was coming, but figured Sam had asked for it.

Marcie's mouth pursed primly. ''Why, they hired a cook, just like every genteel family did in those days.'' Then she sighed. ''Oh, for the good old days.''

Dewey snorted. ''You don't clean your own house and you haven't cooked a meal like this since last Easter, Marcie Lee, so don't go all pitiful on us now.''

Sam laughed, which insulted Marcie highly.

Personally, Harley just wanted the night to be over.

''I come from people who did their own cooking and cleaning,'' Sam said. ''I do my own, between shifts at the firehouse, of course.''

Dewey leaned forward, resting his elbows on the table as he fixed Sam with a curious gaze.

''Sam, what made you want to be a fireman?''

Sam shrugged. ''I don't know. Just always thought I'd like it.'' Then he looked at Harley, wishing he could say something that would take that ''shoot me and get it over with'' look off her face. ''And I do...like it, I mean.''

''But it's so dangerous,'' Dewey said. ''I know this isn't a topic for supper conversation, but were you working in Oklahoma City when that federal building was bombed?''

The animation went out of Sam's face, and when it

did, Harley felt as if something inside of her had twisted and cracked. She had a sudden urge to put her arms around his neck and cradle him to her breasts. He looked so—stricken.

"Yes. I was there."

"Daddy, would you care for another piece of chicken?"

Dewey blinked. Harley was passing him the platter of chicken, and the look in her eyes ended whatever else he might have asked.

"Well, uh, yes, don't mind if I do."

Marcie wasn't interested in jobs as much as she was his past. If only he had some ancestors of which she could brag, maybe then this wouldn't be a total fiasco.

"So...have your people always lived in Oklahoma?" she asked.

Sam shook his head, glad that the subject had changed. The hell that he and all the other rescuers had seen was still there in the back of his mind, ready to slip out in the quiet of the night.

"No, ma'am. My great-grandfather was originally from Boston. He came to Oklahoma when it was still a territory."

Harley felt obligated to add her bit to the lagging conversation.

"My friend Susan's family was originally from Boston," Harley said. "Of course, that was several generations ago. They've long since become true Southerners."

Marcie snorted delicately. "Oh no, Harley June. Susan Mowry's family were carpetbaggers. They didn't come here until after The War of Northern Aggression."

"Mother! For goodness sake."

Marcie sniffed delicately, her nose rising a bit higher in the air.

"It's true, Harley June. Carpetbaggers. The lot of them."

Sam laughed. "If that's the kind of stuff that matters to you, ma'am, then my ancestral family will probably turn your hair gray. The first Clay to hit Oklahoma, the one I said was from Boston, was running from the law. He married a Kiowa Indian woman and had four children with her before his legal wife caught up with him and ran her off."

Marcie gasped, her voice just above a whisper. "And which woman would your lineage be tied to?"

"That would be the Kiowa with the four half-breed bastards."

Harley hid a grin as her father laughed aloud.

Marcie paled. So much for bragging rights on the son-in-law.

"Anyone for strawberry shortcake?" Harley asked.

Sam cut his gaze toward her, his eyes suddenly dark with promise.

"We had strawberries and champagne on our wedding night. Do you remember, darlin'?"

Harley started to deny it when she flashed on Sam

leaning over her, pouring champagne in the valley between her breasts and then licking it off with his tongue. She looked at him then, unaware of the want in her eyes.

"Yes. I remember," she said softly.

Sam's heart skipped a beat. Glory hallelujah. It was her first moment of honesty.

Marcie scooted her chair back abruptly and stalked into the kitchen in disgust. Dewey stood.

"I'll just go help your mama with the dessert," he said.

Sam was still staring at Harley and she felt pinned beneath that dark gaze, unable to breathe.

"Do you really?" Sam asked.

"Really what?" Harley whispered.

"Remember."

She shuddered, letting her eyelids drop for just a moment to shutter the intensity of her emotions. When she looked up, Sam was leaning across the table. She had just enough time to catch her breath before their lips met. The kiss was brief and hot, like heat lightning in a storm.

"Harley, darlin'."

"Hmmm?"

"When we get back to your apartment, we are going to make love. You know that, don't you?"

It was a warning and a promise and Harley shivered, both from fear and longing. Longing for this evening with her parents to be over and fear that making love to Samuel Clay would never be enough to make up for the rest of what was lacking in this marriage. It was a sham, and she suddenly wasn't so sure that she wanted it to be over.

"You didn't answer me, sweetheart," Sam said.

"I didn't have to," Harley said. "Some things you just know."

Chapter 3

Even before Sam and Harley left her parents' house
to go to her apartment, she'd made up her mind to
give their marriage a real try. She wasn't clear on
when the notion had settled, but it was somewhere
between the time he'd stifled Marcie's continual whine
and made her like it, and the joke he'd told that had
her father laughing aloud. She couldn't remember the
last time she'd seen her father that way—his eyes sparkling and slapping his leg in glee from the punch line
of Sam's stupid joke. Something told her that if he
could do that to her parents' staid, cocoonlike exis-
tence, then she needed to think about what their life
might be like.

God knew hers was in a rut. At least it had been

until she'd gotten on that plane to Las Vegas. All too aware of the man in the seat beside her, she gave him a nervous smile and clasped her hands a little tighter in her lap, trying desperately to calm down. By the time their cab reached her apartment, she was trembling, but from anticipation rather than fear.

Sam knew Harley was in a panic. He'd seen it set in the moment they'd said their goodbyes to her parents. By the time they'd shut themselves inside the cab, she'd been a mess.

Now that they'd arrived at her apartment, it was up to him to put her at ease, and he knew just how to do it.

He got out of the cab, and as the driver took his bag out of the trunk and set it down on the sidewalk, Sam reached in his pocket for money to pay.

Harley felt as if she was coming down with the flu. Her teeth were chattering and her stomach was turning somersaults. Every muscle in her body was straining to run, and yet the only place she really wanted to go was into Samuel Clay's arms.

The faint light from the streetlight on the corner exaggerated the size of his shoulders, making him seem broader, almost menacing, as he straightened, then turned to face her. He looked at her and smiled and Harley exhaled softly. It was going to be all right.

Sam picked up his bag, took Harley by the hand and together, they started toward the door to her apartment building. A few steps from the door, she stumbled. His grip quickly tightened as he pulled her close against his side.

"Honey…are you okay?"

She sighed. "I will be."

He gave her hand a squeeze. Moments later they were inside the building and climbing the stairs to the second floor. Harley opened the door and then looked at Sam.

"Welcome to my home," she said softly.

Sam set his bag down just inside the door and gave it a small kick as he took her in his arms. Harley sighed again, only this time it was from the inevitability of this moment.

"The door…lock the—"

Sam reached behind him and turned the dead bolt without looking, unwilling to take his gaze from Harley's face.

"I've dreamed about this nonstop for days."

Harley's knees went weak. "I'm a little bit scared."

"June Bug, the last thing I would ever do is hurt you."

"June Bug?"

"Yeah. We've got a lot of them back in Oklahoma. They're persistent little things, too. They come out at night and spend the biggest part of their lives trying to assassinate themselves against the brightest lights that they can find."

Harley almost smiled. "So, are you saying I have a death wish, too?"

Sam shook his head and cupped the palms of his hands against her cheeks.

"No, but you're damned persistent in claiming you don't remember anything about us, and I can't accept that. I *won't* accept that. I think the more time we spend together, the more you're going to remember."

He brushed her lips with his mouth, letting the sound of her soft moan feed his soul.

"I know you remembered the strawberries and champagne. I saw it in your eyes."

Sam's hands were underneath her jacket and unbuttoning her skirt. When he pulled her close against him, Harley felt the hard ridge of him against her belly and shuddered with sudden longing.

"Yes, I remembered."

He was pulling off her clothes now, piece by piece. His voice was tugging at her senses, his touch making her ache for so much more.

"Then make some more memories with me, Harley June. Make them now, before you forget how much you cared."

Harley reached for his belt buckle.

"First door down the hall on your right."

It was all Sam needed to know.

Harley's bedsprings squeaked. The rhythm matched the hard body sound of flesh against flesh. Sam was sprawled on top of Harley, his long arms holding the upper half of his weight from her body as he drove

home the point he'd been trying to make ever since
that day in Las Vegas when she'd come to in a blue
fog. No matter what else was lacking between them,
it wasn't sexual chemistry.

Harley's heart was pounding, her eyes were closed.
Every fiber of her being was focused on the body-to-
body contact between her and Sam. With her fingernails digging into his forearms, her legs wrapped
around his waist, she was lost in the ride, chasing elu-
sive and mindless pleasure with the stranger who was
her husband. The feeling continued to build, pushing
them to a frantic need for completion.

The end came suddenly. One second it was just a
good feeling and the next thing it was there, ripping
through her body and up her throat in a husky, guttural
groan.

For Sam, it was the trigger that made him lose his
control. In the space of a heartbeat, he was helpless.
The climax was upon him, washing over him in
waves. One thrust. Another thrust—and another and
his mind went blank. Only afterward did he think to
raise his weight from Harley as he gathered her in his
arms and rolled so that she was on top, resting on him.

He tangled his hands in the dark lengths of her hair
as the aftershocks still reminded him of what they'd
done.

"Dear Lord," Sam whispered, and pressed a kiss
on Harley's brow.

She was quiet. Too quiet. Lying silently in his arms.

He lifted his head.

"Junie...are you okay?"

"No," she mumbled.

His heart jerked. In his selfish need for completion, had he hurt her? The thought horrified him.

He scooted her off his chest onto her side, then rose up on one elbow to stare down at her face. Even in the shadows of her bedroom, he could see tears running down her face.

"Baby...what's wrong? Please tell me I didn't hurt you."

Harley shook her head and then covered her face with her hands.

He had to strain to hear her answer.

"No, you didn't hurt me," she said.

"Then what's wrong? Why are you crying?"

She looked at him then, her heart in her eyes.

"I didn't know I could feel like this—be like this. I don't know who I am anymore."

Sam reached for her, encircling her shoulder, then sliding his hand across her back as he pulled her close.

"I do," he whispered. "I know who you are. You're my wife."

Harley shuddered on a sigh.

"But that's just it. Don't you see? How can I be a wife when I don't even know my husband?"

Sam felt her confusion, and if he'd been honest, he would have admitted to some worries of his own. But his greatest hurdle had already been passed when he'd found her again.

"Look at it this way, darlin'. We've got this making love stuff down to a science and the rest of our lives to get acquainted."

"You're a crazy man, you know that?" Harley whispered.

Sam grinned. "Yeah. Crazy for you. Now come here to me, woman, and close your sweet eyes. We've got a big day ahead of us tomorrow and we'd better get some rest."

Harley stiffened. "What's happening tomorrow?"

"For starters, packing what you want to take with you when we fly home. The rest we can have shipped."

"Home?"

"Yes, baby. Home. To Oklahoma City. I've got to be on duty in two days."

"Duty."

Sam smiled. "If you keep repeating everything I say, we're never going to get any sleep."

"You mean being a fireman."

He chuckled. "It's what I do, remember?"

"You fight fires."

Sam sensed where this was going.

"Yes, just like I've been doing for the past fourteen years."

"Have you ever... I mean...were you—"

"June Bug, I was in more danger in Las Vegas

when I pulled you off that poker table than I've been
in any fire. I knew the moment your arms went around
my neck that I was in too deep.''

"Really?"

"Yes, really."

He heard her sigh. "I wish I could remember that."

This time, it was Sam whose voice was tinged with
regret.

"Yes, well, so do I, June Bug, so do I."

The trip to Oklahoma was anticlimactic compared
to the scene Harley's mother had made at the airport
in Savannah. She'd cried and she'd begged and then
resorted to threats, at which time Sam's patience had
run thin. He could tell that Harley was already nervous, and her mother's behavior was adding to her
guilt. Despite the fact that he didn't want to incur his
new in-law's wrath, he was too afraid of losing Harley
to stay quiet any longer. When Marcie grabbed Harley's arm and threatened to disinherit her, Sam lost his
cool.

He stepped between Marcie and his wife, his voice
low and angry.

"Mrs. Beaumont, I do not appreciate listening to
you threaten my wife."

"She's my daughter!" Marcie cried.

"Then quit acting like a bad version of *Mommie
Dearest.*"

Marcie gasped in anger and would have said more but Dewey hushed her instead.

Sam shoved a hand through his hair in frustration and glanced at Harley, who was struggling not to cry.

"Look, I understand your reluctance to see your daughter leave, but no one's forcing her. Don't you want to see her happy?"

"Yes, but—"

Harley took a deep breath and interrupted.

"Then, Mama, you're going to have to trust me to make my own decisions."

Marcie glared, still unwilling to back down.

"I always dreamed of watching you walk down the aisle in our church in Great-Grandmother's wedding dress. The vestibule would be filled with lilies and forsythia and I'd be dressed in pink. It's my best color, you know."

Harley sighed. "Mama, that's your dream, not mine. Besides, lilies are for funerals and I'm thirty pounds heavier and six inches taller than Great-Grandmother was. I could never wear her wedding dress, even if I waited another forty years to get married."

"Hush, Marcie," Dewey said. "It's Harley June's life, not ours." Then he looked at Sam. "I made those calls. According to your boss, you're one of the best firemen on the squad. Your pastor speaks highly of your whole family, and your banker was assuring as well. I am trusting you to care for my daughter, and..." He looked at Harley June. "I am trusting my daughter has enough sense to take care of herself. If things aren't right, she knows how to get home."

Sam sighed. "Fair enough." He glanced at Marcie one last time. "Mrs. Beaumont, it's been a pleasure meeting you, and I've promised Junie that we'll come back to Savannah for Christmas, okay?"

Marcie's anger shifted slightly. "Really?"

Harley nodded and smiled. "Yes, Mama, really."

"Well, then," Marcie said. "I suppose that's that."

Within a few minutes of the cease-fire, the plane started to board. No one was more relieved than Sam when Harley allowed him to take her by the hand and lead her down the walkway toward the plane.

A few hours later, the flight attendant had the passengers making preparations for landing at Will Rogers Airport in Oklahoma City. For Sam, it was none too soon.

"This is it," Sam said, turning into the driveway.

Harley leaned forward in the car, her gaze fixed on the sprawling, single-story brick home.

"It's really nice," she said.

Sam smiled. "Don't sound so surprised."

Harley blushed. "I didn't mean that—"

"I was teasing," Sam said, then he pointed toward the front porch as he killed the engine. "I inherited it from my grandfather. It's a nice neighborhood. You won't be afraid here, I promise."

"It's not the house I'm afraid of."

"I hope you're not referring to me."

There was both shock and hurt in Sam's question and Harley heard it. She looked at him then, still unaccustomed to the fact that this big gorgeous man was actually her husband.

"Just the situation in general," she said.

Sam hesitated then nodded. "I can accept that…at least for now." He leaned across the seat and brushed a kiss across her lips. "It's going to be all right, June Bug."

Harley made herself smile. "So give me the cook's tour, okay?"

They got out and started toward the front porch when someone called out Sam's name. They turned to see an elderly woman across the street, waving at them.

Sam waved back.

She came off her porch and headed for the street before Sam could stop her.

"Sorry," he told Harley. "That's Mrs. Matthews. She's nosey but nice."

"I have survived my mother's raising. I can take anything, remember?"

Sam chuckled. "Your mother's okay."

"She's spoiled and controlling and living in the past. Other than that, I'm sure she's no different from anyone else's mother."

Sam squeezed her hand in warning as Edna Matthews crossed the curb and started up the walk.

"Prepare to be grilled."

"Yes, well, since you're still smoking from what my mother did to you, I'm sure I will survive."

Sam grinned. Harley's tongue-in-cheek comment spoken in her slow, Georgia drawl was priceless.

"Sammy, I'm so glad I caught you," Edna Matthews said, as she huffed and puffed her way to where they were standing, then handed him a small box. "The UPS man left this on your doorstep day before yesterday morning, but Henry's dog got to it before I could stop him. It's a little chewed up. I hope nothing is damaged inside."

Sam took the box. "Thanks a lot, Mrs. Matthews. It's a part that I ordered for my lawn mower, so it should be okay. I really appreciate you being so observant on my behalf."

She beamed. "That's what good neighbors are for." Then she gave Harley a pointed look.

Sam winked at Harley before introducing her to his neighbor.

"Mrs. Matthews, I'd like for you to meet my wife. Her name is Harley June and she's all the way from Savannah, Georgia, so I'm counting on you to make her feel welcome to the neighborhood."

Edna Matthews's mouth dropped. Sam Clay was considered a prime catch. To hear he'd been taken off the marriage market was quite a coup. She couldn't wait to spread the word. She eyed Harley up and down as if imprinting the image for future use and then smiled and held out her hand.

"Harley June? An unusual name to be sure."

"It's my mother's maiden name," Harley said. "It's not uncommon to do that where I grew up."

"I see," Edna said. "Savannah, you said?"

"Yes, ma'am. It's a beautiful city. Have you ever been there?"

"No. My late husband and I preferred the western part of the States. He was partial to Las Vegas and Reno. Have you ever been there?"

Harley wouldn't look at Sam and resisted the urge to roll her eyes.

"Yes, ma'am. I have been to Las Vegas."

Edna beamed. "Well, then. We have something in common already. As for our Sammy, here, you are to be congratulated. He's considered quite a catch."

"I consider myself the lucky one," Sam said, and took the opportunity to end the conversation before Edna invited herself inside as she'd been known to do. "Thank you again for rescuing my package. Next time I have a cookout, you're invited, okay?"

"Why, thank you, Sammy, I'd be honored. I'll bring my Italian cream cake." Then she looked at Harley. "Everyone loves my Italian cream cake."

"Sounds good," Harley said.

"Oh, it's marvelous," Edna answered. "Do you cook, dear?"

"Yes, ma'am. All Southern girls are brought up to take care of their men, and you know what they say. The way to a man's heart is through his stomach."

The moment she said it, she eyed Sam nervously, all too aware that the way to his heart had nothing to do with food.

"We're pretty tired now," Sam said quickly. "Thanks again, Mrs. Matthews. I'll be in touch."

He headed Harley toward the door, hoping that Edna Matthews was going in the opposite direction. He turned to look just as he put the key in the lock and was pleased to see her disappearing into her own house. Then he opened the door, picked Harley up in his arms, and carried her across the threshold.

Harley was unprepared for the symbolic moment and caught herself choking back tears.

"Welcome home, Harley June," Sam said softly, then set her down in the hallway and kissed her.

Harley's heart was pounding when he lifted his head, but Sam wasn't through. He reached in his pants pocket and pulled out a small, gold band, then slipped it on the third finger of Harley's left hand.

"I've been saving this for the right time. Is this okay?"

She stared at her hand, remembering the mixed emotions she'd had the first time she'd taken it off, and then looked up at him, unaware that her thoughts could be so easily read on her face.

"Yes, it's okay."

Sam lifted her hand to his lips and pressed a soft kiss on the band itself, then gave her a hug.

"The guest bathroom is the second door down the hall on the left. As soon as I get our bags out of the car, I'll give you a tour of your new home."

He was gone before Harley could think, but instead of moving around, she found herself staring at the small circle of gold on her finger and wondering how something so fragile could make her feel so bound.

Twenty-four on. Twenty-four off. Twenty-four on. Twenty-four off. Twenty-four on. Twenty-four off, then home four days.

After three weeks of marriage, Sam's work schedule at the Oklahoma City Fire Department was, metaphorically speaking, burned into her brain. On the days that he was gone, she cooked and cleaned and worked outside in the yard like a woman possessed. On the days that he was home, she was a little uneasy, still unable to believe that she was living with a man she hardly knew. She knew Sam was doing his best to make her feel at ease, but it was difficult. His brothers and their families had all come calling just long enough to give her the once-over, express real interest in the fact that she'd been named after the father of all motorcycles, tease her about getting married in Las Vegas and let their children stain the living room carpet with Kool-Aid. Even though she'd tried to explain that Harley was her mother's maiden name, they hadn't wanted to listen.

Sam had taken them to task in a jesting manner, telling them to quit picking on the love of his life, and then treated them all to barbecued ribs at a local restaurant. Harley had been overwhelmed by their boisterous manner and more than a little intimidated by the monumental platters of ribs and the amount of beer that flowed with them.

One of Sam's brothers had passed her a freshly topped mug of the brew, which she quickly refused.

"Hey, Sam," his brother said. "What did you go and do—marry a little Southern teetotaler?"

Harley had turned instantly, giving Sam an "I'll kill you if you tell" look, which made him grin.

To her relief, Sam's answer was less than revealing.

"You just worry about your own wife and leave Harley to me," he drawled, then to her surprise, he leaned over and planted a hard kiss right on the middle of her slightly parted lips.

He'd tasted of barbecue sauce and beer. The swift shaft of want that she'd felt at that moment had pierced clear through to her gut.

He'd seen her expression and whispered in her ear. "Hold the thought."

She'd held on for dear life. That night after everyone had gone home, he'd made the thought well worth her while.

There were still the occasional days when she was

certain she'd made a big mistake in coming with Sam to Oklahoma, but they were becoming few and far between. Most of the time she was going through the motions until he wheeled into the driveway and then came striding through the front door yelling, "Hey, Junie, I'm home."

Life was good. Sex was great. And just when she was getting the hang of being married, she tried to pull a hero routine that would have been better left to Sam.

There was a cat up the tree in their front yard.

Harley had heard it meowing when she'd gone outside to get the morning paper. Thinking little of it at the time, she'd gone back inside. Later, when she'd gone out again to drop some letters in the mailbox, she'd heard it again and took the time to stop under the tree.

She looked up into the foliage and, at first, didn't see it. But then it spied Harley and the meow turned into a loud, plaintive squall.

"Poor kitty," Harley muttered, and shifted her stance just enough that she could see a fuzzy orange cat face peering down at her through the branches and leaves.

The cat meowed again, this time adding a warble to the squall.

"I'll bet you're hungry, aren't you, baby? If you come down from there now I'll get you a big dish of milk. Come on...here kitty, kitty. Come on, kitty. Come on. Come on."

"Waarrrooowww."

Harley dashed back into the house, returning moments later with a piece of bread, thinking that the scent of food might coax the cat down. All she got for her troubles was another squalling wail.

Five minutes and a bowl of milk on the ground later, the cat was still up the tree and Harley's empathy for the situation had gotten completely out of hand. Instead of going back into the house and leaving the cat to come down after the food on its own time, she was convinced that it couldn't come down. Of course the logic that it had gotten up by itself was now completely lost on Harley June. She wanted to help poor kitty out of the tree, at which point, she had another idea—equally as bad as her first one.

There was a ladder in the garage. It hung on the wall above an old bicycle and a pair of Sam's boots that had seen better days. As she dragged the ladder down from the wall, she kept telling herself she could do this. All she had to do was go up the ladder, brace herself carefully as she climbed up through the branches, get poor kitty and then down they'd come.

The first part was simple. The tree was large. The ladder was tall. She went up the steps carefully, and by the time she was halfway up, could already reach the lowest branches of the tree. It didn't occur to her to be worried that the moment the cat had seen her coming up, it had climbed higher, rather than coming down to meet her.

When she looked up to gauge her position and saw
the cat still several branches above her, she frowned,
thinking that the cat must have been higher up than
she'd imagined. Bracing herself by holding on to the
closest branches, she swung a leg out around the ladder and put a foot on the branch. Within moments she
was off the ladder and in the tree.

"Here, kitty, kitty," she called. "Come on, kitty."

"Maaarrroooww."

She hefted herself to another branch, automatically
elevating her position higher up into the tree, at which
point the cat began to hiss.

Harley frowned.

"Look, kitty, don't you want to come down and get
some nice warm milk? Come on, kitty, kitty. Here, kitty."

Harley stretched out her hand. The cat extended its
neck, sniffing in the direction of her fingers.

"That's a good kitty. Come on, kitty."

All she needed was another six inches and she'd
have the cat by the nape of the neck. Confident that
this could be done, Harley moved just a little bit
higher, only slightly aware of the sound of a truck
engine coming to a stop beneath the curb.

The door opened—the driver emerging to the tune
of country music blasting from the interior of the cab
at earsplitting decibels. Harley looked down, saw the
top of a baseball cap on a fat man's head and then to
her horror, watched her ladder being dragged away
from the tree and loaded onto the top of the truck.

"Hey!" she shouted. "That's my ladder! You can't take my ladder!"

The man gave no sign of having heard her above the din of music as he proceeded to tie the ladder down. To Harley's horror, he got into the truck and drove away.

"Stop! Thief!" Harley shouted.

The driver didn't stop and the cat moved up another two branches, this time completely out of sight.

"Oh fine," Harley moaned, got a sudden burst of vertigo and grabbed on to the branches as the ground beneath began to waver and roll.

For several minutes she clung to the tree without moving or speaking while the cat, having tired of something else occupying what had once been its private domain, climbed down on the opposite side of the tree from Harley and proceeded to eat the bread and drink the milk that she'd brought before ambling off down the street in search of quieter quarters.

Harley stared in disbelief, and was then forced to close her eyes again as, once more, vertigo threatened to unseat her.

"Ingrate," she muttered, and then sniffed as a few errant tears blurred her vision.

Sam wouldn't be home until sometime tomorrow and it was too far to the ground to just climb down to the lowest branches and let go. The last thing she wanted was to break a leg or an ankle. Added to that, not knowing anyone in the neighborhood but Edna Matthews pretty much limited the people who would even know she was missing. The thought of being caught up a tree was only less embarrassing than the fact that she'd torn her shorts. Although she was afraid to check the damage, she suspected it was severe because she could feel breeze on her backside where her shorts pocket was supposed to be.

Time passed.

Enough that her legs were beginning to cramp and her fingers were getting numb. Added to that, she needed to pee. It was, except for that morning when she'd come to in Las Vegas and found herself married, the worst day of her life. The way she figured, she had two choices. She could pee her pants and hope they dried before someone actually found her, or she could forget her embarrassment and start yelling for help.

She opted for the latter.

"Help! Help! Somebody help."

On the seventh call, she heard the blessed sound of someone calling back.

"Who's calling for help?"

"Me," Harley answered, and ventured a look down. Edna Matthews was standing on Harley's front lawn looking around in complete confusion.

Edna turned. "Harley, dear, is that you?"

"Yes," Harley shouted.

"Where are you?" Edna shouted back.

"Up the tree," Harley answered.

Edna's mouth made a small *o* as she looked up in disbelief.

"My goodness, dear. How on earth did you get up there?"

"I climbed a ladder and then someone stole it."

"Oh my," Edna said. "Are you all right?"

"No," Harley said, trying hard not to cry. "I can't get down."

"Yes, I can see that," Edna said. "Don't you worry, though. I'll go call for help right now. You wait right there."

She bolted before Harley could answer. Harley laid her cheek against her arm, resisting the urge to laugh. Where the hell did Edna think she could go?

A few moments later, Edna was back. "I called the fire department, honey. They'll be right here."

Harley moaned. Sam. Oh Lord. Something told her she'd never hear the end of this.

"Honey?"

"What?" Harley muttered.

"Not that it's any of my business, but why did you go up that tree to begin with?"

"There was a cat up the tree and I thought he couldn't get down."

"But, honey…how did you think it got up there?"

Harley stifled an expletive. "I guess I didn't think, did I, Edna, or else I wouldn't be in the predicament."

To Harley's relief, Edna did not laugh.

"I think I hear a siren," Edna offered.

"Great," Harley mumbled and closed her eyes.

Chapter 4

When the call went out for Sam's company to roll, he donned his gear without thought, concentrating only on the impending job and wondering what they would find upon arrival. It wasn't until he'd jumped onto the ladder truck that the captain had come running out, yelling that the call had come from his residence. Within moments, every fireman on the rig knew where they were going, and although they cast the occasional nervous glance in his direction as the big red engine raced through the Oklahoma City streets, no one spoke. To a man, they were all empathizing with Sam's shock and fear.

For Sam, the ride was a blur. All he could think was that Harley was in trouble. He'd been anxiously scanning the horizon for smoke, but as they neared his home, he'd come to the conclusion that whatever had happened to Harley, it didn't involve a fire—at least not anymore.

As they turned the corner, he saw Edna Matthews standing in his yard and gesturing wildly. Sam was off and running before the truck came to a complete halt.

"What happened?" he yelled, grabbing Edna by the shoulders. "Where's Harley? Where's my wife?"

"Up the tree," Edna said, pointing up and over Sam's head.

"Up the what?"

"The tree! The tree!" Edna cried. "Someone stole your ladder and she can't get down."

By now, it was evident to all the firemen that no one was in mortal danger. Relief swelled through the crew as they gathered around Sam and looked up the tree.

Sam squinted. He could see a familiar length of bare leg and shoe, but he couldn't see Harley's face.

"Junie. Are you all right?"

Harley rolled her eyes. God, but this was humiliating.

"Someone stole your ladder. I only saw the top of his head but he was driving a big black truck."

"Why did you climb up the tree?"

Harley resisted the urge to scream.

"It's a long story," she said. "Suffice it to say, I want down. Would you please make that happen?"

One of the firemen slapped Sam on the back as another placed a ladder under the tree.

"Sounds to me like she's running out of patience, old buddy. If I were you, I'd save the questions for after she's down."

"Yeah…right," Sam said, and started shedding his bunker gear. He dropped the coat, hat and gloves on the ground and readjusted the suspenders on his pants to make sure they would not get hung up on the limbs. The less he took up the ladder, the easier it would be to help get Harley down.

Another one of the firemen waited with Sam, making no attempt to hide his glee.

"Been wanting to meet your new missus," he said. "Now's as good a time as any, I suppose."

Sam glared. "If you're smart, you will not tick her off."

The fireman grinned. "Hell on wheels, is she?"

"Just steady the ladder and shut up," Sam muttered, and started climbing. "Hang on, honey. Here I come."

"Don't hurry on my account. I've been hanging for the better part of an hour now with no immediate plans to turn loose."

A round of laughter from the men below followed her terse remark. Sam heard her mutter something unsavory beneath her breath and began climbing a little faster. When he could finally see her arms and then her face, his heart skipped a beat. He could see the tear tracks on her face. Whatever he'd been going to say was forgotten in his need to comfort.

"I'm here, now, darlin'. Can you scoot backward toward me about six inches?"

"Yes," Harley said, and did as he'd asked.

When his fingers curled around her ankle and then slid up the curve of her leg to steady her, she resisted the urge to cheer. So she looked like a fool to about a dozen men. So what. She was still going to be down from this tree.

"Easy does it," Sam said. "Now put your foot here."

He placed her foot on the top rung of the ladder.

"Okay…good…good. Now the other foot. It's okay. I've got you. You're not going to fall."

Finally Harley was standing upright, sandwiched between Sam and the ladder that was leaning against the trunk of the tree.

"Thank God…and Edna Matthews," she said, and rested her forehead against a rung of the ladder.

Sam's nose was against the back of her head, his arms encircling her as she stood. Her hair smelled as if she'd washed it this morning, although there were bits of leaves stuck in the curls. He kissed the back of her neck behind her ear and then gave her a quick hug.

"Ready to go down now?"

"Yes, you go on ahead," she said. "I'll follow."

"We'll go together," Sam said.

Harley sighed. "Sam. Please. I'm not hurt. Just stupid. You go first and I'll be right behind you."

He could tell she was embarrassed and figured that arguing with her wouldn't help.

"Okay, if you're sure."

"I'm sure."

He came down the ladder as quickly as he'd gone up. It wasn't until he got down to the ground and looked up that he realized there was a large tear in the seat of her shorts.

"Uh, honey, maybe I'd—"

"Sam! For pity's sake. Allow me the dignity of disembarking from this tree on my own."

"But your—"

It was too late. She was already halfway down before he could warn her that everyone was going to have a pocket-size view of her backside, and in a most unfortunate place.

Harley was halfway down when she heard the first whistle then a couple of men's chuckles. She heard Sam mutter something beneath his breath and the chuckles stopped, but only momentarily. By the time she got to the ground, every man there except Sam had a big silly grin on his face.

"Well," she said, pasting a smile on her face. "I've been wanting to meet the men Sam works with for weeks now, but didn't intend for it to be quite this way."

"Yes, it's real nice to meet you, too, Junie," they chorused.

"Harley," she said. "I'd really rather be called Harley. Now if you'll excuse me, I'm going into the house and call the police to report a stolen ladder." Her cheeks were pink with embarrassment as she glanced at Sam, but her shoulders were straight and her chin was held high. "Sam, we must have the men and their families over for a backyard picnic. We'll grill hamburgers and hot dogs and whoever wants can swim in the pool. You set up a date with the men and just let me know."

"Hey, thanks, Junie... I mean. Harley. We'll look forward to it," one of them said.

Harley glanced at Sam and smiled primly. "Now that the emergency is over, I suppose you'll need to get back to the station. I'll let you know what the police have to say about the ladder."

With that, she pivoted sharply and headed for the house, resisting the urge to run.

Five steps later, a slow wolf whistle sounded, then someone called out in a slow, Okie drawl.

"Hey, Harley...nice tattoo."

She froze in midstep and reached behind her, felt the dangling remnants of her hip pocket and gasped. Without missing a beat, she pulled it up over the bare spot, pasted a smile on her face and turned.

"Thank you," she said primly, then strode into the

house as if it was of no consequence that a covey of men she did not know had just seen her bare ass.

"Dang it, guys, you are not helping matters any," Sam said.

The men laughed among themselves as they began returning their gear to the fire truck and tying down the ladder that they'd used. Just as they were about to pull out, a big black pickup truck came around the corner and then screeched to a halt in front of the house.

The driver bolted from the truck cab, then pulled a ladder from the back of the truck.

Sam frowned. That looked like his ladder. Thinking of what Harley had been forced to endure, he jumped off the fire truck and headed toward the man with single-minded intent.

"What in blazes do you—"

"Look, I am real sorry," the driver said, still dragging the ladder behind him. "My boss sent me to pick up a ladder they'd left behind on a paint job yesterday, but they gave me the wrong address. When I got back to the shop, I got chewed out big time for going to 904 instead of 409 Carolyn Lane. I hope I didn't cause any trouble. You got any idea where the owner is? I'd like to apologize."

"I'm the owner," Sam said, and took the ladder out of the man's hands. "You left my wife stranded up a tree. If I were you, I'd get myself back in the truck and get out while the getting is good."

The driver groaned. "Oh man, I am so sorry. So I guess she's pretty ticked, huh?"

"That doesn't come close."

When the front door slammed, they turned. Harley was coming out of the house on the run.

"That her?" the man said.

"Yep," Sam said.

"Tell her I'm sorry," the man said, and bolted for his truck.

By the time Harley reached the curb he was almost out of sight.

"Why didn't you stop him?" she yelled.

"He brought it back," Sam said. "It was all just a mistake."

Harley stared at Sam as if he'd lost his mind and then put her hands on her hips and gave him a cold, angry glare.

"Fine, then you can be the one to call the police and tell them that the ladder is back. I've had all the humiliation I can stand for one day."

Then she fixed the grinning men with a look that wiped the smiles from their faces.

"Don't you people have someplace to be?"

"Load up," Sam told them. "I'll hang the ladder in the garage and be right with you."

Glad to be out of the line of Harley's fire, the men headed for the truck.

"Don't bother," Harley told Sam, yanking at the

ladder he was holding. "I got it down. I can put it up."

Sam held on tight, refusing to relinquish the ladder and resisting the urge to turn her over his knee.

"I will put it up and you will take a deep breath before you say another word to me," he muttered, then turned and headed for the garage.

It was the first sign of anger she'd ever seen in Sam, and it stunned her. Suddenly, she realized she was standing alone in the yard and Sam was already at the house. By the time she got to the garage, the ladder was on the wall and Sam was turning around.

"You over your hissy fit, yet?" Sam asked.

"I do not have fits," Harley said. "They aren't ladylike."

Sam snorted beneath his breath and then grabbed her by the shoulders and hauled her into his arms.

"Honey, my first impression of you was anything but ladylike, and it was enough to make me want to spend the rest of my life with you, so climb off your high horse just like you climbed down out of that tree and get over it. You were the victim of circumstances and you're okay. If the worst you got was embarrassed, then so be it. You don't know how scared I was when we got the call to this address. I don't ever want to feel that sick and empty again, do you understand me?"

Overwhelmed with shame, Harley could barely

meet his gaze. She hadn't thought about the call from his point of view.

"I'm sorry," she said.

Sam shook his head and pulled her close against his chest, holding her so close she could barely breathe.

"God, woman, I would have thought you'd figured out by now that I love you so much I ache."

He kissed her then, taking what was left of her breath with his words.

"I've got to go," he said quickly, kissing her again, only this time harder and swifter, groaning softly when he had to let her go. "I'll be home this time tomorrow and then we'll have four days together. Don't climb any more trees until I'm here to catch you, okay?"

Too stunned to do more than nod, she watched him jog toward the truck, then watched as they drove away. Only after the big red rig was gone did she turn and go back into the house.

The rooms were cool, quiet and empty. It occurred to her then that without Sam's presence, the house was not a home. He made everything come alive—especially her.

She touched her mouth where his lips had been.

I love you so much I ache.

The room blurred before her eyes. The words had never been said before—by either of them. And now the truth was out in the open and Harley had to think about what she felt for him. Was it possible that in this short period of time that she, too, was falling in

love? She'd been attracted to him sexually. That was
a given. And with passing time, she'd come to realize
that her husband was a man whom people trusted and
admired. But she'd been so busy trying to cope with
the chaos of an unplanned marriage that she hadn't
allowed herself to feel. She took a deep breath and
closed her eyes, remembering her relief as she'd heard
Sam's voice beneath the tree, then knowing as he
helped her onto the ladder that he would never let her
fall. That was trust. But did she love him, like a
woman was supposed to love her man? She wasn't
sure. What she was sure of was that Sam was light
and laughter and kept her safe.

And he loved her so much it made him ache.

The doorbell rang again, as it had off and on for the
last thirty minutes. Harley raced to answer it, side-
stepping two firefighters' wives and a half-dozen kids
and wondering as she did what on earth had made her
invite all these people to their home for a cookout.

She opened the door, recognized the man holding
the cake as the firefighter who'd complimented her on
her tattoo and tried not to blush.

"I'm Charlie Sterling," he said quickly. "This is
my wife, Tisha."

"Come in," Harley said. "Sam's out back cooking
hamburgers and if you all brought your swimsuits, feel
free to jump in the pool."

"Love your accent," Tisha said, and took her cake

from Charlie's hands. "You can go outside and play, but be nice, you hear?"

"Real cute, honey," Charlie said, and patted his wife on the rear as he headed for the kitchen and the patio beyond.

Tisha rolled her eyes and then grinned at Harley.

"He's not quite housebroke yet," she said. "Can't take him anywhere."

Harley laughed. It was the first time since this whole day started that she thought she might have found a friend.

"According to my mama, the best ones are always like that," Harley said. "I've got some beans baking in the oven, so follow me."

"Oooh, you cook, too," Tisha drawled, then spied the other wives and had to stop for a hug and a hello. It was a couple of minutes later before she made her way into the kitchen where Harley was taking a large pan of baked beans from the oven.

"Those smell heavenly," she said.

Harley smiled. "Grannie's recipe, but it makes so much that I never make them unless I have company."

Tisha gazed around the kitchen, noting the changes that had taken place since Harley's arrival.

"We were all here about three years ago for a party, but that was when Sam had the pool put in. Haven't been here since, but it looks like you've fixed the place up a lot."

"Mostly just new curtains and paint. Have to do

something while Sam's gone to occupy my time. I'm thinking about looking for a job, but haven't decided what I want to do.''

"Did you work before you and Sam got married?" Tisha asked.

"Yes, for an insurance agency. Very boring. I'm not doing that again."

Tisha filched a handful of potato chips from a big plastic bowl and started munching as she watched Harley flit about the room. First impressions were usually her strong suit, but she couldn't quite put her finger on who Sam's wife really was. Being the nosey person that she was, she pressed on for answers to satisfy her curiosity.

"You sure pulled a good one," Tisha said.

Harley looked up from the boiled eggs she was peeling.

"What do you mean?"

"Snagging Sam. Taking him off the marriage market, so to speak."

"Oh, that," Harley said, and reached for another egg. She had to get them peeled and deviled before the hamburgers were done or the cookout just wouldn't be right.

Tisha frowned. It wasn't exactly the giggle she'd expected from a newlywed.

"Don't tell me the bloom is already off the rose," she said.

Harley paused and looked up, a slight grin on her face.

"Do you always speak in analogies?"

This time it was Tisha who'd gotten lost in the conversation.

"I don't know what you mean."

Harley's smile widened. "Well, first you tell me I pulled a good one and now you're asking if the bloom is off the rose. Why don't you just come out and say what you mean?"

Tisha swallowed the last chip she'd been chewing and dusted off her hands.

"All righty then, since you asked, how long have you and Sam known each other? He never mentioned you until he came back from Las Vegas and then, according to Charlie, you were all he talked about. As for the bloomin' rose, you aren't as gooney-eyed as I expected a newlywed to be."

"Oh. That," Harley said, and began cutting the eggs in half and dumping the yolks into a bowl.

She didn't know Sam had come into the kitchen until he slid his arms around her waist and kissed the back of her neck.

"Tisha, are you grilling my ever-loving wife about our love life, because if you are, you're gonna be sorry."

"Why?" Tisha asked.

"Because ours is so good it'll make you mad at Charlie, and don't tell me it won't. I know the man.

He bunks next to me at the station, remember? Ten minutes after a meal, he's asleep."

Tisha laughed. "You've got that right. The moon has long since set on the honey part of our life." Then she sighed. "But I have to keep him around. Lord knows no one else would have him."

Harley laughed, more than a little surprised at herself for being so at ease with Sam's public affections.

"What are you making now?" he asked, as he watched Harley mashing a bowl full of boiled egg yolks.

"Deviled eggs," she said. "Do you like them?"

There was a glitter in his eyes as he whispered against her ear.

"June Bug, I like everything you do."

Tisha grinned. "Obviously, you don't know all of his likes and dislikes yet, but that will come."

Sam bit the edge of Harley's ear, well aware that she was struggling not to go limp in his arms.

"Shoot, Tisha. We don't know fudge about each other yet, but we're learning, aren't we, honey?"

Harley blushed, but she was one to give back as good as she got.

"Oh yes, and it helps that I'm such a quick study."

This time it was Sam who was caught by surprise. His eyes widened suddenly and then he burst into laughter.

"And a damned good dancer, too," he said.

Tisha's interest piqued again.

"You were a dancer? I thought you said you worked in an insurance agency."

Harley glared at Sam. "I'm not a dancer and I do...rather, I did, work in an insurance agency."

Tisha leaned across the counter, her eyes alight with interest.

"So, exactly how long did you two know each other before Sam popped the question?"

Harley knew from the look on Sam's face that he was going to tell the story and while it was inevitable that they would eventually find out, she would have preferred they got to know her better first. However, never one to let a man tell something that she knew she could tell better, she blurted out the truth.

"Beats me," she said. "I was drunk at the time."

The expression on Sam's face was priceless, and then he started to grin.

"Let's see," Sam added. "If I remember right, it was about two hours after I pulled you off the poker table where you were dancing and right before you went swimming in the nude in the waterfall at the Mirage."

Harley's face fell. "I didn't."

"Well...actually, you did," Sam said. "But I hauled you out before the cops got there and hid you in the bushes. In fact, that's where I proposed."

Tisha whooped with laughter, which promptly brought the other wives into the kitchen.

"What's going on?" they chimed, but Harley was too horrified by what Sam was telling her to care.

"I was naked in the bushes?" Harley mumbled.

"No, I had your panties and your bra back on by then."

She looked down at the egg yolks and groaned, unaware of the rapt attention of their audience.

"I can never go back to Las Vegas again," she said.

Sam gave her a quick hug. "Naw, it'll be all right. I can assure you that the few people who saw you in the water weren't looking at your face."

"Why didn't you tell me?" she moaned.

He shrugged. "The subject never came up." Then he dug his finger into the egg yolks and took a quick taste. "I think this needs some salt."

"Don't put your fingers in the food," she muttered, almost as an afterthought, and reached for the saltshaker. "Was that before or after I got the tattoo?"

"You have a tattoo?" Tisha squealed. "Where? Can we see? I've always wanted a tattoo but you can't get them done in Oklahoma. Charlie keeps telling me that he'll take me across the border into Dallas, but he hasn't done it yet. What does it look like, Harley?"

Harley looked up, all too suddenly aware that she and Sam had captured quite an audience.

"You must think I'm awful," she said, and bit her lower lip to keep from crying.

"Oh no," Sam said. "You're not awful, darlin'.

You're the best...I mean, the best thing that ever happened to me.''

"Well, whoop-de-doo," Tisha said, and then came around the island where Harley was working and gave her a quick hug. "Honey, the only thing on my mind right now is how to get through the rest of this day with good manners, because right now I'm so jealous of you I can't stand myself.''

"Yeah, me, too," another woman said, and several more chimed in.

"Jealous? I made a complete fool of myself.''

Tisha winked at Sam and then blew him a kiss. "Yeah, but look what you wound up with.''

When Harley realized the women weren't going to turn her into some kind of pariah, she started to relax.

Tisha sidled up close to Sam and tickled him under the chin.

"Sam, honey, did you get a tattoo, too?''

A dark flush suddenly appeared on his cheeks as he swatted at her hand.

"You're a menace to society," he muttered. "And I gotta go flip the burgers. We'll eat in five, Junie. Will you be ready?''

"Aren't I always?" Harley said sweetly, reached for the mayonnaise and mustard to finish the filling for her eggs, plopped in a couple of spoonfuls and then blasted him with a smile.

Sam exited the house to the sound of women's laughter. He was all the way out to the grill before he realized he'd forgotten what he'd gone in the house for.

"Did you find the ketchup?" Charlie yelled.

"It's on the way," Sam said.

Even though it was a lie, it was better than admitting that he'd gotten caught in a trap of his own teasing.

Chapter 5

Something began to change between Sam and Harley after the barbecue. For Harley, it had been her baptism of fire and one that she'd survived quite nicely. When she realized that Sam's friends and co-workers had not judged her harshly for the manner in which they met and married, she quit judging herself. She began to see Sam, not as a mistake, but as her friend and husband. On the days when he was home, there were times when she forgot that she hadn't known him all her life. Occasionally, she was reminded of the strangeness of her situation, but even then was leaning toward the theory that marrying Sam was the best mistake she'd ever made. He was a tender lover and a fair and just husband. But it was the day she broke down in tears after a phone call from her mother that she learned Sam also considered himself her guardian angel.

She was in the bathroom washing her face and blowing her nose when Sam found her.

"Junie! What's wrong, honey? Are you sick?"

Harley took one look at the sympathy on his face and burst into tears all over again.

"No," she sobbed, burying her nose against his chest as he took her in his arms.

When Harley cried, Sam got physically sick. It was a phenomenon he had yet to get used to. His stomach was churning as she wrapped her arms around his waist.

"Then talk to me, darlin'. Why are you crying?"

"Mama," Harley mumbled.

Sam frowned. "You're missing your mama?"

Harley shook her head and pulled back.

"No! Nothing like that," she said. "She called and—"

Her chin quivered again and she shook her head, unable to finish. But Sam saw enough to read between the lines.

"Your mother made you cry?"

Harley sighed and then nodded.

"What the hell did she say?"

Harley shrugged. "That I've embarrassed her forever…that her reputation is ruined."

"Bull."

Harley's tears ceased. In all the time she'd known Sam Clay, she'd never heard him curse. And when he handed her a washcloth and told her to wash her face, she was so stunned by the anger in his voice that she did as she'd been told. While she was washing her face, Sam stalked out of the bathroom and headed toward the living room.

His hands were shaking in anger as he dug through the desk drawer for the number to Dewey Beaumont's home. He found it and dialed, punching in the numbers with short, angry jerks, unaware that Harley had followed him into the room. Two rings later, Harley's father answered the phone.

"Hello, Dewey, this is Sam. Is Marcie there?"

The delight in Dewey's voice was obvious.

"Sam! Great to hear from you, son. How are things in Oklahoma?"

"They're fine, thank you. At least they were until a short while ago when your wife called and made your daughter cry."

There was a brief moment of silence and then Sam heard Dewey curse beneath his breath.

"I'd like to speak with Marcie if she's home," Sam said.

"She'll be right here," Dewey said. "And for what it's worth, when you get through with her, I'll be batting cleanup, if you know what I mean."

"Thank you, sir. I would appreciate it."

"You tell Harley that her daddy loves her and is proud of her, too, you hear?"

"Yes, sir. Now may I please speak to Marcie?"

"Hang on."

There was a brief moment of silence, after which Sam heard a series of short steps, then an absolute bellow as Dewey shouted out Marcie's name. If he hadn't been so angry, he would have grinned, imagining the look of shock on Marcie's face from being shouted at by her husband.

Back in Savannah, Marcie Lee was so stunned by her husband's behavior that she came running out of the library, convinced that a calamity was about to occur.

"What on earth!" she gasped, as Dewey took her by the arm.

"Sam is on the phone," Dewey said. "He wants to talk to you."

Marcie's mouth pursed in abject disapproval at the tension in her husband's fingers.

"You're hurting my arm," she said primly. "And you didn't have to shout. It's so uncouth."

"Oh, I think maybe I did," Dewey muttered. "And when you're finished speaking with Sam, come into the library. You and I are going to have a talk."

"Dewey, I will not be ordered about in my own—"

"Sam's waiting," Dewey said, "but I won't be so patient."

He strode off toward the library without waiting to see Marcie's reaction.

Marcie, on the other hand, was so stunned by Dewey's unusual behavior that she found herself hurrying to the phone.

"Hello? Sam? Is something wrong with Harley June?"

"Yes, ma'am, there is, actually."

Marcie gasped. "I knew it. I just knew it. There she is so far away from all who love her and—"

"Marcie… Ma'am…pardon me for being so blunt, but I need you to shut up now."

Marcie gasped. "You can't talk to—"

"Yes, ma'am, I can. I can when it comes to protecting my wife."

"Protecting? What on—"

"You made her cry."

Four little words. But they had the effect of a bucket of cold water on Marcie's bruised senses.

"I don't know what you mean," she said, and knew he could tell she was lying.

"Yes, ma'am, I think you do. I don't know what you said to your daughter, but I would suggest you not say it again. Harley is a wonderful woman and a damn good wife, so it stands to reason that she is a good daughter, as well. Therefore, I cannot understand why a mother would purposefully say hurtful things to someone they're supposed to love. Can you?"

Marcie started to tear. She cried real pretty and

knew it. But as the first tears started to fall, she realized that they weren't going to do her any good. No one was there to see them.

"I didn't mean for—"

"But that's just it," Sam said. "I think you did. And I'm telling you right now to stop it. Harley is your daughter, not the means to your social calendar. If our getting married has cheated you out of some big social event that you've always dreamed of, then I suggest you invite all your friends to an absentee reception, play that video we sent you last week as part of the night's entertainment, eat, drink and be merry on our behalf and let them see that your daughter is still in one piece and relatively happy. At least she was until you called. Do I make myself clear?"

Marcie was unswervingly single-minded, but part of her upbringing had been to acknowledge a true "head of the house" and from the tone in her new son-in-law's voice, she had far overstepped her bounds.

"Yes, dear, you do. Please accept my apologies and then put Harley on the phone. I'll tell her the same."

"No, ma'am. I don't think so, at least not today. Harley's heard the sweet sound of her mother's voice just once too often today. You call next week when we're all in a better frame of mind, okay?"

Marcie sniffed appropriately and then delicately blew her nose, wanting Sam to know that she was crying.

"Yes, I will do that. You tell Harley I'm sorry, though. Will you do that for me?"

Marcie rolled her eyes as she hung up the phone. That hadn't gone well at all. And then she remembered Dewey was in the library waiting and stuffed the handkerchief back in her pocket. Something told her that the more tears on her cheeks, the better off she would be when she faced him.

Sam's anger was still simmering as he hung up the phone. He turned around and saw Harley standing in the door. Unable to read the expression on her face, he caught himself holding his breath. Would she be mad at him for talking to her mother that way, or would it be okay?

"June Bug, I—"

"Sam."

"What?"

"You are forever my hero."

Tension slid out of him all at once.

"You aren't mad at me?"

"Hardly."

Then she crossed the room, wrapped her arms around his neck and kissed him soundly.

Sam's body responded with instant need.

"Yes," Harley said.

Sam lifted his head and grinned.

"I didn't say anything...yet."

Harley's eyelids lowered as she leaned against the hard ridge behind his zipper.

"Oh, yes, you did." She swayed her hips slowly from side to side, knowing how quickly they could give each other pleasure.

Sam groaned. "Damn...Harley...let me get us to the bed."

"Too far," Harley whispered, and slid her hand between their bodies.

Seconds later, they were tearing off their clothes and sliding to the floor.

Harley had a brief moment of lucidity as Sam rolled her on her back and she looked up at the light fixture in the hall. There was a long thin strand of spiderweb dangling from the ceiling. She tried to make a mental note to clean it later, and then felt Sam's tongue dipping into her belly button and lost her train of thought. All she remembered was that she'd been right all along. It *was* too far to the bed.

Harley was stretched out on a chaise lounge by the pool, watching a pair of robins in the shade tree overhead, barely aware of the condensation from the ice-cold lemonade in her glass running between her fingers. Tiny bits of sunlight filtered through the canopy of leaves forming her shade, glittering like tiny diamonds against the green. She adjusted her sunglasses on her nose and then sighed.

Today was September 1st. Labor Day weekend. Three months ago today she'd come to in that Las Vegas motel and found herself married. Who could have known how much difference the ensuing ninety-two days would have made in her life?

Sam would be home tonight and then would be off for four days. She could hardly wait. There was so much she had to tell him. She closed her eyes, picturing his face—the way his eyes crinkled up at the corners when he smiled, the way his muscles bunched and rippled as he walked, the way his mouth felt on her lips when he was kissing her good-night.

She shuddered on a sigh. Yes. She had fallen in love. Head over proverbial heels in love. And it was about time. After all, a woman should be in love with the man who was going to be the father of her child.

A faint breeze shuffled the hair against her forehead and she stifled a soft moan. It reminded her of Sam's breath on her face as they made love.

Goodness. Making love. If she'd had half a brain, she should have known that chemistry like that had to come from something other than lust. They'd been made for each other. Sam had seen it from the start. It had just taken her longer to get past the shock of what she'd done to see the man with whom she'd done it.

Now, they were going to have a baby.

Sam's family would be happy for them and her parents would be beyond excited. After the dressing-down Sam had given her mother a month ago, things had been absolutely perfect. Marcie and Dewey called regularly once a week but always had positive things to talk about. Without knowing the details, Harley could tell that the level of power within her childhood home had shifted, but she didn't care how it had happened. All she knew was that her parents seemed happier.

Of course some things would never change. Marcie still saved aluminum foil and took home packets of salt and pepper from fast-food restaurants, insisting that Dewey use them on his morning breakfast while saving the salt and pepper in her fine crystal shakers for company.

As she lay in the lounge chair contemplating the impending changes in her body and her life, she heard the faint but unmistakable sound of sirens in the distance. Her stomach clenched and she sat up with a jerk.

Fire sirens.

She'd long since learned to distinguish them from police or ambulance. And while she knew this was a part of Sam's life that he truly loved, it took everything she had not to show how much she feared his chosen work.

"Hello, dear. Having yourself a nice morning, I see?"

Harley turned and tossed her sunglasses aside. Edna Matthews was waving at her over the backyard fence.

"I rang your doorbell. When you didn't answer, I thought you might be out here," Edna said. "I hope you don't mind the intrusion, but I brought you that recipe you've been wanting.''

Thankful for a reason to think of something besides fires, Harley hurried to the backyard gate to let Edna in.

''You know we never mind a visit from you,'' Harley said, and held up her half-empty glass. ''Would you like to join me in some lemonade?''

''Thank you, dear, but not this time. My sister is on her way over to pick me up. We're going to the mall. There's a giant Labor Day sidewalk sale. Want to come?''

Harley thought of all the crowds and the heat and quickly declined.

''No, but thanks anyway. Maybe another time.''

''Can't say as I blame you. It'll be a mad crush, that's for sure, but I've always been a sucker for sales. Anyway, here's the recipe. It's quite easy, although you don't need to worry about details like that. You're such a marvelous little cook.''

Harley grinned as she took the recipe. ''Only one of the useful things my mother taught me. It's right up there with knowing how to pick ripe watermelons and keep the curl in my hair on rainy days.''

It wasn't the first time Edna had heard Harley speak of her mother and her unique requirements for being a proper Southern lady. She chuckled.

''I can't wait to meet your mother. She sounds like quite a girl.''

"That she is," Harley said. "Have fun with your sister and remember to use sunblock. It's very hot outside today."

"Already applied it," Edna said, patting the lines and wrinkles in her pudgy face. "Well, I'm off. Take care, dear. I'll talk to you later."

Harley was still smiling as she entered the house. She laid the recipe card on the cabinet and put her sweating lemonade glass in the sink. Surprised that it was almost noon, she set out a bowl of tuna salad that she'd made the day before and decided to have a sandwich. While she was eating, she began mentally planning the meal she would make for tonight. It had to be special. All of Sam's favorites. He would know when he saw what she fixed that something was up, but she wasn't going to tell him until after they'd eaten. She knew exactly what she was going to say and the way she would say it. I love you, Sam Clay, more than I ever believed it possible to love, and we are going to have a baby. And the moment she thought it, something skittered through her mind that took the smile off her face and sent shivers up her spine.

Harley jumped up from the table and spun around as if someone had just tapped her on the shoulder, but there was no one there. Hugging herself against the sudden dread in her heart, she strode to the patio door. The serenity of their backyard was still in place. The clear, crystal blue water in the pool sparkled brightly in the noonday heat. The pair of robins that had been in the shade tree earlier were now hopping about on the lawn and there were a pair of butterflies in the flower bed having a meal of their own. Nothing had changed, but Harley knew something was wrong.

And then her gaze slid up beyond the treetops where a large black column of smoke was quickly spreading against the sky. Her heart skipped a beat. Something very large was on fire. Remembering the sirens that she'd heard earlier, she clutched her hands against the middle of her stomach and closed her eyes in prayer. Seconds later, the phone rang. She dashed to answer.

"Hello."

"Harley, it's me, Tisha. Turn on your TV."

"Why?"

"Just do it."

"What channel?" Harley asked.

"Any local channel. It doesn't matter. They're all there."

Harley ran for the living room, carrying the phone as she went. Seconds later she had the remote in hand. The picture came on just as she sat down. The image was a mesmerizing hell. Flames as tall as a three-story building were eating through the roof of a massive, single-story structure. Firefighters were silhouetted between the camera and the fire while long columns of water crisscrossed in the air in a dubious effort to put out the flames.

"Oh my God," Harley whispered. "Is it Red company?" referring to the crew on which Sam worked.

''They're there, but so are a bunch of others,'' Tisha said. ''It's a four-alarm, honey, but try not to worry too much. The guys have been together for years without coming to any harm. I know this is your first big one, so I thought I'd better call you and tell you not to panic, okay?''

Suddenly Harley's hands were shaking too hard to hold the phone to her ear.

''I don't feel so good,'' Harley said. ''I can't talk anymore.''

She disconnected before Tisha could say anything more and then sat in front of the television without moving, glued to the unfolding drama of the fire. That it had occurred at a very large supermarket during business hours had also complicated the firemen's ability to proceed in an orderly fashion. Because of the holiday weekend, a large number of people had to be evacuated from the building, and the parking lot had been packed with an unusual number of vehicles. Everyone had been shopping for Labor Day celebrations. It couldn't have happened at a worse time.

Harley watched, wanting to cry and knowing it would solve nothing. She kept telling herself this was part of Sam's life. It was something she had to get used to. Finally, after more than an hour, programming resumed with only the occasional bulletin updating the viewing area on the disaster. She told herself that the lack of coverage had to mean that everything was going okay, but there was that knot in the pit of her stomach that had nothing to do with fear. It was a helpless knowing that someone she loved was in danger.

The parking lot was a mess. Police had cordoned off the area directly around the building to give emergency vehicles easier access, but the people who'd been in the store were still stuck at the perimeter of the area, unable to get to their vehicles and leave while others were being treated for smoke inhalation and hysteria. The temperature of the day was in the high nineties. Coupled with the intense heat from the fire, many firefighters were being treated for heat exhaustion, as well.

Sam and Charlie had been part of the evac-crew and were nearly blind from heat and exhaustion. Sam had stripped off bunker gear, and was bent nearly double, holding on to his knees to keep from falling while Charlie downed a bottle of Gatorade. The wind was strong, giving power to flames already out of control, but as it blew, it also caught spray from nearby hoses, sending a welcoming drift of mist onto their overheated bodies.

Sam straightened with a groan and took the bottle of Gatorade someone handed him. It was his second, but the much-needed electrolytes in the drink were replenishing fluids and minerals he badly needed. As he turned around, two more units from nearby station houses were arriving. He breathed a sigh of relief, knowing they could use all the help they could get.

Suddenly, a woman pushed her way past the roped-off area and began running toward the firemen, screaming as she ran.

"My son! My son! I can't find my son."

Sam's heart stopped. A trapped victim was one of a fireman's worst fears. Their captain caught her before she had gone too far, and as Sam watched, saw her gesturing wildly toward the engulfed building, then saw her fall to her knees, screaming as she went.

Tossing aside his drink, he retrieved his bunker gear and headed for their captain. Charlie was right behind him.

"Sir?"

Captain Reed turned, his expression grim.

"She says her son was in the bathroom when they began evacuating the store. She says that when she tried to go after him, they wouldn't let her go, but assured her that store personnel were checking all the offices and bathrooms and that she could find him outside."

"But she didn't find him, did she, sir?"

Reed glanced down at the prostrate woman and then back up at Sam.

"No."

"How old is he?"

"Twelve."

A muscle jerked in Sam's jaw as he gazed back toward the burning building.

"Where are the bathrooms located?" Sam asked.

Captain Reed shook his head. "Oh, no, you don't. The front of the building is already engulfed."

"Yeah, but maybe we can get in from the back," Charlie said. "I was there only a couple of minutes ago. There's a lot of smoke, but I didn't see any flames."

The mother heard what they were saying and clutched at Sam's pant legs in deep despair.

"Please! Please let them try. He's my only child."

"Captain?"

Captain Reed hesitated briefly, then yelled for the manager of the store who'd been standing nearby. When he heard his name being called, he came running.

"Where are the bathrooms located?" Reed asked.

The manager looked panicked. "In the back of the store. Why?"

"We think we've got someone trapped."

"Oh, I don't think so. My assistant manager checked. He assured me that all the rooms were empty."

"Where is he?" Reed asked.

The manager turned, quickly surveying the area, then shouted. A short, stocky man of about forty came running.

"Henry, did you check all of the offices and bathrooms before you left?"

Sam could tell by the look in the man's eyes that he had not.

"I tried," Henry said. "But the smoke was so thick I—"

"Dear Lord," the manager muttered, then gave Captain Reed a horrified look. "I didn't know! I swear I didn't know!"

"Ma'am, what's your son's name?" Sam asked.

"Johnny. His name is Johnny."

Sam looked at Charlie and then grabbed the manager by the arm.

"Come with us," he said. "Show us the back door closest to the bathrooms and give us a layout of what's inside as we go in."

The man hurried to keep up with Sam and Charlie, shouting as they ran.

"Two in! Two out!" Captain Reed shouted, and two firemen quickly moved with them, dragging hose lines as they went. Within seconds they were at the back of the building and hooking up to another hydrant while Sam and Charlie put their bunker gear back on. Sam checked his SCBA, making sure that the Self-Contained Breathing Apparatus had the full thirty minutes of compressed air, then settled the visored-helmet on his head.

"Take these," Captain Reed said, handing Sam and

Charlie two-way radios. "I want to know what's happening at every turn."

Sam nodded and thrust the radio in one of his voluminous pockets. He knew where he had to go to reach the bathrooms. If God was with him, and if the boy was still inside—

Then he stopped. He wouldn't let himself think past those two ifs. He couldn't think of Harley, or let himself panic at the thought of never seeing her again. All his focus was on the direction he had to go and the boy who might still be inside.

"Ready!" he shouted, and then he and Charlie raced toward the back door as a spray of water began raining down upon their heads.

As they opened the back door, billowing clouds of black smoke emerged from the opening along with flesh-searing heat. Sam paused inside and looked back for Charlie. He was right beside him, as were the two firemen outside the door with the hoses. The two out would follow with the water for as long as the hand lines would reach. After that, Sam and Charlie were on their own.

Ignoring everything but the task at hand, Sam said a quick prayer and felt for the wall.

Chapter 6

Relying on what the manager had told him and the constant spray of water at their backs, Sam put his hand flat against the wall. Using it as a boundary, he began a mental countdown of the distance they needed to go.

Charlie tapped him on the shoulder to let him know he was there beside him. At that point, Sam keyed the hand radio.

"We're in," he said.

Reed's voice bounced back, giving Sam and Charlie the illusion that they were not alone.

"Good, but don't take any chances. You don't have any time to waste. Do one thorough sweep of what's not burning and get the hell out."

"Yes, sir," Sam said, then he and Charlie dropped to their knees and began crawling through the smoke with the imprint of the layout stuck fast in their minds. Two firefighters just inside the doorway continued to man the hand lines, keeping water on Sam and Charlie's backs.

According to the manager, the first two doors they would pass were offices. They would be locked. Then there would be a space set back from the straight line of the wall where the box crusher sat. The opening was ten feet in length and about twenty feet deep. They had to bypass that to reach the next section of wall and the first thing they would come to would be the store's walk-in freezer. Next door on the right would be the men's bathroom. If the boy was where his mother said he would be, he'd be in there, or at the least, close by.

Sam crawled with his flashlight in one hand while keeping the other one on the wall as a guide. Water from the hoses aimed at their backs kept raining down around them, but the effort did little to dilute the smoke. At any moment, Sam knew the whole back of the building could erupt just as the front had already done, and when it did, their chances of getting out safely lessened drastically. Charlie was still with him, holding on to Sam, while following along behind.

Again, Sam shouted out the boy's name, and again his words were muffled by the mask of his SCBA as well as the roar of the fire. He didn't hold out hope of being heard. A few seconds later, he felt a doorknob against the wall and tried to turn it. It didn't give.

The first locked office.

This was good. It meant they were on the right track. He paused momentarily, tapping Charlie on the shoulder and pointing to the door so that Charlie also understood where they were at.

Charlie tapped him on the arm and nodded. They resumed their trek.

A few feet farther Sam felt the second knob. It, too, was locked. But, while they were proceeding according to plan, they had crawled out of the range of the water's spray which had intensified the heat. Before Sam had time to adjust to that fact, he suddenly ran out of wall. He stopped, replaying the instructions he'd been given.

This had to be the space where the box crusher was. It should be about twenty feet deep and at least ten feet in length before he'd find any more wall. Trusting instinct and the manager's directions, he started to crawl, well aware that the farther they went, the closer they got to hell.

A few feet more and once again he felt wall to his right. Charlie tapped him on the leg, indicating that he'd felt it, too. Sam kept on moving, the flashlight's beam little more than a wink in the dense, acrid smoke.

Sam tried to slow his breathing, knowing that at the rate he was going, the compressed air in his self-contained breathing apparatus wouldn't last more than fifteen minutes. They couldn't be far from reaching their goal. All they had to do was keep moving. But the distance from the wall to the next landmark was farther than he imagined. Just when he feared they might be lost, he felt a long, metal handle. Adrenaline spiked.

The freezer. This had to be the walk-in freezer. Only a few more steps and he should be at the door to the men's bathroom. Please, God, let the kid still be inside.

"Johnny! Johnny! It's the Oklahoma City Fire Department. Can you hear me?"

Even as he called out, he knew hearing any answer would now be impossible. The hiss and roar of the fire was like an oncoming storm, and the constant explosions of aerosol cans and cleaning supplies in the front of the store sounded like ground warfare. He swept his hand along the wall, expecting at any moment to feel the doorknob to the men's bathroom, but there was nothing but smooth surface beneath his glove. The muscles in the backs of his legs had started to jerk from the tension of crawling and his gut was in knots. So if he was still on the right track, then where the hell was that door?

One second he was questioning their path and the next he was clutching a doorknob. The men's bathroom! It had to be the men's bathroom! Rocking back on his heels, he grabbed Charlie's shoulder and then slapped the wall. Charlie nodded to indicate he'd seen it too.

Sam made a motion, then he and Charlie stood abruptly. Yanking the door open, they moved inside, quickly sweeping the flashlight beams in every corner. Almost instantly the room filled with smoke, but they had visibility long enough to know that there were two stalls besides the urinal, and they were both empty.

Ah God.

Charlie pointed toward the door. Sam nodded and they immediately turned, retracing their steps out of the bathroom. Either the manager had told him the wrong door, or the boy had tried to make a run for it and failed.

They dropped back to their knees, seeking respite from the thick and boiling smoke. The heat was intense now, seeping through their bunker gear. Everything inside Sam told him to run, to get the hell out while there was still time. His gloves were so hot, he imagined them melting into his skin. Staying any longer was going to be suicide, but oh God, he wanted to find the kid.

He thought of the mother—picturing her waiting—picturing her expression if they came out alone. Just one more sweep. They'd go back the way they came, but down the other side of the wall. Maybe they'd get lucky.

"Let's get out of here!" Charlie yelled.

Sam nodded, but took Charlie by the arm as he pointed.

"Down the other side as we go out!"

"Yeah!" Charlie shouted.

Sam grabbed the hand mike to tell their captain.

"Captain! It's Sam! We can't find the boy. We're coming out down the opposite side of the wall."

A spate of static cut through the noise inside the building. Sam knew Captain Reed was answering, but couldn't make out anything except the words "now." Then he heard Reed shout "breaking through" and his blood ran cold. The fire must have gone through the ceiling in back.

He pocketed the radio and shouted at Charlie.

"We gotta get out now!"

Charlie nodded and together they began to move. Seconds later, Sam realized he was no longer crawling on concrete. Even through the thickness of his gloves, he could feel the outline of a body on the floor.

"Charlie! We've got him!" Sam shouted.

Charlie crawled up beside Sam.

"You take his legs. I'll get his shoulders," Charlie shouted.

But before they could move, a fireball exploded. Sam looked up just as a wall of flame came billowing toward them. Slapping Charlie's headgear, he screamed.

"Fireball! Get down!" then threw himself on top

of the unprotected boy, pulling him under just as the fireball roared overhead.

The horror of what was above him was equal to the fear of the too-still child beneath him. His mind was reeling. Was the kid already dead, and if he wasn't, how could they keep him alive? They couldn't go out the way they'd come in and there was no other exit except through the fire, which now was no option at all.

And then the answer came as suddenly and clearly as if someone had spoken right in his ear.

The freezer. Get inside the walk-in freezer.

He looked up, reaching for Charlie as he did and then his heart almost stopped. There was a large chunk of smoking metal on the floor that hadn't been there moments before—and Charlie wasn't moving.

"Charlie! Charlie!" he shouted, but Charlie didn't respond. Now Sam had two victims to worry about besides himself.

He scanned the area frantically as burning debris began to rain down on their heads. The freezer couldn't be more than four or five feet behind them. He grabbed his hand mike.

"Mayday! Mayday! We're trapped near the middle. I found the boy but Charlie's down. Repeat! I found the boy and Charlie's down!"

Another loud explosion rocked the building. Sam looked up. The ceiling was awash with flames, beautiful, deadly curls of orange and yellow rolling along the surface of the ceiling, like surf upon the shore—defying gravity while consuming everything combustible in its path.

Rollover—and it was out of control.

He keyed the hand mike again.

"Captain, we're going into the freezer!" he shouted. "In the walk-in freezer."

Then he stuffed the mike back in his pocket, grabbed the back of Charlie's coat and one of the boy's legs and started scooting himself backward, dragging the bodies as he went.

The muscles in his back were on fire, he didn't know whether from strain or heat. Although he kept on pulling, progress was slow and he felt that too much time had passed. Certain that he'd veered off course, he let out a shout of relief when he suddenly hit solid wall. He turned loose of Charlie and the boy long enough to feel behind him, and when his fingers curled around the handle on the freezer, he said a quick prayer of thanksgiving. Someone was guiding more than his thoughts.

The freezer opened easily. Sam slid the boy in first, his inert body moving easily and lifelessly along the smooth, cold surface, then he reached for Charlie and dragged him in, too, quickly slamming the door behind him.

Still on his hands and knees, he took off his headgear, lowered his head and fell face forward onto the floor, his heart hammering inside his chest.

The cold against his cheek was like water to a man dying of thirst. Relief from the intense heat of the fire outside was coupled with the knowledge that the power was off inside the freezer, which meant no new air would be circulating. If things didn't go right, they could just as easily suffocate before they were found, but that was a worry for another time.

Sam struggled to get up. He had to know if the boy was breathing. He had to check on Charlie's injuries. But the silence inside the freezer was almost mesmerizing. Only the faintest of sounds penetrated the thick walls. If they died, then so be it. At least their families would have something to bury besides a couple of bones and some ashes.

Finally, he got to his feet and began feeling along the floor, wishing he hadn't dropped his flashlight. Sweeping his arms out in front of him, he found the first body. It was Charlie. Removing his gloves, he ran his fingers along Charlie's neck, searching for a pulse. It was there, strong and steady. He ran his hands all over Charlie's body but couldn't feel any blood. What he did feel was a definite dent in Charlie's helmet that hadn't been there before. All he could do was hope that Charlie had only been knocked out.

His next concern was the boy. He found him quickly, and tested him for a pulse. Unlike Charlie's, the boy's life was hardly there. The pulse was weak and thready and he could barely detect any signs of breathing. He felt along the floor for his SCBA and quickly slipped it over the boy's head. Whatever air was left in the pack was better used for the kid than for him. With a weary groan, he sat down with a thump. Without light or first-aid equipment, there was nothing more he could do but wait.

Within seconds, Sam began to feel the cold. Confident that Charlie was protected by his gear, his focus shifted to the boy. He opened his coat, gathered the boy up in his arms and pulled him tight against his chest.

"Johnny, can you hear me? You're safe now, but you've got to stay with me. Your mother's outside and she's real worried about you. You're gonna have to be tough, son. Tougher than you've ever been before."

Knowing there was nothing more he could do, Sam clutched the boy close against his chest. As he sat, he thought of Harley, remembering the laughter in her eyes and the way they made love. Knowing that her life would go on if he died and resenting the hell out of the fact that his might end before they'd had a chance to make this marriage thing right.

Outside, Captain Reed had gotten just enough of Sam's last message to know they were in trouble. He spun, shouting as he ran.

"I want the Rapid Intervention Team in here now."

Firefighters sprang into action, stringing new hose lines and grabbing SCBAs as they moved toward the back of the building.

"What's happening?" Johnny's mother screamed. "Did they find my boy?"

Captain Reed shouted at a nearby policeman.

"Get this woman out of here now! The area is too dangerous for civilians."

The woman grabbed hold of Reed's arm, her eyes dark with fear and shock.

"I don't move until you tell me what you know," she said. "That's my son. I have a right."

Reed hesitated and then covered her hand with his.

"Ma'am, it's not good. All I heard my firefighters say was that they'd found him but they're trapped. I don't know what his condition is. I don't know if he's alive or dead, but unless I can get my men out, they're all going to die. Please go with the officer. He'll take you to a safer place and I swear that when I know something definite, I'll tell you first."

"Dear God," she whispered, and dropped her head as the officer led her away.

Reed resisted a shudder. He had no time to give in to his own emotions. Lives depended on rational decisions. He moved toward the fire, giving orders as he ran.

Harley had known for almost an hour that something was wrong with Sam. Every breath she drew was painful and every second that ticked away was time lost with the man she loved. She sat without moving, staring blankly at a phone that didn't ring. Sam couldn't die because she hadn't told him that she loved him. Life couldn't be that unfair.

Sometime later the doorbell rang, but she couldn't bring herself to answer. Then knocking sounded and she heard the familiar sound of Tisha Sterling's voice.

"Harley! Harley! It's me, Tisha. Are you in there?"

Harley shuddered. Her body was weak with fear, but her need to know was strong. Slowly, she made her way to the door and then opened it.

Tisha grabbed Harley by the shoulders.

"We've got to go! I got a call," she said. "It's—"

"Sam's in trouble," Harley said.

Tisha frowned. "Who called you?"

"No one," Harley said, staring blankly at a space over Tisha's shoulders.

"Then how did you know?" Tisha asked.

Although she was unaware of moving, Harley's hand drifted toward her heart.

"I feel it."

"Get your purse and come with me. I'm not waiting for a call from Captain Reed. Charlie's in danger, too, and I've got to know what's going on."

Harley shuddered again and then turned around, staring blankly at the room.

Tisha screamed with frustration and bolted for the hall table where Harley usually kept her purse. Sure enough it was there. She grabbed it on the run and then headed for the door, yanking Harley with her as she ran.

* * *

The Rapid Intervention Team was fighting a losing battle. Walls had already collapsed on the north side of the building and the steel arches of the long, metal roof had long since caved in.

Franklin Reed was sick to his stomach. He was forty-seven years old and wanted to cry. Ever since the rollover, he'd been second-guessing his decision to let Sam and Charlie go in. If he hadn't they'd still be alive. And they were dead, of that he had no doubt. They would have long since run out of air in their SCBAs. He kept telling himself that they had probably succumbed to smoke before the fire had gotten them, but he didn't know that for sure. Media vans from local television stations were lined up a good four blocks away, but he could feel the long-range lenses trained on him. For that reason and for that reason only, he kept his emotions masked. When he grieved, it would not be in front of a camera.

As he looked away, he saw movement from the corner of his eye and then started to frown. The cops had let two women under the blockade and they were coming toward him. He recognized Charlie Sterling's wife but not the woman she had in tow.

"Damn it," he said to no one in particular. He didn't want to have to tell Patricia Sterling that her husband was most likely dead.

* * *

The air was full of smoke and noise and the moment Tisha and Harley crossed the police barrier they found themselves walking in water.

Harley let herself be dragged along, but she wasn't looking at the tall, stern-faced man in uniform waiting for them at the end of the block. Her focus was on the flames silhouetting him against the sky.

"Oh God," she whispered, then stumbled.

Tisha caught her by the elbow.

"Don't stop," she said, her eyes bright with unshed tears. "And don't look at the fire. Captain Reed will tell us what we need to know."

Reed came to meet them.

"Patricia, isn't it?" he said, touching Tisha on the arm.

Tisha's chin wobbled, but she made herself smile.

"Yes, sir, and this is Sam's wife, Harley."

"You shouldn't be here, you know."

"Where else would we be?" Tisha asked.

Reed shrugged and then glanced at Harley. He took her hand and knew immediately that she was unaware she'd even been touched. Her eyes were wide, her pupils fixed and dilated as she stared in disbelief.

"Mrs. Clay. I'm sorry we have to meet under these circumstances. I tried to make the cookout you and Sam had last month, but my youngest son broke his leg that day playing baseball. My wife and I spent the afternoon and most of that evening in the emergency room. You know how it is."

Harley blinked. "I'm sorry," she muttered. "What did you say?"

Reed sighed and shifted his gaze to Tisha.

"I'm assuming someone called you or you wouldn't be here."

"What can you tell us?" Tisha asked.

A muscle jerked in Reed's jaw. Unconsciously, his grip tightened on her arm.

"Sam and Charlie went in after a kid who'd gotten trapped."

Tisha moaned and then pressed a finger to her lips to keep from screaming.

"And?"

"They found the boy but didn't make it out," he said. "Last message we had was a Mayday from Sam. He said something about being trapped and then most of the other words were too garbled to understand. We sent the RIT team in immediately, but they were unsuccessful." He took a deep, shuddering breath. "I'm so sorry."

Tisha covered her face and then went to her knees. Almost immediately, Harley's hand was on Tisha's head.

Reed saw Harley's eyelids drop as she swayed on her feet. Thinking she was going to faint, he caught her by the shoulders, then found himself caught in the undertow of a blank stare.

"They're cold," Harley said.

"Ma'am... Harley, is it?"

Harley nodded, then smiled. "But Sam likes to call me Junie."

Reed sighed.

"Harley, let me help you to a—"

"No, I'll wait here for Sam," Harley said. "He's just cold. Somebody needs to get him a blanket."

Reed's eyes filled with tears. "Mrs. Clay, please. You and Patricia need to come with me."

A frown creased the surface of Harley's forehead as she abruptly pulled out of his grasp.

"You're not listening to me," she said, her voice rising with each word. "They're not dead. They're cold."

The store manager had been nearby, listening to what they'd been saying, and then suddenly, a thought occurred to him.

"Captain Reed. Captain Reed!"

Reed turned. "What?"

"What if she's right? We couldn't make out the last part of the fireman's message, but remember you thought he was shouting for someone to free them. What if he was saying freezer? The walk-in freezer is right beside the bathrooms. What if they took shelter in there?"

For the first time since the roof went in, Captain Reed felt a glimmer of hope. It wasn't based on anything but a young wife's refusal to give up hope and the small bit of truth in what the manager was saying.

It wasn't much, but he'd seen miracles before with far less reasons. He pointed to Tisha and Harley.

"Stay with them," he said, and started toward the fire at a lope.

They were sitting in water, which didn't surprise Sam because the world had surely melted from all the heat. Once he thought he'd heard Charlie groan, and he'd called out to him, letting him know that he was there. But Charlie hadn't responded and so he'd opted to save his breath.

The boy was breathing. Sam knew because he could feel the faint rise and fall of his chest. He also knew that the kid had certainly suffered from smoke inhalation and was in dire need of medical attention, and yet all he could do was hold him in his lap. Frustration coupled with acceptance. They'd come so close. It was damned unfair that it would end like this.

He took a slow, even breath, inhaling the smell of thawing meat and wet paper along with badly needed oxygen. Their headgear was empty of compressed air and the oxygen inside the freezer was depleting fast. He was getting sleepy—so sleepy. Once he thought of getting up and trying the door, just to see if the fire was over. But if it wasn't, fire would be the last thing he saw and he didn't want to die that way, knowing the thing he'd given his life to fight had won out in the end. So he'd stayed inside the freezer with the boy cradled in his arms, listening for the moment when breathing would finally cease, wondering if his would be the first to go.

Don't forget me, Junie. I sure won't be forgetting you.

The boy was so heavy in his arms and he was tired—so tired. He let his head fall back against the wall and closed his eyes. They burned some, but itched even more. His mind wandered again and he had to focus on why his eyes were bothering him. Oh yes. Just a hazard of the smoke. He needed to rest—but just for a minute.

Seconds ticked by and ever so slowly, the boy slid out of Sam's arms and down into his lap as his arms went limp. Except for the constant drip of melting ice, it was quiet—deathly quiet.

Captain Reed's hand mike crackled with static and then he heard a fireman shout.

"We found them!"

He keyed his own mike.

"In the freezer?"

"That's a positive, Captain. We're bringing them out right now."

"Are they alive?"

"They've got pulses."

Reed's knees went weak.

"Thank you, Lord." When he turned around, Harley Clay was there. "They found them, Mrs. Clay. They're alive."

"Yes," Harley said.

Reed stared at her for a moment, and then took her by the hand.

"Harley?"

"What?"

"How did you know?"

"That Sam was alive?" she asked.

He nodded.

"I could feel him...here," she said, and put her hand on her heart.

Reed shook his head. "Excuse my language, but I'm thinking that's a sign of a damned good marriage. You two are to be congratulated on making such a good choice."

Harley nodded, her chin quivering as the Captain walked away. The longer she stood waiting for the men to be evacuated, the lighter her heart became.

Choice?

Maybe. But it wasn't good sense or choice that had first led her to Sam, it had been the champagne. After that crazy ceremony she didn't really remember, then yes, it had been about choices. She'd certainly chosen to stay with him when every instinct she'd had told her it was a mistake. Now they had the beginnings of a wonderful marriage and a baby on the way. Thank God Sam was alive to hear the news.

Suddenly, there was a stirring of people near the doorway and she knew they were bringing them out. She started moving toward the waiting ambulances, desperate to see Sam's face. He would be all right. She knew that just as she'd known he was still alive.

Tisha was there, too. Still crying, but now with tears of relief. Harley moved past her toward the first stretcher.

It was the boy. She looked down, staring past the oxygen mask to the thin, smoke-streaked features of a man/child's face. Pride for what Sam and Charlie had done brought tears to her eyes. No matter how the boy's fate ended, they'd given him another chance at life.

The second stretcher was coming now. She ran to meet it. It was Charlie, his head swathed in bandages.

"Is he going to be all right?" she asked.

"Yes, ma'am," a paramedic said.

She clutched her hands against her middle and turned toward the smoking building, waiting for them to bring out the man who'd claimed her heart.

Seconds passed. Long, interminable seconds in which her breath caught and started a dozen times, and then she saw them coming with the last stretcher and started to run.

"Sam."

He heard her voice and opened his eyes. Harley was running beside him, trying to keep up.

"Junie?"

"I love you, Sam. I almost waited too long to tell you, but I'm telling you now."

Peace settled within Sam in a way he'd never

known. He reached for her hand and she caught it, still moving with the men who'd brought him out.

"Thank you, June Bug."

She started to cry, hiccuping on sobs as she trotted to keep up with the men's longer strides.

"Don't cry, honey," Sam said. "I'm not hurt. Just got a little smoke."

"I'm not crying," Harley said.

Sam wanted to laugh, but his chest was too sore and tight.

"Then you're leaking," he said.

Moments later, the firemen lowered him to the ground beside a waiting ambulance. One of the men patted him on the shoulder.

"I need to get another gurney, then we'll load you up in a couple of seconds, Sam."

"Take your time," Sam said. "I've got all I need right here beside me."

Harley dropped to her knees. Ignoring the streaks of soot and smoke, she laid her cheek against Sam's grimy face.

It took all the strength Sam had, but he got his arms around her neck. His voice was quiet, but the truth of what he said told Harley far more about what he'd gone through than she wanted to know.

"I wasn't sure I'd ever get to do this again," he said.

Harley started to cry.

"Ah, God, Junie, don't cry. You'll have me bawling, too."

She kissed him then, tasting fire and smoke and the man who was her husband.

"Sam?"

"What, honey?"

"I'm going to have your baby."

Shock rocked Sam where he lay. He stared at her in disbelief, gazing at the familiar curves of her mouth, at two very small freckles on the bridge of her nose that she continually denied existed, remembering the way she sighed when he slid inside her, knowing he'd given her all he'd had to give.

He thought of how close he'd come to not hearing this news. Her face blurred, but he quickly blinked away tears.

Ah God.

"Sam?"

He grabbed her hand and pulled it to his lips, almost too moved to speak.

"Thank you, Harley, for giving us a chance."

"Thank me? I should be the one thanking you," she said. "You came after me when I got scared and ran. You loved me when I was afraid to love myself. You're my hero, Sam Clay, now and forever."

He shook his head. "I'm no hero. I'm just a man, and only God in heaven knows how much I love you."

Harley wanted to hug him but was afraid she'd

squeeze a part of his body that was hurt, so she settled for another brief kiss.

"I'm getting you all dirty," Sam said, and pointed to the streak of black that was now on her chin.

Harley shivered. She wanted to strip him naked just to make sure he was unharmed and he was worrying about getting her dirty? If he only knew. Not wanting him to see how close she'd come to coming undone, she made herself smile.

"I've been dirty before. I seem to remember you telling me something about our wedding night and strawberries and champagne."

"That wasn't dirt. That was good, messy sex."

Harley wanted to laugh. The fear she'd lived with all afternoon was almost gone, but it was still too fresh to allow much room for joy.

"Sam?"

"What, honey?"

"When you're well, there's something I want to do."

"Anything," he said.

"I want to marry you again. I don't want to go through life without remembering our vows."

Sam's eyes filled with tears. With a few simple words, Harley had shattered what was left of his control.

"It would be my pleasure," he said.

Harley grinned.

"Oh, yes, Sam, I promise you it most certainly will."

Epilogue

"Harley June, are you sure you want to do this?"

Harley smiled at her mother and patted her cheek as they waited for the minister to appear.

"Yes, Mama, I'm sure."

Marcie made herself smile when she wanted to scream.

"It's just so...so..."

"Tacky. The word is tacky, Mama."

Marcie sighed. "Yes. Well. I'm sure you know what's best."

Harley grinned. Mama had come a long way in the past five months just as they all had. Charlie had suffered a concussion from the fire but had quickly recovered. The boy Sam and Charlie had rescued was

alive and on the road to complete recovery. The baby
she was carrying was healthy and due the day before
Valentine's Day. The way she figured it, she could
afford to cut her Mama some slack.

And she had to admit, the Love Me Tender wedding
chapel left a lot to be desired. It was a cross culture
of architectural nightmares, somewhat between *Little
House on the Prairie* and *The Best Little Whorehouse
in Texas*. Fake flowers hung from rustic beams inside
the small chapel, interspersed among what appeared to
be chasing Christmas lights wound around two fake
pillars near the pulpit. There was a flashing neon cross
over the pulpit, while the pulpit, itself, was draped in
purple satin with a picture of Elvis embroidered on the
front.

Sam stood nearby, his hands in his pockets, deep in
conversation with Harley's dad. The two men had
taken to each other like ducks to water and the coming
attraction of a grandchild had cemented their bond
even more. Ever since the day Sam had taken Marcie
to task for making Harley cry, she deferred to him with
batting eyes and homemade pound cakes, betting on
the philosophy on which she'd been raised to see her
through. If feminine wiles didn't work on a man, feed-
ing him would.

The baby kicked and Harley laid her hand on her
tummy.

"Patience, sweet thing," she said softly. "We're
waiting on the preacher man."

No sooner had she spoken when music began to play. The familiar strains of "Love Me Tender" filled every tiny space inside the room.

"Here we go," Harley said, and patted her mother on the back.

In the midst of the chorus, there was a loud popping sound at the altar and then a large puff of smoke, through which the preacher appeared; complete with black hair and sideburns, and wearing a white satin jumpsuit. He gave his embroidered cape a dramatic flourish, not unlike that of a cast-off vampire and began to sing along with the song.

"Good Lord!" Marcie muttered, and cast a nervous eye at Harley.

"Mother," Harley said warningly.

"I'm just startled, that's all," Marcie said, trying not to glare back at her only child.

Sam caught Harley's eye and winked. Harley stifled a laugh and winked back. So this was what she couldn't remember. No wonder.

"Mother, it's time," Harley said.

Marcie gathered her matron of honor bouquet tightly against her middle and lifted her chin. In that moment, Harley got a glimpse of her great-great-grandmother Devane standing on the steps of her plantation home and slapping General Sherman for riding through her yard. There was something to be said for Southern women besides their gentle speech and impeccable manners. They had backbones made of steel.

Marcie started down the aisle toward the hip-hunching preacher, thinking she should be carrying a gun for protection, not a handful of daisies. To her relief, the song ended and the preacher stilled before she reached the altar. She caught Sam's gaze and then looked at Dewey and sighed. They were actually smiling. It figured. Men had no sense when it came to decorum.

More music swelled within the room as a taped version of "The Wedding March" rocked the walls. They all turned to look up the aisle.

Harley was coming toward them carrying a bouquet of white roses in front of her burgeoning belly. The hem of her pink maternity dress brushed gently against her knees as she walked and Sam's heart swelled inside his throat. At this moment, nothing else mattered. He had it all.

And then Harley was holding his hand and smiling at him as they turned to face the preacher.

The words came and went, the same as they had before, and Harley would later realize she still didn't remember saying her vows to Sam. All she'd seen was the love in his eyes—and all she'd heard was the beating of her heart.

Suddenly, the preacher slapped the Bible down on the pulpit and lifted his arms up to the ceiling.

"I now pronounce you husband and wife," he shouted. "Thankyouver'much."

Suddenly, "You Ain't Nothin' but a Hound Dog,"

blasted from the loudspeakers. The preacher looked wild-eyed and bolted for the back where the sound equipment was housed.

Dewey snorted.

Marcie gasped and dropped her bouquet.

Harley laughed out loud.

Sam took her in his arms and kissed the laughter, trying hard not to cry.

It was the best damned day of his life.

MARRYING A MILLIONAIRE
Dixie Browning

* * *

To Lee.
Love at first sight is no myth.

Dear Reader,

Bits and pieces from different parts of my life came together for this story. Once upon a time I worked briefly in a department store. Ha! Experience! I've painted and decorated furniture; I'll paint anything that doesn't move out of the way.

This past spring I attended a reunion of descendants of the keepers of Hatteras Lighthouse, where a ring of stones from the original base had been engraved with all their names. The circle of stones—our own version of Stonehenge—struck me as a wildly romantic place for a wedding.

Ah, but that would have been too easy, wouldn't it? So I added a younger couple and their ideas of love, threw in a few added elements and ended up with "Marrying a Millionaire." One pair of lovers ends up marrying. Guess which.

See you at the circle,

Dixie Browning

Chapter 1

Grace McCall tilted the newspaper page to the light and studied the picture of a well-dressed man accepting a plaque from the head of a charitable foundation. He really was a handsome man. Was it any wonder he'd starred in an occasional X-rated fantasy?

Pity he was such a stuffed shirt, she thought, setting the can of paint directly on the impressive figure of her employer, Chandler Daye, CEO and chief stockholder of Daye Department Store.

Sitting cross-legged on the floor of what had once been a potting shed, Grace carefully touched her brush to the freehand version of a morning glory vine twining across the front of the chest of drawers, the wooden knobs cleverly disguised as buds. She would have to put at least two coats of clear varnish over the knobs once the paint dried to be sure it didn't rub off with use.

From somewhere inside the house, a door slammed. Next came the sound of a radio turned up full blast. Whatever happened to singers who respected the songwriter's work and at least tried to carry the tune?

Whatever happened to tunes that were worth carrying?

The generational gap strikes again, she thought ruefully.

Leaning back on her elbows on the newspaper-covered floor, Grace admired her handiwork. Over the past few years her style had evolved from stenciled traditional patterns to whimsical freehand designs. "You're good, gal. You're really getting good," she gloated softly.

Over the noise of the CD player, Susie screeched from the back door, "Grace! Gra-ace, I'm home!"

Saturday morning classes were the absolute pits, according to eighteen-year-old Susie, a fashion design student at the local community college. Personally, Grace enjoyed Saturdays. Nearly all her weekends were spent here in the potting shed, painting furniture. Either that or out hunting for more to paint at various flea markets, dumps and yard sales.

"I'm out here," she called back. As much as she loved her much younger half sister, aside from a mutual absentee father, they hadn't a whole lot in common.

"Yuk, this place stinks." Susie, her small nose turned up in disgust at the paint fumes, stood outside, a canned cola in one hand, a candy bar in the other. And that was another thing, Grace told herself. Susie's metabolism could handle any amount of high-calorie abuse. As lean as she was, at thirty-six, Grace had to watch each calorie to see that it didn't end up in an inappropriate place. For the past few years, thanks to her sedentary job, her hips had begun to spread. On someone who had always been reed thin, every additional ounce showed. According to Susie, she looked like a snake that had just swallowed an egg.

Tactful her sister was not.

"So, how'd the project go? Did you get an A?"

"Oh, Gracie, nobody grades like that anymore." The young woman in the skintight leather bell-bottoms and the fake-fur bomber jacket heaved an exaggerated sigh. "Besides, who cares? The class is boring. I mean, anybody who's really serious about fashion design is in New York. Maybe I could, like, you know— transfer my credits?" Susie bit off a big chunk of chocolate, still managing to look wistful with her cheek squirreled out.

Grace shivered and fastened another button on her old flannel-lined denim coat. They'd been down this road before. Evidently they were headed down it again. Every class was boring unless it was centered around Susie McCall. "Honey, we both know New York's out of the question right now." The tuition at the community college was all they could afford, even with Susie working part-time. "Either come in and close the door or go out. I'm freezing in here."

"You need to breathe, don't you? I'm just offering you some fresh air."

It was fifty-three degrees outside. Warmer would have been better for drying paint, but if she was going to get enough pieces together for the huge spring community yard sale, she couldn't wait for warm weather.

"By the way, I'm going out tonight," Susie announced.

"Any details you'd care to share?" Grace sealed up the leaf-green and reached for the small can of the stamen-yellow enamel.

Susie started to toss her candy wrapper away, then shrugged and crammed it into her pocket. How could anyone manage to make a simple shrug look like an exotic dance, Grace wondered. The fact that she practiced in front of a mirror didn't lessen the effect. Susie was…simply Susie. Some people were mature at eighteen—some weren't. It wasn't a value judgment so much as a statement of fact.

"I'm going out with Buck," said Susie, slanting her a look from eyes that were bluer than any morning glory, and nearly as large.

Grace waited. There was a challenge lurking somewhere in the simple declarative statement. Going out was a given. It was Saturday night.

Buck? Susie's friends had names that ended in the letter *I*. Maggi, Timmi, Marci, Patti. Susie occasionally signed her own name that way. Grace never did, preferring the old-fashioned spelling. "Um…football player?" she ventured.

"Buck *Daye*," the curly-haired blonde said impatiently. "And don't tell me I can't, because I'm eighteen years old."

You're also flaky, impulsive and stubborn, Grace wanted to say, but didn't. Ever since her widowed and newly remarried father, Amos McCall, had given her an adorable, golden-haired baby sister, Grace had loved this child—this young woman, she corrected. Grace herself had been barely eighteen at the time, the same age Susie was now.

But had she ever been that young?

She didn't think so.

She'd quickly fallen in love with the infant. Everyone did. From the day Susie had gummed her first wet smile, everyone had exclaimed over how *cute* she was. She'd been a cute toddler, a cute kid, a cute teenager— she was still cute, from her Barbie-doll figure to her mop of chemically enhanced curls, to her turned-up nose and her rosebud lips.

The trouble was, she'd skated by on her looks and bubbling personality for so long, she had never matured beyond a certain point. All Grace's efforts to set

a good example were ignored. Which was hardly surprising. Who would want a skinny female who was
valiantly fighting off the onslaught of middle age as a
role model?

"Am I to assume he's one of the department store
Dayes?" Grace asked dryly. Of course he was. There
weren't that many of them in the area, and they were
all related. "You do realize this is rather awkward for
me, don't you?"

Susie shrugged. "I don't see why. It's not like
Buck's uncle knows who you are. He must have hundreds of people working there at the store, and anyway, like who cares? Nobody pays any attention to all
that old class stuff anymore. Besides—" She broke
off and flashed an engaging grin that would have
melted the stony hearts of the Mount Rushmore quar-
tet. "Oh, Gracie, he's just so-o-o cool! We're going
to this party tonight and I stopped by and bought a
new skirt—it's red leather. It'll go great with my new
boots."

Which meant it was short. Probably barely legal.
Which also meant it was expensive, but Grace couldn't
find the energy to demand that she take it back. Suddenly, she was bone-tired. It was turning colder—
probably going to freeze tonight. She'd have to take
her cans of paint into the kitchen and hope the things
she'd just painted didn't get ruined. She was no chem-
ist. The instructions on the label—at least those that

were large enough to read—recommended painting on a warm dry day.

In January? Get real, as Susie would say.

"That's a pretty rich crowd you're playing with, honey—way out of our league."

"Get real," the younger woman said right on cue. "You'll like him, Gracie, you really will. He's got this smile that shows where he chipped a tooth playing soccer—it's to *die for!*"

"Oh, my, a chipped tooth. That's definitely a basis for a serious relationship," Grace said gravely. Hoping Susie knew she was joking. Communications weren't always easy when sisters were a full generation apart. Especially when one sister was a wildly popular eighteen-year-old and the other was a stodgy thirty-six-year-old whose idea of a good time was scouring the dumps for cast-off furniture.

There were days, Grace thought, when she felt older than dirt. Thirty-six was hardly ancient—she knew plenty of women who were young and vital at fifty, and even sixty and beyond. The trouble was, somewhere along the line she had settled into a rut, opting for security. Now that Susie was practically grown and Grace was free to start living her own life again, she'd forgotten how.

Across town, Chandler Daye dressed for the coming meeting. In this case, it consisted of donning a dark gray suit with a faint pinstripe. He selected a conser-

vative silk tie, knotted it before the mirror and ex-
amined his freshly shaved face.

He looked bored.

He *was* bored. Once every quarter for the past fourteen years, ever since his father's sudden death had
landed the family business squarely on his shoulders,
Chandler had gone through this same drill. Dinner at
Great-Uncle Dockery's mansion—the old man actually called it that—with the entire family in atten-
dance. Great-Aunt Henrietta, Cousin Mortimer, the
twins, Cousins Perry and Patsy—octogenarians, all.

All but Buck, who invariably came up with some
excuse not to attend. One of these days, Chandler told
himself, his young nephew would fall heir to all this.
The store, the stock, the cousins and aunts and uncles.
He hadn't a single doubt that they'd all live on to
hound another generation.

It would do the boy good, though. Having just
turned twenty-one, Buck was old enough to begin settling down. Ever since his parents had been killed by
a drunk driver going the wrong way on a one-way
street, Chandler had done his best to be a steadying
influence. He himself had been only twenty-six when
he'd inherited the store, lock, stock and relatives. That
had quickly knocked the youth right out of him.

He could have sold it, of course. There'd been several interesting inquiries, but with a flock of stock-
holding relatives peering over his shoulder, questioning his every decision because Daye Department Store

was not only their sole source of income but their sole interest in life, he hadn't had the heart to sell out.

So he'd left the Navy and given up his dream of flying small, fast fighter jets off the pitching deck of an aircraft carrier. And, incidentally, of making love to exotic women in exotic ports.

Instead, he'd accepted a lifetime commitment to a cause in which he'd never been particularly interested. As for making love to women, exotic or otherwise, the last time he'd made love to any woman had been nearly a year ago during a retail convention in Detroit, when the executive director of a chain of outlet stores had invited him up to her room to see her brochures.

He yanked the knot of his necktie and grimaced at his face under the thick crop of gray hair. All the Daye men were gray by their fortieth birthday. He was right on schedule. "Daye, you're a real jerk. At the rate you're going, in another few years you'll be staring geezerhood in the face, and what have you got to show for it?"

With that unsettling thought, Chandler Daye jogged down the polished golden oak stairs, collected his briefcase and had one hand on the door when Buck called from the kitchen.

"Hey, Uncle Chan, don't do anything I wouldn't do, y'hear?" He was gnawing on a drumstick. Buck had his own apartment near Research Triangle. He divided his time between there and Chandler's house.

"You wouldn't want to trade places, I guess."

Chandler's jaded look said it all. He was in for a night of unbearable tedium, and both men knew it. "Nah, I guess not."

"Man, you couldn't handle what I've got planned. There's this knockout—this babe—this—"

"Woman," Chandler finished dryly. "Does she have a name?"

"Susie McCall. I mean, she is, like, *wow!*"

"'Like wow' can be hazardous to your health."

"Oh, man, she's not like that. I mean, we don't— you know—"

"Not yet, you mean. Look, just don't forget what I told you."

"Yeah, I know, all the stuff that can happen and all. Look, man, it's not like I'm still a virgin or anything. I'm long past the age of consent, you know."

Yeah, you're twenty-one, spoiled, immature and too damned popular for your own good. Chandler thought it, but had better sense than to say it. Instead, he nodded and left, warily eyeing the dark gray sky. Snow, he wouldn't have minded. Freezing rain was the pits.

"I saved it for you," said Cleo Watson, Grace's closest friend in the billing department at Daye's Department Store. "It" being the business section of the *Durham Herald* that showed tiny head shots of the employees who had recently been promoted or recognized in some way.

Grace's name and face stared back at her. She'd

been recognized for having collected the most pledges for the annual fund drive of a local children's charity. She couldn't afford to give much money, but she was generous with her free time.

"Thanks. Did you see the piece on the front of the business section last Friday?"

"You mean, the picture of his hunkiness accepting that award?"

"His what? Cleo, the man's a stuffed shirt!"

"Yeah, but oh, what that shirt's stuffed with," sighed the fiftyish matron, mother of three, grandmother of two.

Grace laughed, folded the page announcing her small recognition and stuck it in her purse. Not that there was any reason to save it. Susie wouldn't be interested, and there was no one else.

A week later Grace settled in front of her computer, still concerned about the conversation she'd had at breakfast with her sister. Actually, it had been more of a confrontation, if not an outright challenge. Susie had been out past midnight every night for the past week. Being eighteen didn't mean that she couldn't get into trouble, as Grace had reminded her more than once.

"You could get stranded without a ride home."

"Oh, big deal. If I had my own car—"

"We've been over all that before, Susan."

"Fine! Like, I'll call a cab, okay? Besides, I can always get someone to drive me home."

"But what if that someone turns out to be...well, not nice?"

"Gra-ace! Give me some credit."

"I read the newspapers. I listen to the nightly news."

"Well, quit it. It's not healthy." Susie had flashed that irresistible smile at her, and Grace had sighed and surrendered.

"Okay, so I care—so sue me. Stuff happens, honey. I just don't want it to happen to you."

"Stuff happens," Susie teased, laughter dancing in her morning glory-blue eyes. "You've been reading T-shirts again, haven't you?"

The night before that she'd come home at a quarter past three. Grace had been waiting up. Susie, her clothes awry, her lipstick gone, had been highly indignant. "You're bizarre, you know that?" Bizarre was her latest favorite description. The week before it had been "archaic."

"If bizarre means I care what happens to you, then you're right. I am."

"It's embarrassing! Gracie, I'm eighteen years old! I'm an adult, for God's sake!"

"Don't swear."

"Don't swear," the younger woman had mimicked. "Honestly, like this was the—the—fifties, or something! I mean, all those old-fashioned TV families like the—the Mayberries.''

"Mayberry was a place, not a family.''

Susie had flung her new leather coat, charged to Grace's store account, onto the floor. "I don't care! And for your information, Buck and I might just get married, if that's what it takes to spend some—some quality time together!''

"Quality time? Do you mean…in bed?''

Susie shrugged. "At least if we got married, we wouldn't have any old stogie nagging at us for staying out past nine o'clock.''

"That's fogy, not stogie. And three o'clock in the morning is a bit past 9:00 p.m.'' At least she had better sense than to use the classic warning, not while you're living under *my* roof.

"We were just having fun,'' Susie protested. Having gone through belligerence and indignation, she'd reached the sulky stage. She did it so beautifully, complete with damp eyes and trembling lower lip. "You never want me to have any fun. You're just jealous because I'm beautiful and you're not. I mean, can I help it if you're not like, popular? I mean, maybe if you didn't always smell like paint—''

Grace had lain awake for hours that night, wondering when adolescence ended and adulthood began. And just how far a sister's obligation extended. By the time Susie was old enough to think seriously about marriage—threats made in anger weren't to be taken

seriously—Grace would like to think she'd be mature
enough to choose wisely. Susie's mother had not set
a very good example, walking out on her husband and
young daughter, leaving the child to Grace and her
father to care for. Especially as her father had already
been getting...strange. Which might be the reason his
wife had left him.

Not that Grace had anything against lay preachers,
but seven nights a week? Two or three hours a night?
Salvation, maybe, but at what cost?

The light on her phone began blinking, jerking her
back to the present. She grabbed it as if it were a
lifeline. "Ms. McCall, Mr. Daye would like to see you
in his office."

"Me? Are you sure it's me he sent for?" But by
then the connection was broken. "Jerk," she muttered,
standing to peer over the top of her cubicle. "That
was his majesty's secretary. I'm supposed to go upstairs."

"He probably wants to congratulate you for the, you
know—the award and all?"

That was it, Grace thought, relieved. She could do
with a few strokes this morning. Worrying about Susie
and her involvement with that boy was keeping her
awake nights, which was affecting her concentration.
If it had been anyone else—someone settled, older,
with a decent job, it might not be so bad. But she'd
made it her business to check out this Daye fellow,
and from all reports, he was Susie's male equivalent.

A playboy. A party creature. Spoiled rotten, with no visible means of support other than the fact that he was one of *the* Dayes.

The McCall family was dysfunctional enough without help from an outsider.

In all the years Grace had worked at Daye's Department Store, she had never had occasion to go near the executive office, but everyone knew Mr. Daye's secretary's reputation. The woman was a shark. Rumor had it she was in love with her boss, even though she had to be at least ten years his senior.

Pausing outside the elevator, she touched her hair, brushed away an imaginary wrinkle in her gabardine skirt and glanced at her fingernails. Purple and green. No amount of scrubbing with lemon juice or paint remover would get the last bit of color from her cuticles, it simply had to wear off.

The woman seated behind a French Provençal desk glanced up and offered her a smile that revealed beautifully capped teeth, but no real warmth. Grace felt the first prickle of uneasiness.

"Take a seat, Ms....uh, McCall. Mr. Daye will be with you in a moment."

Stiffly, Grace lowered herself onto one of the three chairs. What if she wasn't about to be congratulated for being a model citizen—for reflecting well on Daye's Department Store? What if she was about to be fired? Granted, her computer skills might lag behind some of the younger clerks, but for the past seven years she'd managed pretty darn well for someone who had never wanted to work in an office in the first place.

For as long as she could remember, Grace had wanted to be an artist. She had drawn and painted, her mind on some distant future when she could afford to study art, to buy artist-quality materials instead of the cheaper student grade.

Well. That was then. This is now, she thought as half a dozen scenarios, each less welcome than the last, played through her mind.

It couldn't have been more than a few minutes, but it felt like hours when the piranha in the silk suit said, "He'll see you now, Ms. McCall."

Grace bounced out of her seat, touched her hair again, and brushed the same imaginary wrinkle from her skirt. She curled her fingers into her palms and pushed open the door with her knuckles.

He was seated behind a massive desk. He didn't bother to glance up. Oh, my. What was that old saying about snow on the mountains? There was plenty of fire in *that* particular furnace, she'd be willing to bet on it.

Was he really studying something on his desk, or was he deliberately trying to make her nervous? He didn't have to try very hard.

Back in the days when she used to be called into the principal's office, usually for not paying attention in class—she'd always had a tendency to daydream—

she'd have been fighting tears by now. For some reason, she had never dealt well with authority figures.

He still didn't look up, which gave her plenty of time to study the man she'd seen only at a distance before today. He was well worth the study.

According to the office grapevine, he'd just turned forty. His hair looked older; the rest of him—at least what she could see—appeared far younger. He had the kind of looks that would be right at home on the cover of a men's fashion magazine. Too masculine to have modeled for any of Michelangelo's sculptures. Although...

Just stop that right now, McCall.

"Ms. McCall? Sit down, please."

It was clearly an order, even with the please tacked on. She sat, knees together, feet together, hands curled in her lap to hide her stained fingernails.

"I assume you know why I sent for you."

"I do? I mean...is it about the Children's Fund?" Grace felt as if a chunk of cold concrete had settled in the pit of her stomach.

"More the children's fun," he said, meeting her eyes and smiling grimly.

She waited. Should she know what he was talking about? Whatever it was, he obviously wasn't happy about it.

While she waited for him to connect the dots, she couldn't help but notice his remarkable eyes. Pale gray with black rims. Pity his smile never got that far. He was looking at her as if wondering if he'd seen her somewhere before…like on a wanted poster in the post office.

Chapter 2

"It might interest you to know that my nephew won't come into his money until he's twenty-five years old." The statement came out of the blue.

His nephew. "Buck Daye?"

He didn't respond, just pinned her to the wall with those cool gray eyes that matched his hair. With his unseasonable tan, the combination was lethal. "I believe your, uh—sister—has shown some interest?"

Steady, reliable, unflappable Grace, oiler of troubled waters, came to a fast boil. "I *beg* your pardon." She surged to her feet. "Are you implying that my sister is interested in your nephew's money?"

The look he shot her could almost have been called admiring if it weren't for those iceberg eyes. "Bingo," he said softly.

"For your information, my sister is not only beautiful, she's—she's—" Grace scrambled for something to show her sister in a better light. Sensible? Hardly. Hardworking? That might be a stretch. Ambitious wouldn't cut it, either. At the moment her ambitions were to be an actress, a fashion designer, or to marry a rich man. "She also happens to be wildly popular. It's no wonder your nephew is interested, but you can tell him for me, he'll have to take a number and wait if he wants to date my sister."

Oh, Lord, she'd just perjured herself. Maybe not perjury, which had to do with courts, but she had deliberately misled, which was just as bad in her book. The two had been seeing each other for at least two weeks, maybe longer.

The maddening man continued to stare at her as if she were something on a slide under a microscope. Biting her tongue, Grace said with what she considered commendable dignity, "If there's nothing more, Mr. Daye, I'll get back to work."

She made it as far as the door, congratulating herself for not taking a swing at him for his insulting insinuation. At the door she turned. Regally, she said, "Oh, and by the way—tell your nephew my sister is supposed to be in no later than one o'clock. She's still a student, you know."

Chandler leaned back in his black leather ergonomic chair and stared at the paneled door after she'd closed it behind her.

Quietly. Far more effective, when he knew damned well she'd wanted to slam it. He didn't know what he'd expected—big, bleached hair, too much makeup. A woman who looked like the hustler he half suspected her of being. It would be a damned shame to bleach and tease that thick, dark crop of hair. If she wore makeup—and of course, she must—it was subtle. But the quick color that had stained her elegant cheekbones was nature's own.

She was good, he'd hand her that. If the two McCall sisters were up to something—and odds were better than even they were—then she was damned good!

Slowly, he reached for the phone. "Nancy, get Dick Lennon on the line, will you?"

"The investigator?"

"Security firm. I've been, uh—thinking it's time we upgraded our system around here."

Well, hell. The blasted woman had him lying to his own secretary!

Grace whipped through a morning's work, her fingers flying faster and unfortunately, more inaccurately than ever on the keyboard. "Oh, darn," she muttered for the third time after reversing a set of numbers. Dyslexic, she wasn't. Disgruntled, she most assuredly was. The very idea of hinting that her sister was only interested in a man for his money. Susie loved everyone, and everyone loved Susie. Grace hadn't lied when she'd told Chandler Daye that her sister was wildly popular. She'd always been popular with both sexes and all ages, from the cradle straight on. There wasn't an unkind bone in her body.

Careless, perhaps, but never deliberately unkind. She never held a grudge for more than a few hours. Little Susie Sunshine. That's what Grace used to call her.

It was only to be expected that Susie liked to dress well. If she'd been six inches taller, and with a smaller bust, she could easily have been a model. As it was, she helped pay her own tuition by working part-time at the college, but both women depended on Grace's discount at the store for clothing.

Occasionally Susie would charge something at another store, one that catered to her age group. Daye's suited Grace just fine, because her needs were modest, her tastes conservative, but at Susie's age, modest and conservative were to be avoided at all costs. Understandably, she preferred to dress like all her friends, with the right look and the right label. Oh, yes—labels were extremely important. They even wore them on the outside, to prove they were…well, something or other. Conformists, if nothing else.

Not for the first time, Grace wondered what kind of person Buck Daye really was. Handsome? That was a given. Popular, naturally. But what were his core values? Twenty-one was awfully young in a man. In her estimation, a man didn't even begin to get ripe until he passed thirty.

Too many young men tried to prove their manhood or macho-hood, or whatever it was called, by drinking too much, driving too fast and experimenting with things best left alone. He could outgrow all that. Most men did, sooner or later. Most, but not all.

Grace didn't envy parents of young children, trying to raise them to be decent citizens in spite of the kaleidoscope of temptations out there.

There'd been temptations when she was growing up, too. She'd been born smack-dab in the middle of the notorious sixties, after all. Like so many young men of his generation, her father had protested the war, but once he'd gotten married he'd settled down and gone to work on a tobacco farm to support his family.

Two children and two wives later, he'd ended up becoming an evangelist.

As for Grace, she had gone directly from being a shy schoolgirl to a dull-as-mud spinster. Or to put it in more PC terms, an independent woman of a certain age.

She returned her thoughts to the problem at hand. Susie had been seeing Buck Daye for almost a month and had yet to bring him home to meet her family. Not that she brought many of her friends home. It wasn't, as she'd assured Grace, that she was ashamed of where they lived, but so many of her friends lived in exclusive neighborhoods, attended private schools and belonged to country clubs.

The closest thing to a country club Grace could claim was a brief membership in the 4-H club back in junior high. Their house was a small brick bungalow built in the late thirties. Any possible charm it possessed was in the landscaping. Flower seeds were cheap, and Grace had taken cuttings, with or without permission, from all the neighbors and even a few public gardens. As vices went, she considered hers harmless enough.

By the time Grace got home from work she was still fuming about her boss's implication that Susie was nothing more than an opportunist. Obviously, he suspected Grace of putting her up to it, hoping to use her connection to the family business.

Susie was already there, sprawled on the sofa, a bag of popcorn open on the floor beside her. She was watching one of the raunchier channels on television, and Grace restrained herself from mentioning all the really wonderful programs on the Discovery and the History channels.

"Hi, hon—you're home early."

"I hate that dress on you," Susie said by way of greeting. "It makes you look old."

"Then I'd better hurry up and change into my blue jeans. Did you start anything for supper?"

"I thought we might order pizzas."

"I have some in the freezer. We can add other things on top."

"I like take-out better."

"I like grilled salmon and fresh asparagus better, too, but we'll settle for store-bought pizzas, okay?"

Susie shrugged and helped herself to another handful of cheese-flavored popcorn, scattering a few kernels on the floor. "Whatever. I'm going out later tonight, anyway."

"No homework?"

"Gra-ace," the younger woman protested. "I'm not a school kid."

Grace knew better than to comment. Stepping out of her shoes, she began unbuttoning her taupe gabardine dress. "Buck again?"

"We're going to a party. There'll be plenty to eat there. But first he's got to go by and see his uncle." Susie rolled her eyes expressively.

The gesture was easy enough to translate. Relatives were a drag. "Honey, you're not actually serious about him, are you?"

"Get real, I'm only eighteen. Why settle down before you have to?" Susie said airily. "I mean, like you're only young once, right?"

Eighteen, the magical age. It could be manipulated to suit the occasion. "Like, true," Grace said dryly.

Susie responded with that irresistible smile. "Why didn't you ever get married, Grace? You're almost pretty when you fix yourself up."

"Gee, don't spread it on so thick, I might not be able to scrape it all off. As for why I never married,

I already have a family. What would I need with another child?"

Susie grinned. "I don't know—like, maybe because
you did such a terrific job raising me, you want to try
for an encore?"

Before Grace could think of a suitable comeback,
her sister went back to watching some young hunk
with a greased body and washboard abs shake his
booty. His tootie? Whatever they called it now, Grace
thought, oddly depressed.

Collecting her shoes, she headed down the hall to
the bedroom. Why *had* she never married? It wasn't
for want of opportunity. She'd been engaged twice,
but by then her father had taken up missionary work
and gone overseas, leaving her with a volatile teenager
to raise. Neither of the men she'd been dating at the
time—nice men, really—had been interested in taking
on a ready-made family.

And she had to admit, she hadn't been particularly
heartbroken either time. Instead she had willingly
taken on the job of providing a wholesome role model
for a sister who would far rather choose her own. As
if any teenaged girl in her right mind would chose to
pattern herself after a dull-as-mud office worker when
there were dozens of pop stars wearing barely-there
bras and tight, low-cut jeans, competing for the adu-
lation of the twelve-to-twenty set.

As soon as Grace changed, she went out to the
kitchen, turned on the oven and got two small cheese

pizzas from the freezer. While the oven was heating, she dashed out to open the door to the shed. Might as well get some fresh air in there before she went to work. Last weekend's yard sale find had been a six-drawer chest in perfect condition except for several missing drawer pulls, layers of ugly dark varnish and several cigarette burns. She'd been able to buy it for twenty-five dollars. By the time she was finished, she could probably sell it for at least two hundred. Antiqued green, she thought as she chopped onion onto the pizzas and reached for a jar of banana peppers. With a simple scroll design and the solid brass drawer pulls she'd rescued from another piece that was too far gone to restore.

Half an hour later, Susie bounced up from the table, leaving three-quarters of her pizza on her plate. "Gotta run. I'm meeting Buck at the mall. May I take your car?"

"He could have picked you up here."

"I'll fill the tank," Susie offered, knowing full well that it would only need a gallon or so.

"Don't be out too late, hon. I worry."

"Gra-ace, I'm eighteen years old," Susie said for the umpteenth time.

"And have been for all of a month and a half. Give me time—I'll get used to your being so decrepit."

Susie slid a kiss off her sister's forehead, grabbed her keys and hurried outside. A moment later when Grace heard her seven-year-old tan Chevy scratch off on the graveled driveway, she closed her eyes in a silent prayer. *Daddy, you'd better put in a good word for your baby where it counts. I'm not sure I can do this job by myself.*

The next morning, when an unnatural hush fell over the office, Grace glanced up from her computer. And up and up and up, past navy worsted with a fine pinstripe, a bronze-and-navy striped tie and a plain white shirt. Lord, the man was handsome! Never mind he was maddeningly arrogant, suspicious and what Susie called an old stogie. Sensing his approach, she lowered her face and pretended to work.

"Ms. McCall, I'd like to talk to you about—" Suddenly, every face in the office was turned their way. The silence was deafening. "—about the company picnic."

The company picnic was in May. This was only late January.

"In my office, if you please."

The chunk of concrete settled in the pit of her stomach again. The moment he left, Cleo was around the wall, grinning from ear to ear. "Anything you want to confess, girlfriend?"

"I don't *know* anything to confess, and stop grinning like that! If I don't come back in ten minutes, call nine-one-one."

"That bad, huh?"

Grace's shoulders fell. "'Fraid so. I think I'd better dust off my resume, just in case.''

Sympathetic eyes followed her as she rose, closed out the file she'd been working on and headed for the elevator. If she possessed a suit of armor, she'd be buckling it on about now. As she didn't, she touched her hair. Not that any amount of touching would help. She had thick, unruly hair the color of polished walnut. Not so much as a faint glint of auburn. Permanents made it unmanageable, so she indulged herself with a really good cut every six weeks, rationalizing that she saved enough to afford it. Susie spent a fortune on perms, coloring, highlighting and maintenance.

Her dress was okay—nothing special, but then, she didn't need anything special to sit in a cubicle all day in front of a workstation. As usual, her nails were paint-stained, but dammit, she hadn't asked for this interview. If he was offended, he could just—

No, he couldn't. She wasn't about to let herself be fired just because her sister happened to be dating his nephew. Not in this enlightened day. There were government agencies that dealt with unfair practices in the workplace.

Employees' picnic, my foot, Grace thought as she stepped off the elevator and greeted the secretary's piranha smile with one of her own that was every bit as false. "Shall I go right on in?"

"Door's open," the woman said grudgingly. She obviously took her job as keeper of the gate seriously.

Grace enjoyed the minor triumph of breezing past her into the inner sanctum.

This time he didn't make her cool her heels by pretending to be busy. "Come in, Ms. McCall. Have a seat."

She took her time choosing a chair, sat and carefully crossed her ankles. Never show fear in the face of the enemy—she'd heard it all her life.

Or was it never look a strange dog in the eyes? Her defensive skills weren't up to par, mostly because she'd so rarely needed to use them.

"I took the liberty of looking into your sister's, uh—affairs."

Grace came up out of the chair in a single flowing movement. "You did *what?*"

"What did you expect, Ms. McCall, when a girl of your sister's, uh—means, goes after a man of my nephew's caliber?"

Her green-tinged fingernails tightened into her palms. Struggling to get a grip on her temper, she glared at a dead fish that had been mounted and hung on the wall. Not until the urge to strangle the man with her bare hands began to subside did she sit back down. She took another deep breath. At this rate she was going to hyperventilate.

He was obviously waiting. So let him wait. When she was good and ready, she said calmly, "That is the most insulting, outrageous thing I have ever heard, Mr.

Daye. Susie is too young to *go after,* as you so delicately put it, anyone.''

"She's eighteen, I believe."

"Just barely. She's young for her age." Young in some ways. Older than Grace in others.

"Old enough to know what she's doing, I suspect."

"What about your nephew? Is he underage? Is he so clueless he can't defend himself against—against unwelcome advances?"

"It doesn't work that way, Ms. McCall, and I suspect you know it. Buck's only twenty-one. In a boy, that's practically adolescent. At any age men can be easily fooled, and your sister, I believe, is considered…fairly attractive?"

"I told you that. Look, we've already covered this same territory. Why did you call me up here again?" In other words, why was he badgering her with the same old accusations? "And the word is beautiful, Mr. Daye, not just fairly attractive. And smart. And—and popular. And sweet. I told you the other day that everyone who's ever met my sister adores her. Ask any of her friends. Ask your nephew," Grace said triumphantly. "Or is he too dimwitted to—"

"No need for name-calling, Ms. McCall," Chandler Daye said quietly.

Oh, he was a smooth one, all right, Grace fumed. With that thick crown of pewter-colored hair and those clear silver eyes. And that perfectly gorgeous tanned face. Even furious, she couldn't take her eyes off him.

"What do you want me to do, forbid her to see him?" she asked when she could harness her temper enough to speak calmly. "You know what they say about forbidden fruit."

"You're right, it would probably be counterproductive. I tried bribery by offering Buck a couple of weeks at his favorite ski lodge in Colorado."

"And?"

"And he asked if he could take your sister with him," he replied with a rueful smile. This time the smile reached his eyes. Fleetingly. "Ever done any fishing, Ms. McCall?"

She shook her head. Fishing for minnows in New Hope Creek probably didn't count.

"Trying to manage a pair of headstrong, hormone-driven youngsters is roughly comparable to hooking into a fifty-pound red drum on ten-pound test line. Using a fly rod."

Grace sighed. She had a pretty good idea what he meant. She was no happier about the situation than he was. Susie was entirely too young to consider marriage, but that was hardly the worst thing that could happen if she got in over her head.

"I'll try to talk to her, Mr. Daye. I can't promise anything, though."

He stood, indicating that the meeting was over. "You do that, Ms. McCall. Believe me, it would be to everyone's advantage."

In other words, Grace inferred, she was to warn her

sister off the precious Daye heir. She bristled again, but held her tongue. Just barely.

Chandler watched her leave, only the swirl of skirts around her shapely calves offering an indication of her true feelings. Why *had* he called her up here to go over the same questions they'd already covered? Because he was a glutton for punishment?

He'd done it without thinking. He *never* acted without thinking. Even so, he considered he'd handled the interview about as well as anyone could. Maybe he was losing it.

Or maybe he was just envious....

At Buck's age, he'd been pretty wild, too. A young Navy flier in training to save the world, having himself a hell of a good time while he was at it. Then his father had suffered his first stroke. Seven months later, he'd had another one. Three years later, Chandler had inherited the store.

From time to time he still thought about the life he might have led, given a choice. But not often. One of the hard lessons he'd had to learn was that indulging in what-ifs was counterproductive. What was...*was*.

He opened the folder lying on his desk. Dick Lennon, friend, security expert and private investigator, was checking into the McCall sisters' background. Nothing particularly surprising so far...father a tobacco farmer turned preacher, lost wife number one, remarried, lost wife number two, joined up with a missionary group and went overseas, leaving behind two daughters, ages thirty-one and thirteen at the time. Hadn't been back in several years, although he still retained his U.S.A. citizenship.

Not much of interest about the older sister. Engaged twice, once to a medical student, once to a software designer. Both engagements had ended amicably. Both men, since married, spoke highly of her. Even more telling, so did their wives. She picked up old furniture at yard sales and thrift shops, refurbished it and resold it at a profit.

Good for her, Chandler mused. While he prided himself on paying top salaries, in retail, even the top rates were comparatively low.

Funny thing, he thought, gazing unseeingly out the window at a graying sky...he couldn't recall the last time he'd been as intrigued by any woman, and she wasn't even—

That is, she wasn't really...

Yeah, well. Maybe his social life needed ratcheting up a few degrees.

Placing the report in his personal file, he considered the younger woman. Susan Jean McCall was a student at a nearby community college. Evidently, Grace hadn't exaggerated. The girl was popular with both sexes, young and old alike. Not even the faculty had anything to say against her other than the fact that she wasn't particularly studious.

Chandler had a pretty solid suspicion, based more on experience than evidence, that the younger sister was out to snare herself a wealthy husband. The older one, too, for all he knew.

Good luck to them both, he thought wryly—only not in his backyard.

Oddly enough, Chandler found his thoughts returning to Grace McCall more than once during a day that was fraught with the usual irritations, mostly minor, one or two fairly major. The fact that he thought of her now as Grace surprised him. Funny how quickly she'd become a real person in her own right instead of merely a means of protecting his nephew.

Grace McCall. Thirty-six and single. Hardly beautiful, but certainly attractive. Good hair, direct eyes— nice speaking voice, well modulated, even when she was in fighting mode.

Her hands, though, could use some attention. Hadn't she ever heard of rubber gloves?

Three times during the following week, Grace glanced up from her computer to find Chandler Daye standing directly behind her. Each time her fingers froze and her normally cool, sensible brain blew a fuse.

Oh, he always had some excuse, but she didn't believe him, not for a minute. He was harassing her.

"Just happened to be passing the office and thought I'd look in and see if there was anything, um…" He let it drop, but they both knew what he meant.

The third time it happened, Cleo had teased her unmercifully.

"He's got the hots for you, girl. Go for it!"

"Hots, my foot, I'm tempted to reported him to the police," Grace grumbled.

"For what? Honey, if that's harassment, I'll take a large helping. That is one gorgeous dude. Kind of on the pale side for a lady of my persuasion, but mm-mm!"

He was more than gorgeous, that was part of the problem. How did a compass describe magnetic north? No matter how much she tried to put him out of her mind, he refused to go. Dammit, last night she'd even dreamed about him!

Oh, he was always perfectly polite, only Grace knew better by now than to take him at face value. The man was up to something. If he was hoping to catch her diverting company funds into her own account, he was flat out of luck. She was tempted to quit and find another job, but she couldn't afford to, not after working at Daye's for seven years. Until Susie left school and found a full-time job of her own, they needed the money as much as they needed the discount and the store-wide sales that were open to the employees a day before they opened to the public.

Now, if only Daye's would open a grocery department...

Grace was still irritated when she got home that evening. Not that Chandler Daye had said anything more pointed than, ''Morning Ms. McCall. How's that sister of yours?''

Still, it had been enough to ruin her whole day, knowing that what he really meant was, had she talked Susie out of setting her sights on his nephew?

Or rather, his nephew's trust fund. Grace would be the first to admit that her sister was materialistic, but she was certainly no predator. Like most girls her age, she liked nice things and enjoyed having a good time. What was so wrong with that? From all reports, his nephew was no paragon of mature virtues, either.

Supper was cooking. That was the first hint that something was in the air. Susie was many things, but domestic she was not.

''Hi, hon. We're having pizza again?'' The boxes were out on the counter, already opened.

''I thought you'd be glad. I mean, the chicken and all that other gunk in the freezer has to be thawed first, right? I just got home a little while ago.''

Grace waited a moment for the other shoe to fall. When it didn't, she turned the oven up from three-fifty to four-fifty and went into the bedroom to change out of her work clothes into her paint clothes. The last time Susie had volunteered to cook supper had been three weeks ago, when she'd shattered the budget by charging those horribly expensive boots to Grace's credit card.

Over pizza that was loaded with strange things and

burned black on the edges, Grace waited. It was coming—something major, to judge by the way her sister avoided her eyes.

Finally, Grace pushed away her plate full of burned crusts. "Want to tell me about it? Whatever it is, you'll probably feel better to get it off your chest."

Chapter 3

"We're going to get married. Buck and me."

"Oh, no. No way." For once, Grace didn't bother to correct her sister's grammar.

Susie flung down her napkin and flounced to her feet. "I knew you'd say that, I just *knew* it!"

"Sit down." Grace glared. Susie continued to sulk. "Sit down, Susan, and have the courtesy of telling me what this is all about."

"I just told you what it's all about, we're going to get married."

"Why?"

"Why?" Susie's arms flew out in a dramatic gesture. She had dramatic gestures down to a fine art. "Like, why does anybody get married? Because we love each other, that's why! And because you make such a big deal of it if I don't come home at eight o'clock every night!''

"That's not true. Have you thought about where you're going to live? What does Buck do for a living? You do realize, don't you, that I've never even met the—the man?'' She'd started to say "boy," but that would have been a major mistake.

"He doesn't have to *do* anything, he's like, got the store. And for your information, he's got this humongous trust fund.''

"Lovely," Grace retorted. "Is that the big attraction?''

"Gra-ace! Buck can't help it that he's like, rich. Does that mean he has to be a monk or something? I know lots of rich men that get married. Lots of times, too.''

"And why do you think that is?''

"Well, like maybe because they fall in love lots of times. How do I know? But Buck's different.''

Grace sighed. There was such a thing as beating a dead horse. "All right, suppose you do get married, what's he going to do until his trust fund becomes available? Who'll pay the rent? You? Who'll buy groceries?''

"Oh, get *real*. At least we won't have to paint cheap, junky furniture for a living.''

Before Grace could swallow the hurt, Susie dropped to her knees and laid her head in her sister's lap. "Oh,

Grace, I didn't mean that. Honestly, I think the stuff you paint is—I mean, like at least it's different.''

Grace laughed past the lump in her throat.

"Didn't Daddy marry your mama when he was only eighteen, and she was even younger than that?''

"Yes, and look how that turned out,'' Grace said dryly. She still remembered the noisy battles before her mother had died of an aneurysm.

"Well, but he was a lot older when he married my mother—they both were—and look how *that* turned out. Age doesn't have anything to do with it.''

"Honey, you know the statistics.''

Falling back on her knees, Susie stared at her, blinking those impossibly blue eyes. With a face like a troubled angel, who could resist her, Grace wondered. That was the root of the problem.

"Buck and I aren't statistics, we're—we're *us*.''

"Has Buck talked to his uncle yet?''

"He's going to tell him tonight.''

Grace took a deep breath and puffed out her cheeks. Oh boy. Maybe she wouldn't go to work tomorrow. She'd never in her life called in sick unless she really was, but there was always a first time.

Across town, Chandler Daye paced the floor, pausing every few rounds to glare at his nephew. "You're too young.''

"Who says?'' Buck shot back.

"*I* say, dammit!''

"Dad was only twenty-four when he and Mama got married."

Taking a deep breath and flexing his shoulders, Chandler tried a different tactic. "How much do you know about this…young woman?"

"I know I'm like, you know—crazy about her. I know she's smart and ambitious and beautiful and I'm the luckiest man alive if she'll have me."

"Are you sleeping with her?"

Handsome Buckridge Daye, the absolute coolest dude in Durham County, blushed like a twelve-year-old caught with a copy of *Playboy*. Chandler took it as a good sign. At least the boy could still be embarrassed. "Hey, man, she's on the pill. We're careful."

Did Grace know? Chandler wondered. Of course she did—she'd probably been the one to advise her. He didn't know if he was relieved or disappointed. Both, he guessed. Obviously he was spending far too much time with a bunch of octogenarian relatives and not enough with his own peers, if he could be shocked at the idea of sex between two consenting adults. These days, abstinence was considered a novel theory, even among school kids. *Particularly* among school kids.

"Are you seeing her tonight?"

"We're going to this party over at Jimmy's."

Jimmy being the youngest son of a state senator. Chandler happened to know—he'd made it his business to know—that it was a pretty wild bunch, but probably no wilder than the one he himself had run with at that age. "We'll talk about this later," he said grimly.

As threats went, it was pretty lame, but it was the best he could do without making things worse.

Grace did her best sanding when she was upset. At the rate she was going, she'd be down to bare wood in no time.

Married? Susie was nowhere near ready for marriage. If that boy thought she was ready to take on the responsibility of a family, then that only proved how little he knew. What her sister was, was sweet, spoiled and about as mature as the average fifteen-year-old. Grace had to take responsibility, as she'd been the sole guiding influence for the past five years since both parents had abdicated their duty. Even before that, as she'd been a willing baby-sitter. So maybe she was inclined to be overprotective. Raising a child under any circumstances was a scary proposition. When that child happened to be both immature and totally irresponsible, it was impossible not to worry.

She sanded and fumed, paused to change to a finer grit and sanded some more, thinking of arguments that might make an impression. The skyrocketing divorce rate? In the good old days—or the bad old days, depending on your perspective—couples married for better or worse. Even when it actually came to worse, they were far more apt to stick it out.

Which might or might not be the best course, Grace
conceded. The trouble was, there weren't any one-
size-fits-all answers. Look at the examples in her own
family. Susie took after her mother. Iris had been
sweet, pretty and totally self-centered. Why she had
ever married a dirt-poor farmer with an adolescent
daughter was still a mystery. Although Amos McCall
had been strikingly handsome, even Grace recognized
that. He'd passed on his good looks to his youngest
daughter.

Grace had taken after her own mother. Not exactly
homely, just...ordinary.

Lapsing into a daydream in which her drab brown
hair turned to a rich auburn, her eyes turned emerald-
green instead of plain brown, and she magically went
from an A-cup to a C-cup, Grace continued to sand.

At first she thought what she was hearing was thun-
der. Lightning wasn't unheard of in early February,
but the weatherman hadn't mentioned the possibility
of thunderstorms.

A moment later she realized someone was pounding
on the front door of the house. "I'm out here," she
yelled through the window she left cracked for venti-
lation. Probably the paperboy, collecting for the week.
Or the neighbor from whose Cape jasmine bush she'd
borrowed a few more cuttings last week. Who could
blame her when the things rooted so ridiculously easy?

Before she could uncoil from her cross-legged position on the floor, the door was flung open and Chan-

dler Daye glared at her through the opening. Catching his breath, he stepped back. "This place needs airing out," he informed her.

"Don't come in if it bothers you." Oh, great, he *would* have to catch her in her baggy, paint-stained clothes, with dusty hair and filthy hands.

"Breathing these fumes—all this dust—it's not healthy."

"Thanks for your concern. I didn't know you cared." Sarcasm wasn't her style. She only resorted to it when she was acutely uncomfortable. In her cluttered old shed, wearing a three-piece suit and striped silk tie, he looked as out of place as a racehorse in a pigpen.

"Dammit, Grace, do you know what those kids are up to?"

"You mean getting married?"

Propping the door open, he stepped warily inside, looked around for a clean place to sit and gave up. Bracing his well-shod feet apart, he crossed his arms over his chest. "Well, what are you going to do about it?"

Moi, she wanted to say, but didn't because faux sophisticated responses also weren't her style. A firm believer in plain speaking, she didn't even have a style. "Talk to your nephew, he's the one who proposed."

Actually, she was only assuming that. Susie could easily have lured him into it.

"Look, do we have to stay out here? Could we go someplace where we can breathe and talk this thing over?"

Still seated on the floor, a sanding block in one hand, a paint-stained rag in the other, Grace looked up at the man—and up, and up. Tall and lean, he looked as if he spent his days involved in some active, sun-drenched sport instead of sedately seated behind a desk.

As gracefully as she could manage—which wasn't very—she scrambled to her feet and said, "Come on, then. Now that you've seen my shed, the house probably won't come as any big shock."

Actually, it wasn't all that bad, for what it was. And what it was, was tiny, old and cheap. She had some nice furniture, things she'd picked up and refinished. The sofa wasn't among them. That was pure thrift shop, with a ready-made slipcover that didn't quite fit.

"Have a seat," she said grudgingly. "The paint's dry." She indicated an oak captain's chair that was by far the most comfortable chair she owned.

"How long have you known?" he demanded.

"About their plans? No longer than you have, at a guess."

"I mean that they're sleeping together."

Seated on the ottoman she'd reupholstered in blue denim, Grace leaned over and covered her cheeks with stained palms. "Do we have to talk about this?"

"I think it's time someone did."

"They're both of age," she reminded him. "These days they're probably taught Sex-Ed in grade school."

"Barely. What, it doesn't bother you? That they could end up getting pregnant and ruining their lives over some crazy infatuation?"

"How do you know it's only infatuation?" Before he could answer, she exclaimed, "Of course it bothers me! You think I want my sister to have to marry some—some empty-headed playboy whose idea of a good time is seeing how fast he can drive without getting pulled over by the highway patrol?"

He jumped up and began pacing. There wasn't room to pace. When he bumped against a table, threatening her fake Tiffany lamp, they both reached out to catch it at the same time. Their hands touched and Chandler jumped back as if he'd been burned. From the way he glared at her, you'd think she'd deliberately staged the encounter.

"You think I want my nephew to marry some flea-brained gold digger?"

That did it. Burned the last shred of insulation clean off her temper. "Listen, you—you—" Not usually given to profanity, she couldn't come up with a suitable description. "My sister might not be a straight-A student, but that doesn't mean she doesn't have a perfectly good brain! And for your information, the term gold digger went out with women's suffrage. As you would know if you weren't a dried-up, stick-in-the-mud, stuffed shirt *reactionary!*"

They were both breathing hard. All she could see was those iceberg eyes of his, glaring at her. All she could smell was the faint whiff of some crisp, masculine scent, mingled with the smell of paint remover.

When his gaze dropped to her mouth, she lowered her eyes to his lips, half expecting to see them form the words, "You're fired."

Instead, he said gruffly, "Go get cleaned up. I'll take you out to dinner and we'll talk about this—this problem, in a calm, civilized manner."

"I've already dined. Thank you," she said, trying for haughty but failing miserably. She wasn't dressed for haughty.

"Yeah, I see," he mocked, glancing through the opening to the kitchen, where three quarters of a burnt pizza remained to be thrown out.

"That's—that's for the possums," she informed him. Normally, she cleared the table as soon as a meal was over, but tonight she'd been too upset. She'd felt the urgent need to sand.

"You shouldn't feed wild animals, it encourages them to invade the neighborhood."

"So? They're entitled. We invaded their neighborhood first. Besides, possums are God's creatures, too. They deserve to eat."

He shook his head slowly. It occurred to her that aside from looking stunningly sexy in a well-bred way, he also looked tired. And worried. Not to mention larger than life and twice as handsome. Seeing him at the store was one thing. Seeing him in her own living room was a little too personal for comfort.

"Go scrub your hands and brush the sawdust out of your hair, Grace. We need to talk. I figure in a public place, we might manage to get through a productive discussion without actually coming to blows."

The restaurant was obviously one of those hideaway places known only to a privileged clientele. Chandler Daye was greeted by name and led immediately to a secluded table for two. On the way, he nodded to a few other diners, but didn't stop to speak. Or to introduce her.

Embarrassed, probably. The thought stung. If she did say so herself, she cleaned up pretty darn well when she took the time to do more than run a comb through her hair and put on tinted lip balm.

Tonight she'd made him cool his heels while she'd showered off any lingering hint of paint remover. Then she'd blow-dried her hair and palmed on a dab of the stuff that was supposed to make it behave, but never quite did the job.

Dressing had been the easy part. Other than the dresses she wore to work and her Sunday outfit, she didn't have much choice. Black slacks and turtleneck, worn under a gray knit tunic, less than half price with her employee's discount in the January sales. Chic, casual—and he probably knew to the penny how much she'd paid for every stitch she was wearing. Well, shoot. She couldn't win for losing.

They ordered—he suggested the grilled swordfish, and she nodded—and then he got down to business. "Can you talk to your sister?"

"Of course I can talk to my sister. We talk all the time."

"You know what I mean. Buck's nowhere near ready to settle down. When he comes to his senses, he'll realize that. It would be a tragedy if it happens after they're married, with a baby on the way. Lives can be ruined that way."

Irrationally, she wanted to argue, but he was absolutely right. "Me, too. I mean, Susie, too. I want her to wait until she finds the right man. With all due respect—"

"Meaning no respect is due, right?" He smiled. She ignored the impact and forged ahead.

"—with all due respect, your nephew is definitely not the kind of man she needs. He's—"

"Whoa. Back up a minute. With all due respect, what the devil do you know about my nephew? He says he's never even met you."

"He's what—twenty-one? That's the male equivalent of eighteen in a woman. Or is it fifteen? Whatever, it's common knowledge that men mature a lot later than women. That is, if they ever do."

His eyes narrowed, cool gray slits set in a bronzed

face. From a distance he was devastating. Seen at close range, he was…

Fortunately, their dinners were served before she could complete the thought.

Over the delectable grilled seafood they talked about the new spring window displays and about baseball, which she knew a little about and politics, about which she knew nothing. He told her about a recent fishing trip during which he'd caught a swordfish, and she said, "At least when I feed the possums I don't put a hook in their dinner."

"Touché." He chuckled, sending warm ripples throughout her body, then suggested they get back to the subject at hand. "Got any ideas of how you might deflect your sister's interest?"

Grace wanted to suggest he work on his nephew, but there was no point in deliberately antagonizing the man. They were both shooting for the same goal. "Sending her to New York to study fashion design might distract her, but short of that, I can't think of anything."

"So we send her to New York."

Grace bristled. It occurred to her that she'd been doing a lot of that lately. Indignation was causing her far too many sleepless nights, lying awake and thinking of all the things she'd like to say. She was half-tempted to say, Great—be my guest! Instead, she said, "In the first place, we can't afford it, and in the second place—"

"Would you consider accepting a loan?"

Ignoring him, she continued. "In the second place, she's not that good. And if you tell her I said that, I'll never forgive you."

"Word of honor," he said solemnly, but there was a gleam of amusement in those cool gray eyes that she found all but irresistible. "So…any other ideas?"

"What about Buck? Can't you bribe him to leave her alone?"

"Grace, this is a mutual thing we're talking about here. He's not exactly stalking her, for God's sake."

When had they become Grace and Chandler instead of Ms. McCall and Mr. Daye, she wondered. "I know that. All right, let's just accept the fact that they think they're in love and try our best to slow things down until they come to their senses." She sighed as the sheer hopelessness of fighting against raging hormones and human nature struck her.

Chandler studied the woman seated across the small table with growing interest. Was she on the level? He was about ninety-nine percent sure she was. He'd set out this evening to find out if the two women were scheming together, but seeing her in her natural element, he had to conclude that whatever else she was, Grace McCall was genuine. She was definitely not his idea of a gold digger.

A *reactionary?* What the hell had she meant by that crack? He was as progressive as the next man— wouldn't have stayed in business as long as he had against all the mall competition if he hadn't been capable of moving with the times. Big-box stores were closing down every day, and his wasn't all that big a box. Three-and-a-half stories high, it took up less than half a block, including parking.

Reactionary, indeed.

So he drove her home, walked her to the front porch, took her key and opened the door. There was nothing that said a millennium man couldn't have decent manners.

She thanked him and said good-night.

He said it was his pleasure. Surprisingly enough, it was true.

Kiss her, you fool!

Fortunately, he wasn't quite that big a fool. Instead, he said, "Look, maybe something will occur to one of us in the next few days. Let's sleep on it and see what we come up with."

Chapter 4

According to Dick Lennon, the ex-private investigator turned security expert Chandler had hired—actually, he'd only called in a favor, as the two men went all the way back to prep school—Grace McCall had never had so much as a traffic ticket. No big surprise there.

The younger sister hung out with a gang that included dropouts, students and a few recent graduates from Duke and Chapel Hill, including Buck. Little Susie had managed to keep her button nose clean while a few in the group had been busted for possession. Three had been nailed for shoplifting, all of them kids whose parents could buy and sell half the shops in the mall. Did it on a dare, according to the report. Dick had called the shoplifting stunt a rite of passage. Proof of manhood.

Chandler called it proof of jerkhood, but then, what did he know? Holed up in his office, he was starting to think like his great-uncle Dockery.

His thoughts strayed from the younger McCall woman to the older one—something they'd been doing too often lately. Sexy lady. The effect was intensified by the fact that she hadn't a clue about how turned on he was by that prim façade.

Not that he'd mentioned any of that to Dick Lennon when he'd stopped by the office the day before. Instead, he'd said, "Look, if you come up with any bright ideas about how to handle my nephew, speak up, will you?"

"Maybe you could interest him in joining the Navy and seeing the world," Dick replied. "I seem to remember you were headed that way before you turned in your wings and settled for a desk."

"You willing to trust our nation's security to a guy who majored in partying, minored in girls and graduated with top honors in both? I don't think so."

"Hey, he's not a bad kid. From what I hear, he's got great taste in women. The McCall girl's pretty popular." Back to the McCalls. "Nobody, not even her female friends, had anything to say against her. That's pretty rare, you know. Usually in a mixed group like that, you find a few cats. Jealousy, I guess. But this McCall girl's got friends like you wouldn't believe. Ever think Buck might've lucked onto something good?"

"In a few years, possibly," Chandler responded. "Hell, he still eats that pink and blue kid cereal for breakfast. With chocolate milk."

A few minutes later Chandler had seen his friend out, after promising to get together later in the week for a jog through Duke Forest. At their ages—forty and forty-one respectively—staying in shape took more time and effort each year.

Now, turning toward the window, he watched a 747 jet pass slowly from view, headed south. He briefly wished he was on board, headed for parts unknown. Then he sighed and asked his secretary to summon Ms. McCall to his office. Again.

Five minutes later, as Grace came through the door, he thought, *We've got to stop meeting like this.*

There was fire in her eyes today. She lit into him before he could even wish her a good-morning. "Did you send someone snooping around my neighborhood, asking questions about Daddy?"

It never occurred to him to lie. "Just a few questions, discreetly asked. By the way, your next-door neighbor accused you of mutilating his gardenias."

"My— He what? They're Cape jasmine. I only took— I never even— Well, for heaven's sake!" Grace dropped onto the chair and glared at him. She'd come upstairs with an axe to grind, and what did he do? Put her on the defensive for something that wasn't even worth mentioning. "I took a cutting or two, that's all. They needed pruning, anyway."

"You pruned it pretty good, according to your neighbor."

"I'm sure if I'd asked, he'd have given me permission."

"So why didn't you ask?"

"Because—well, because everyone knows stolen cuttings do better. I can personally vouch for that."

"Led a life of crime, have you?" Leaning back in his chair, Chandler tried and failed to suppress a grin. Steady, responsible, diligent—those were the words used most often to describe Grace McCall, according to Dick's report. The lady appeared to be doing her best to be a good influence, but Chandler couldn't help teasing her. She was just too tempting a target. He watched her turn huffy, then collapse into uncertainty. He'd always been good at reading people. With Grace, it wasn't even a challenge. She was an open book.

Which should have told him something, only he hadn't been ready until now to believe it. Hadn't been ready to trust her. Hadn't wanted to like her quite so much. *Definitely* hadn't intended to get interested in her sexually. This situation would have been easier to manage if both sisters had been out-and-out hustlers— or if they hadn't been quite so attractive. According to all reports, the younger sister was a real knockout.

The older one's looks were more subtle, somewhat less arresting.

He settled for asking if she'd come up with any brilliant ideas. "We'd better come up with something fast, Grace. They're starting to get down to brass tacks about this wedding thing."

"I've warned her over and over about how risky marrying too young can be. I've reminded her of the statistics regarding age and failed marriages." To his amusement, the familiar look of uncertainty flickered across her face again. "Actually, I'm not sure what the statistics say, but at their age, it's bound to be significant...don't you think?"

"Divorce is too easy these days," he said solemnly. *These days?* Next thing, he'd be talking about the good old days. Yeah, he really had to do something about his social life. Times like this, he felt like he was headed up a down escalator.

"On the other hand," she said earnestly, "you have to admit that staying in some marriages is worse than moving on. I mean, if a woman's not careful she can mistake infatuation for love and get into serious trouble before she comes to her senses."

Tilting back his chair, he studied her thoughtfully. "On still another hand, we both know people who married right out of high school and stuck it out for the next fifty or sixty years."

She nodded. Was she aware of the fact that when she was feeling uncertain, she tended to lace her fingers together and twirl her thumbs?

"Just out of curiosity, Grace, what do you figure it takes to make a marriage work?"

"Respect," she replied promptly. "On both sides. Of course, you both have to work at being the kind of person who deserves that respect."

He had to give her credit, although it wasn't the answer he'd been expecting. "That's it? What about, uh—sex?"

"Well, for heaven's sake, that's a given," she said.

"A given. Right. You, ah—do know they're sleeping together?"

She nodded again, her gaze straying to the window behind him as if she were vitally interested in cloud formations. "Mr. Da—"

"Chandler."

"I'm sure they're careful. I mean, they teach the stuff in school, for heaven's sake."

"The stuff?" He did it deliberately, wanting to see the swift color rise to her face. He wasn't disappointed.

"Safe sex," she mumbled.

Did the woman have any idea how young she looked when she was embarrassed? Just how tempting it was to tease her? How tempted he was to...

Yeah, well. Fortunately, he was old enough to resist temptation.

The next day it all came apart at the seams. Literally. Grace came home from work to find Susie sitting on the floor, a layer of off-white satin covering her lap, plus a third of the living room rug. She glanced up when the front door opened with a mouth full of pins and a thousand-watt glow in her eyes.

"What on earth—?" Grace dropped her purse and tossed the mail at the table—and missed.

"Mumph—" Quickly, Susie spat the straight pins into her hand, and beamed up at her sister. "Isn't it just the most gorgeous thing you ever saw? It's called *Candleglow,* and you know what? I got it on sale! It had this teensy-weensy little stain on the skirt, but by the time I get these lace medallions sewed on, nobody'll ever notice."

"Oh, honey…" What on earth was she supposed to do now? She'd never been any good at snatching candy from babies. Which might be a part of the problem.

Half an hour later, feeling as if she wanted to curse, cry and throw something breakable at the nearest wall, Grace left a message on Chandler's home phone. "This is Grace McCall. Call me immediately."

She waited twenty minutes and tried again. "This is Grace McCall again. Would you please call me the minute you get in, Mr. Daye? It's really urgent."

The third time she called and received the brief invitation to leave a message she slammed down the receiver and grabbed her purse and car keys. She knew where he lived. Knew the area, if not the exact house.

It was one of those cul-de-sac places off Whitfield Road that backed up onto Duke Forest. Her family doctor and his wife lived in the same area, and she'd gone to their twenty-fifth anniversary party.

After several wrong turns, she located the house with the help of a county map. It was a sprawling rock and wood affair on several acres, with a pond in front and lots of huge rhododendrons, tall pines and holly bushes. There were only a few lights on inside, none at all outside. Taking a deep breath, she jammed her thumb on the doorbell, reminding herself that she was here on perfectly legitimate business.

Personal business, but still...

The door opened and she found herself confronted by a man she scarcely recognized as Chandler Daye, III. His eyes were deeply shadowed, his shirt as rumpled as if he'd been sleeping in it for a week. Both his hair and his face had an equally slept-in look.

"It's you," he said. Snarled would be a more accurate description.

She took a step back. "I guess I've come at an inconvenient time," she said apologetically.

He nodded, winced, and said, "As long as you're here you might as well come inside and get it off your chest. At least that way, maybe my phone won't be ringing every five minutes."

Grace prided herself on handling stress exceptionally well. Over the years she'd had plenty of practice. This business with Buck and Susie was the mother lode, however, and she had no intention of bearing it alone.

"She's bought a wedding dress." It was part challenge, part accusation. She knew she was being unfair, but she couldn't help it. Things were moving entirely too fast.

Swearing softly, Chandler turned and led the way to a room that struck her as both quietly elegant and comfortably untidy. "Sit down. Buck's not here. I haven't seen him in a couple of days."

Immediately on the defensive, Grace said, "Well, don't blame Susie. She's home alone putting her own designer touches on a gown she charged to my account. Which means it can't be returned."

"What do you want me to do, reimburse you?"

"I just want you to put a stop to this nonsense before it goes any further."

"Right. It's all Buck's fault. I'm sure he's somewhere trying on a new tux. Bound to be. Can't let the bride outshine him." His tone was snide, bordering on nasty, but he looked so miserable she couldn't take offense. This wasn't the same Chandler Daye she'd confronted across the space of a massive walnut desk. Or even in her own living room.

"Are you…all right?" she asked tentatively.

"Hell no, I'm not all right. Since you asked, my head's about to destruct. I'm not sure if it's about to explode or fall off—the latter, I hope, since there'll be less peripheral damage."

"Well, don't take your headache out on me. I didn't cause it, your nephew did." Sympathy or not, this was no time to falter in her mission.

"Wrong. My great-uncle Dockery caused it. Not that it's any of your business, but on top of trying to keep my nephew from ruining his life, I've got Uncle Dock to deal with."

"Your great-uncle wants to get married, too?" He gave her the kind of look the remark deserved, and she shook her head and murmured an apology. "Sorry. It's just that I'm at my wit's end."

Evidently he understood, because he relented. "Yeah, I know the feeling. Uncle Dock's threatening to sic the governor on me—the *governor,* for God's sake! He claims we're buying too many Chinese imports—all but accused me of being in the pockets of the Chi-coms, can you believe it?" His bark of laughter had the ring of hopelessness.

She blinked and stared at him in disbelief.

"Yeah, I know. But to help clue you in, Uncle Dock also claims to have dated one of Teddy Roosevelt's daughters. Claims she was crazy about him, but her father broke it up." He shook his head in resigned amusement.

"But can't you—that is, there must be a tactful way to…"

"To what, tell an old man he's losing it?" Suddenly, he looked less like an opponent than he did a weary man who was tired of fighting alone. "He's

ninety-three years old, Grace. Most of the time he's
sharp as a tack, it's just that he has these occasional
lapses—flights of fancy, I guess you could call them.
Trouble is, while he's lapsing he can stir up more trouble than a courtroom full of lawyers can handle.''

"Have you taken anything?"

"Not one penny beyond my salary, but I can't convince him of that. He thinks I'm being paid off by
Chairman Mao himself. Did I mention he's a bit behind the times?'' Flexing his shoulders, he looked
thoroughly miserable.

"No, I meant for your headache." Without thinking, she stood and moved to the back of his chair.
Placing her hands on his shoulders, she began to mas-
sage with fingers made strong by years of sanding furniture the old-fashioned way.

*This is Mr. Daye, for heaven's sake—and you're
touching him!*

He leaned forward to afford her better access.
"God, that feels good. And yeah, I took something for
the pain. Prescription stuff that usually works in half
an hour or so.''

"I probably shouldn't have bothered you, but I just
didn't know what else to do."

"No reason you shouldn't—we're in this thing together. Yeah, right there," he said, letting his head fall
forward. If he had any idea of how the feel of those
rock-hard muscles and that warm, damp flesh was affecting her, he'd run screaming into the other room

and lock the door behind him. For someone who prided herself on being a confirmed realist, she'd been having some pretty bizarre thoughts lately.

Chandler sighed, tempting her to slide her arms around him and hug him until the pain went away, the way she used to do whenever Susie ran to her with an ouchie.

Talk about a mothering instinct run amok!

"Look, I'll talk to Buck when I see him, but I'm afraid there's nothing I can say that hasn't already been said."

For once in her life Grace was tempted to utter that catchall word, "whatever," and go on touching him for the foreseeable future.

"Yes, well…you don't have to bother seeing me out, I know the way."

He didn't argue.

Chapter 5

"Why can't we get married in Duke Chapel? Oh, please, Gracie, it would be so cool!"

"Our church," insisted Grace, feeling an instinctive need to remove as much of the drama as possible from the occasion. She probably should be relieved that Susie wanted to be married in a church at all. "Our parents were all married at Cedar Hill," she reminded her.

On second thought, that might not be the greatest recommendation. She'd been afraid Buck and Susie might elope, but playing the starring role in her non-returnable *Candleglow* satin wedding gown at the famous chapel was evidently too tempting.

"But Buck says—"

"I don't care what Buck says, you're lucky we're letting you get married at all." Oops! Foot-in-mouth disease strikes again.

Predictably, Susie clouded up. Huge morning glory-blue eyes filmed over, full lower lip thrusting out in a trembling pout. Grace tried to think of a way to repair the damage without actually giving an inch. She simply didn't think she could handle a tantrum at the moment. It had been one of those days at the office, where everything that could go wrong, had gone wrong. Murphy's Law.

Or was it the Peter Principle?

Both, probably. With a few Grinches thrown in for good measure.

"Okay, but Buck's on his way over." Susie settled into pouting mode. She did it so well.

"It's about time. I've never even met him, you know."

"You'll have to tell him, I can't."

"Fine," Grace said calmly.

"He's not going to understand." Tears on demand. It was a remarkable talent, but Grace had seen it too many times.

"Then you can explain," she said firmly. "And you might want to go wash your face before he gets here—that is, unless he likes you with mascara running down your cheeks."

Susie never wore mascara. With her inch-long, hedge-thick lashes, she didn't need to. But Grace thought if she didn't have a few minutes to take off her shoes and change her bra—the damned label felt as if it had been sewed on with barbed wire—she'd scream.

The distraction worked. Leaving Susie examining her face in the mirror over the mantel, she had barely made it to the bedroom when the doorbell sounded. She'd give them a few minutes for Susie to pour out her troubles and let Buck kiss them away, then she would go out and settle whatever needed settling. The trick was to walk a fine line—to use every delaying tactic she could think of without driving them to elope.

Then she heard a familiar baritone rumble. Chandler?

Couldn't be. He was probably sacked out at home, suffering the aftereffects of last night's headache. With relatives coming at him from all sides, the man really needed a crash course in stress management.

Maybe she should introduce him to furniture refinishing.

She slipped on her peach-colored sweats. So they were faded and stained. So they fit like a collapsed tent. Did she care?

All right, so she cared. She didn't have to let him know she cared.

"Hi, Chandler," she said airily, sauntering into the living room a moment later. "I didn't realize you were here."

She was tempted to feel her nose, to see if it had grown another inch.

"Grace." He nodded, his gaze sweeping over her coolly. "I understand you've never met my nephew. This is Buck Daye. Buck—Ms. McCall."

It took her a moment to react. She'd heard all about him—even seen him a few times from a distance, when he'd come to pick up Susie. Buck Daye would definitely qualify as a hunk in any woman's dictionary. He was flat-out gorgeous without being in the least effeminate. Obviously, the Dayes' gene pool had enough of the right stuff to go around. As for any children Buck and Susie might produce...

Don't even think *about it!*

"It's nice to meet you, Buck," she murmured, trying not to gawk. No wonder Susie thought she was in love. The young man was nearly as striking as his uncle, in an entirely different way.

"Nice to meet you, too, ma'am."

All this and manners, too, she marveled. Evidently, his formative years had not been a total waste.

It was Chandler who called the meeting to order. "I understand there's a long waiting list for Duke Chapel."

Actually, Grace didn't know if there was or not. She had an idea Chandler didn't, either, but she took the cue. "Well then—maybe we could book something for next fall," she suggested brightly.

"But Gra-ace, you said we had to get married in

our church. It's nowhere near as neat, but at least we won't have to wait.''

What was that old Hamlet saying about being hoisted by one's own petard? She had no idea what a petard was, but she knew the meaning of trapped. Helplessly, she glanced at Chandler.

Looking every bit as devastating as his nephew would look once he reached his potential, the older man said, ''Why don't we all sit down and talk this thing over like sensible adults?''

Because only two of us qualify, she was tempted to say. Although lately she'd had cause to wonder about her own maturity. If she was going to fall in lust with a man, why did she have to pick someone she worked for? There were rules against that sort of thing—with good reason. ''Um—what was that?''

Oops—caught in the act.

''I said,'' Susie repeated with exaggerated patience, ''even if we do have to get married at Cedar Hill, I'm not going to have our reception in any old church basement.''

Chandler looked at Buck. Buck looked at Susie for clarification. Then Chandler said, ''A basement?''

''It's not exactly a basement,'' Grace explained hastily. ''Our assembly room happens to be located on the ground floor, but the church lot slopes so that actually, it's not even underground. At least, not all of it.''

Buck shook his head. "No way. Us Dayes don't do basement receptions."

"*We* Dayes," Grace murmured, and then could have kicked herself. She'd been automatically correcting Susie's grammatical lapses for so long, she did it without thinking. Face flushed, she bounced up off the ottoman and said brightly, "Why don't I make us some, uh—iced coffee?"

"That would be good," said Chandler, recognizing her embarrassment and coming to the rescue. "I'll help."

In the kitchen, she turned to him, eyes suspiciously blurred. "I'm botching everything, aren't I? If you needed any more evidence that Dayes and McCalls don't have a single thing in common, I guess you have it now."

Chandler leaned against the kitchen wall. It was painted a pale, warm yellow, with a border of roosters and matching gingham curtains. Plebeian plus. His kitchen, she happened to know, was pickled pine, with lots of stainless steel and gleaming black appliances.

"Are we making a mistake, Grace? About those two, I mean?"

"A mistake?" She ran a measuring cup of water and set it in the microwave, then got out the milk and instant coffee. He probably had one of those fancy machines that turned out designer coffee on demand. She didn't. Using ground instead of instant was about as special as it got in her kitchen. Susie drank hot chocolate. From a mix.

"The glasses are up there," she said, busying herself with the preparations. She wished she had something besides store-bought gingersnaps to serve along with it.

"I mean about whether or not they're ready for marriage." He set out four glasses. At least she had enough unchipped ones that matched. "I'm beginning to think they might be pretty well suited."

"You mean they're equally immature? Fine, but what if when they grow up, they grow in totally different directions?"

"Odds are, they will. People usually change as they grow older. That probably explains why so many marriages fail."

She nodded and got out an ice tray. Chandler took it from her and popped the cubes neatly into a bowl, then divided them among the glasses.

Grace said, "That makes it all the more important to wait until some of the growing's done, don't you think?"

"Not necessarily."

Turning, she confronted him, puzzled and a bit alarmed. "You sound as if you've changed your mind—as if you're willing to risk it."

"Grace, it's their risk we're talking about here, not yours, not mine. They're legally of age, remember? Can you think of a single time in your own life when you learned from someone else's experience? Most people I know don't even learn from their own.''

He was standing too close—so close she could see those fascinating dark rings around his silvery irises. His eyebrows were black, which made the color of his hair and eyes all the more startling.

She felt her bones begin to dissolve. Her lips softened and parted... ''Experience?'' she whispered, struggling to keep her mind on what they'd been discussing. ''Oh. Well, I learned something when my father remarried so soon after my mother died. And I learned even more when Iris—his second wife—walked out on him.''

Learned that happy endings occurred only in fairy tales and romance novels.

Chandler was standing so close she could feel the heat of his body. Hadn't he ever heard of the thing called personal space? She'd always hated having her own invaded—it made her feel vaguely threatened.

She didn't feel threatened at all now. She felt—

''Hey, are you guys making coffee, or what?'' Buck called from the living room.

''Coming right up,'' Chandler called back. And just like that, the highly charged moment dissipated. Grace told herself it wasn't disappointment she felt. He hadn't been going to kiss her or anything like that, for goodness sake. This was about Susie and Buck, not Chandler and Grace.

* * *

A week later Grace was considering quitting her job, selling her house and following in her father's footsteps. Well...maybe not joining a group of missionaries who saved souls and taught modern agricultural methods, but relocating far enough away that her problems couldn't follow her. She was tired to the point of saying, "Okay—go ahead, do whatever you want to do when and where you want to do it. Just don't come crying to me when your pretty bubble bursts, because I never believed in bubbles in the first place."

Three things kept her from saying it. One, it was selfish. Two, it sounded so silly. And three, she'd be lying. Pretty, shiny bubbles in the air. Daydreams. In spite of everything, deep down in a secret corner of her heart, she still believed.

The wedding was set for March fifteenth, which in Grace's estimation, was indecently rushed. Compromise being the name of the game, the ceremony would take place at Cedar Hill Church, with a reception to follow at the Dayes' country club. Grace knew where it was—she'd admired the huge magnolia trees and even considered digging up a few of the seedlings that had sprouted on the adjacent highway right-of-way.

Susie, wearing her *Candleglow* satin gown with a lace-edged veil, would look like a Christmas tree angel. That is, if she didn't wear the thing out first by trying it on every day before the mirror and practicing angelic expressions.

Grace would have to buy something suitable. She really didn't need the expense, but neither did she want Susie to be ashamed of her maid of honor. Susie wanted her to wear pink—all her bridesmaids were going to wear pink, because pink was so flattering.

To Susie, at least. Which was what mattered.

It was also totally impractical. What Grace needed was something she could cut off to street length and wear to church afterward. Something that wouldn't make her look quite so much like a beanpole with hips. Something that would set off her ordinary features, her ordinary coloring and turn her into—if not a beauty, at least one of those women who were considered interesting in spite of their lack of it.

Yeah, right, she thought, echoing what Susie would have said if she'd known what Grace was thinking. She reminded herself once more that this was about Susie, not about Susie's spinster sister.

In spite of all the encouraging magazine articles about the joys of being a single woman, she felt depressed. Where was the joy of growing old alone, mired in a boring job with no prospects for improvement in sight?

"Why not whine about it, McCall?" she jeered softly. "Whining always helps."

Over the next few days things were quiet at work. No more calls from the executive office. No more tearful ultimatums from Susie, who went around beaming at everyone, from their cranky neighbor with the Cape jasmines to the paperboy, who at thirteen, was completely smitten. Grace no longer fussed at her for staying out until all hours. Why bother? The horse was already out of the barn.

Of course, it would be nice to count on at least nine months after the wedding before their problems began to multiply, but *"que sera, sera,"* as some sage had once remarked. Yogi Bera? Doris Day?

She'd never been any good at Trivial Pursuit.

Chandler called to ask her out to dinner at the end of the week. Sorely tempted, Grace declined. She didn't dare risk further exposure as long as she kept having X-rated daydreams starring the two of them in a king-size bed. So all right, she was wildly attracted to the man. Other than the fact that they were both somewhat old-fashioned and both happened to be responsible for younger relatives, they had nothing at all in common. He was Mr. Moneybags. She was Ms. Penny Pincher. Her father was a tobacco farmer turned evangelist turned missionary; his people were old family, old money. She painted and sold used furniture in her spare time—he went deep-sea fishing. Probably played tennis and golf and all those other gentlemanly sports.

He probably even fenced. Picturing him in a leotard

and face mask, wielding a ball-point sword, she sighed and surrendered to another nonproductive daydream.

On a Saturday eight days before the wedding was to take place, Susie burst into Grace's bathroom—actually, they had only the one bathroom, which caused no end of problems. "Oh, Grace, guess what!"

Grace, her face coated with pink mud that was guaranteed to erase fine lines, peered out from under the towel draped over her newly shampooed hair. "You've decided to get a teaching degree."

"Gra-ace!"

"Enlist in the army? Join a nunnery? Follow in Daddy's wandering footsteps?"

"We're going to get married at the lighthouse! I never wanted to get married at Cedar Hill, anyway— I mean, it always smells like varnish and that yucky furniture polish they use."

Carefully, Grace lowered the lid and sat down. "You what?"

"The lighthouse! I mean, you know—like where we met and all?"

"And all what? Honey, give me a hint. Is this a— a nightclub or something?"

"No, silly, it's the Cape Hatteras Lighthouse—the National Seashore Park thingy. Don't you remember last summer when I went to this house party with a bunch of friends and we drove down to Hatteras to watch the lighthouse being moved, and I met Buck there? I told you all about it, don't you remember?''

Deep breath. Don't hyperventilate, just breathe nice and slowly. "Susie, I remember perfectly well when you went to the house party, but it was—you said it was all girls?''

"Well, it was. I mean, mostly. Traci's father has this big old place at, you know, Duck? And she gets to take all her friends there at least twice a year between seasons?'' Statements in the form of questions. Meaning—are you listening this time? "Anyway, they're all going to be there for a whole week, so they can come down to the wedding, and Buck says—''

"Whoa. Back up a minute.''

Susie backed up. She re-explained and then went over it all again, about how way cool it would be to, like, actually get married on the site where they'd first, you know, like first met?

A few hours later Grace repeated the whole absurd plan to Chandler, who had already heard it from his nephew.

"Do you think we could just say no?'' Grace asked, knowing they could say it until they were blue in the face, for all the good it would do. "Did you know— I read this somewhere—they just recently changed the law in North Carolina that said fourteen-year-olds could marry? Or maybe it was even younger than that. With parental consent, of course.''

Chandler looked tired again. With Uncle Dockery

threatening to throw him to the wolves on one side and an unwanted wedding on the other, it was no wonder. "Grace, the more we insist," he said quietly, "the more they're going to insist right back. Did it ever occur to you that if we hadn't protested in the first place, this whole thing might have died a natural death?"

"Great. Now he tells me," Grace said dryly.

They were seated at her kitchen table. Her hands were on the table. She was picking at a speck of dried paint with her thumbnail. He reached over and covered both her hands with one of his. "Let's take things one at a time, shall we? First of all, they're certainly of age. I have several men about Buck's age working at the store. They're all serious, ambitious men, ready to take on the responsibilities of marriage. A couple of them are already married, I believe."

Were you like that? she wanted to ask. For all she knew, he could have married. It seemed as if half the marriages these days ended in divorce. If he still had a wife, they'd have known about it at the office, but maybe he had an ex-wife somewhere in the background—maybe even more than one. Any woman would consider herself fortunate to...

"What?" She'd been caught daydreaming again. Really, she had to come out of the clouds.

"I said, this place they're talking about—when they moved the lighthouse back to keep it from falling into the ocean, they left a circle of granite stones where it originally stood. Stones from the base, I believe. It's turned out to be a sort of cult thing. Stonehenge-by-the-Sea.''

"Good Lord. They want to get married on a pile of stones on the beach? In the middle of March? In a *satin wedding gown?*"

"Not a great start, huh?"

"I just wish they'd thought of it sooner. I suppose if I had to choose between a romantic wedding that held meaning for both parties and a huge extravaganza that stressed out everyone involved, I'd choose the romantic one, too. But at this late date..." She could only sigh.

"Me, too. So what do we do, let 'em take the ball and run with it?"

"Is that a football analogy?"

"You want baseball? How about score tied, bottom of the ninth, two out, bases loaded and the pitcher up at bat?" He grinned, and she wondered if he remembered that his hand was still covering hers. His palm felt perfectly dry. Evidently, the contact didn't have the same effect on him as it had on her.

"Look, Grace, for better or worse, they're ours. If we love 'em—and we do—" He looked at her as though he could see right through her ordinary brown eyes into her palpitating heart. "Then we'll go along with this thing, no matter how foolish it strikes us. Otherwise, we'll lose them both. At least, that's my opinion," he finished.

"You're probably right. Susie's never been particularly consistent. What if they change their minds again?"

"Then we'll deal with it." His thumb was stroking her knuckles. It had been years since she'd had sex, but it felt alarmingly like foreplay.

"Right." The word emerged as another sigh. "Well, at least maybe you can get in a day of fishing."

He squeezed her hands, released them, leaving her feeling oddly bereft. "Grace McCall, you're a woman after my own heart."

Bingo. I'm after your body, too, but then, that's my problem, not yours.

Not trusting Buck with the practical details, Chandler arranged with the Park Service for the wedding to be held on Park property. Through her own pastor, Grace got the name of a local minister and made arrangements for him to perform the ceremony. When Buck came to collect Susie that Friday night, his wide white grin was an orthodontist's dream. "Hey, guess what, ladies—Uncle Chan's rented us a beach cottage for our honeymoon. A whole week! Man, does that ever rock, or what?"

Susie leaped at him, squealing with excitement. "Oh, that is so way cool! And you know what? We can invite the gang down for a few days. I mean, Traci's always going on about her daddy's place at Duck, but—oh, gee, how many bedrooms will we have? Like, is it one of those humongous places we saw down there? Oh, wow,'' she ended reverently.

A house party? Grace thought. For a *honeymoon?*

She saw them off, wondering wistfully what had ever happened to the love songs and schmaltzy romances she'd grown up with? Was everyone into rap music and space aliens these days? And group honeymoons?

Twenty minutes after they'd left, Grace dug herself even deeper in debt by arranging for a wedding supper to be delivered to the cottage Chandler had rented. Never let it be said that McCalls couldn't hold up their end.

As March had come in like a lamb, the outlook for the next few weeks was not too encouraging. Grace was keeping her fingers crossed that the weather would cooperate. She had her car serviced the day before they were to leave. Susie had been campaigning ever since she'd turned sixteen for a car of her own— actually, she wanted a pickup truck. Grace had told her that when she could afford her own insurance premiums, they would talk about it again.

Other than the occasional grumble, that had been the end of it. Susie never lacked for rides.

They argued over who would ride with whom. Susie wanted to ride with Buck, not with Grace. Grace wasn't at all eager to drive alone to a place she had never even been, but she wasn't about to make an issue of it. She'd made too many issues, as it was, and look where it had got her.

A compromise was decided on. They would meet at the rest stop on Roanoke Island and Susie would ride the rest of the way with Grace. "I can show you all the neat places on the way. We could even go by Traci's cottage, only that's not exactly on the way, but I mean—"

Grace smiled and nodded. She was learning. The drive would take about four hours. If the wedding hadn't been set for sunset, she might have saved herself the cost of an additional night at the motel and driven back home the same day. As it was, by the time the wedding supper was over, it would be too late and she'd no doubt be exhausted from smiling and pretending this wasn't the most harebrained stunt she had ever been a part of in her entire uneventful life.

Instead of live music, they planned to use the CD player in Buck's convertible to play music from the movie *Titanic*. Grace only hoped it wasn't an omen. She knew better than to offer an opinion. When Susie had announced two days ago that she'd invited all her friends to the reception, taking it for granted that one would follow the ceremony, Grace had calmly called the caterer and renegotiated.

Susie, listening in, said, "Is it going to cost too much? But you did say I could have a reception, didn't you? I mean, what's a wedding without a party, right?"

Right. Four hundred dollars and rising. Oh, well— she could always take out a loan. What had she been thinking—a wedding supper for just the four wedding participants?

Duh. Another of Susie's classic expressions.

Chapter 6

By the time the rendezvous took place, Susie didn't even beg to be allowed to ride the rest of the way with Buck, which Grace thought was somewhat surprising. But then, she'd given up on trying to figure that pair out. They continued south along the Outer Banks, talking very little. The edge seemed to have gone off Susie's feverish excitement.

On reaching the village of Buxton, Grace followed the directions she'd been given over the phone. Pulling up before the weathered one-story building, she said, "Wait here and I'll register and get a key."

"Gra-ace, this place sucks! Do we have to stay here?"

"It's the closest motel to the lighthouse that had a vacancy." Also the cheapest.

"It smells like fish."

"Honey, it's only for one night. Tomorrow you'll be moving to the high-rent district, remember?"

"I wonder which cottage is ours." Susie was quick to sulk, but just as quick to get over it. "Remember all those big cottages we passed on the way down the beach? I remember seeing some last summer that are even bigger. I remember this one humongous place that was like a palace or something."

"I wouldn't count on a palace, honey. I'm sure Chandler rented something nice—it's his wedding present, after all. But you hardly need a dozen bedrooms for two people."

"Yeah, but wouldn't it be cool? We could do it in every bedroom and then start on—"

"Susan McCall!" Grace bit back a giggle. "How about unloading the car while I go get us registered?"

"Hey, this place rocks, man." A few miles away, Buck pulled up behind his uncle's Lexus and ejected himself from the seat of his own convertible. "Way cool! Thanks a bunch."

The cottage was only a modest four-bedroom affair with a hot tub and a rooftop sundeck, but it was ocean-front as opposed to ocean-side, with its own private boardwalk over the dunes.

The two men carried the luggage inside. Chandler had brought fishing clothes as well as his tux. If he was going to be best man at a formal wedding, no matter where it was held, he was damn well going to do it in style. Like it or not, he represented the family business, which was struggling to maintain certain outmoded standards in a rapidly changing world.

Personally, he considered the whole idea ridiculous, but then what did he know? He was still at the awkward age, somewhere between whippersnapper, according to Great-Uncle Dockery, and geezerdom, according to Buck, who at least was polite enough not to mention it.

The weather was only slightly overcast. It could go either way. He'd reminded his nephew that March was prime time for nor'easters along the mid-Atlantic coast. Black tie and white satin might stand up to a chilly breeze, but a wet, howling gale was something else.

"I better call Sooz to see if they got in yet. Do you have the number of that place they're staying?"

He had seen her less than an hour ago. "Drummer's Court. Look it up."

Some twenty minutes later Buck hung up the phone. "I told her we'd pick 'em up at seven and go out to supper. There's this great place down at Hatteras. Humongous crab cakes."

"Fine. I'm going to check out a few things first. See you later."

What he intended to check out was the latest fishing report. There was a pier not too far away, and miles of promising surf. While he was out he might even

jog a few miles on the beach to work the kinks out of
his system. Not that the drive had been all that bad,
but the weeks leading up to it had been stress squared.

For dinner, Grace dressed in the black outfit with
the gray knit tunic. Not until she'd worn it a few times
did she realize that oxford gray wasn't the most flattering color for someone with her skin tone.

Navy blue was hardly much better, but after getting
estimates on the cost of a buffet super for twelve, she
had given up any notion of buying a new gown for
the wedding. Her old navy dinner dress would have to
do the honors. With the beach, the nearby lighthouse,
the starring couple and Chandler in all his spectacular
glory, who'd be looking at the maid of honor, anyway?

Besides, unless it warmed up considerably, she'd be
wearing a coat.

"They're here," Susie called over her shoulder as
Grace peered at the cloudy mirror and wondered if the
foundation she was wearing emphasized the fine lines
at the corners of her eyes. "God, I hate for them to
see this dump. Buck's real picky about stuff like that."

Grace bit back her impatience. One more day, and
Buck and his bride could deal with each other's pick-
iness. "Honey, Chandler knows exactly how much I
earn. He'd have thought we were being extravagant if
I'd booked us at one of those places that charge an

arm and a leg. Besides, most of them don't even open for the season until Easter weekend.''

"All the same— Oh, hi, dogbreath.'' Susie swung open the door.

Dogbreath?

Over the heads of the younger couple, Grace's gaze met Chandler's. His eyes sparkled with amusement. His lifted brow implied, "It's a generational thing.''

"If you're ready,'' he said, "I've made reservations for seven-thirty. I figure it'll take us about fifteen minutes to get there.''

They drove separately, Grace and Chandler in Chandler's car, the younger couple in Buck's red convertible. With the top down. "Is freezing your ears off supposed to prove something?'' she asked. For some reason she was in a snarly mood.

"Sign of manhood. I take it Susie doesn't worry about her hair blowing.'' Chandler ignored her snappishness, and for some reason, that helped ease the tension.

"I don't think she worries about anything, unless it's an untimely zit. But then, she's only ever had two in her entire life.''

His chuckle finished smoothing her hackles. "Hey, life's not fair. Look at it this way—by this time tomorrow, we'll be over the hump.''

Traffic was light. He turned onto Highway 12 and headed southwest. Remembering something from the office grapevine about his once having been a Navy flier, Grace watched his hands on the steering wheel, picturing him in the cockpit of one of those sleek, monster machines. Before she could stop it, her imagination took off on a flight of its own.

Stamping out the fantasy before it could catch fire, she said, "I understand Buck wants to travel before they settle down."

"I have an idea they're still working on a few details. Last night I tried to sound him out about coming to work at the store, but for some reason he was in a foul mood. Wedding jitters, I guess. Maybe a week down here with no distractions will help."

Unsaid, but clearly understood was the fact that he doubted it. Grace did, too. These past few days Susie had been almost too cheerful. Excitement was only to be expected, but there'd been something about the way she'd babbled on and on about their plans for the future that made her wonder if perhaps the two disagreed about their future plans.

Susie had said on the trip east, "If we decide to go to Africa on safari, remind me to take Daddy's last address, will you?"

"Africa? You're thinking of going all the way to Africa?" Grace had thought of traveling as far as maybe Busch Gardens, or Epcot Center.

"Buck's got this friend who went there last year, and he said it was way cool."

She told Chandler about it now, and asked if he had any idea what their immediate plans were. He grinned, and she could feel her face heating up. "What I meant was, has Buck said what he eventually wants to do? I know he has a degree, but does he plan on using it?"

"In other words, what are his prospects," Chandler said dryly.

"Somebody has to ask, Daddy's not here to do it. And anyway, Susie's more like a daughter than a sister."

Chandler pursed his lips thoughtfully. Grace couldn't look away. He had beautiful lips for a man. On a woman they would be...

Sheer bliss, she thought, and sighed.

They passed through Buxton and Frisco, the wooded parts of the island, and headed down the beach toward Hatteras. A few miles down the highway, Chandler said, "I'll be glad when it's over. I'm going to stick around for a few days afterward—maybe I'll get a room in that place you're staying. Don't tell the kids, though, I wouldn't want them to get the idea I was trying to oversee their honeymoon. I'll be on the beach or the pier most of the time." He glanced at her, looking both tired and amused. Or maybe resigned was a better description. "Might even charter a boat. Want to come along? I'll share my tackle with you."

Before she could shut off thoughts of the two of them spending long days...and nights...together, Chandler pulled into the parking lot of a waterfront restaurant. There was no sign of Buck's Beamer.

''We can wait here or go inside and get a table.''

She would much rather wait right there, in the cozy warm comfort of his car, but before she could suggest they'd better go inside, he switched off the engine, unsnapped his seat belt and turned toward her. ''Grace—I might as well warn you that if we stay out here, I'm going to kiss you.''

Was he a mind reader, she thought wonderingly. And then her pulse went wild as the sheer inevitability of it struck her.

It was almost as if she'd been expecting it—as if she'd known that sooner or later, it would come to this. Only it had never occurred to her that it worked both ways. Because, logical or not, there was something between them that was too powerful to resist.

Powerful and still growing, she thought a moment later as he unhooked her seat belt and pulled her over into his arms. The kiss was all she'd imagined and more. His skin smelled faintly of soap—he had obviously taken time to shower, but he hadn't shaved since morning. She could feel the slight stubble, even though she couldn't see it. Against her own skin the sensation was exquisite. Shivery. Like lightning stabbing through her body, electrifying her most private and sensitive parts.

If a kiss can do this much damage, what would it be like to make love to this man?

''Whatever happened to bench seats in a car?'' Chandler grumbled a few minutes later. He was having trouble with his breathing. Actually, neither of them had much breathing room. Grace was wedged between the steering wheel and his chest, her hips sagging into the well. It was uncomfortable, but with his arousal throbbing against her stomach, she wasn't about to move away.

Resting her forehead against his chest, she felt his chin brush against her hair. He was laughing softly.

Laughing?

"Would you look at who's making out in a car?" he said with a soft chuckle. "Whatever happened to middle-aged dignity?"

"Who're you calling middle-aged?" Grace made a move to extricate herself, but he held her fast. And really, she wasn't trying all that hard.

"Stay here a minute more. I like the way you fit in my arms."

She liked the way she fit, too, but she would have liked it much better on a soft, horizontal plane—preferably a mattress. "Warn me the minute you see Buck's car. If Susie catches us like this, I'll never live it down."

"Hasn't she ever seen you…?"

"Not like this. In a car, I mean. Besides, I don't really—"

He knew what she didn't really do. Dick's report summed up her love life in a single word. Zilch. Which was a damned shame, not to mention a monumental waste.

But as long as she was here....

Taking her face between his hands, he kissed her again. Soft, exploratory kisses, brushing over her eyebrows, suckling her earlobes, gently nipping her lower lip. After long, intoxicating moments she found her hand inside his shirt front. Realized that somehow, her bra had come unfastened.

Instinct led, and wordlessly, they followed. By the time they realized that their seven-thirty reservations were down the tube, and that the younger generation had yet to put in an appearance, Chandler was in no condition to think rationally about anything.

"Too many layers," he said, reluctantly easing his hand from under her layers of turtleneck, tunic and dangling bra.

"Sorry. It never occurred to me to dress for a seduction scene." A rumpled scrap of satin and lace was small comfort after the warmth of his palms on her small, incredibly sensitive breasts.

Chandler shifted uncomfortably, wondering what she'd say if he were to slide over into her seat, ask her to remove her pants and straddle him. Quite aside from the nerve it would take, the calisthenics would be awkward, if not damn near impossible for someone as out of practice as he was. He didn't know whether to apologize and invite her into the back seat, or take her back to the motel.

"They're not coming," she said, her voice muffled against his shirt.

No, but I am. Damn close to it, anyway. How the devil had he got himself in a fix like this? If the Chamber of Commerce could see him now, they'd take back every award they'd ever given him.

"I think we'd better go find them, don't you?"

Reluctantly, Chandler helped her right herself. They were both breathing as if they'd run a four-minute mile. The way he felt now, he might even manage it, if only out of frustration.

"Need a hand?" he asked. She was struggling to right her clothing.

"No, thanks. Do you?"

Oh, yeah. Preferably a dainty, long-fingered hand with paint-stained cuticles. Right where it would do the most good.

Driving back up the beach a few minutes later, Chandler asked quietly, "You want an apology?"

"No." And then she looked at him curiously. "Do you?"

"You're kidding, right?"

"Weren't you the one who called Susie a gold digger not long ago, intimating that I was no better?"

"Ouch." Long pause. Intermittent beams from the lighthouse swept across the treetops as they entered Frisco Woods.

They pulled into her motel. Buck's car was nowhere in evidence. Then Chandler backed out and headed for the cottage he'd rented, where the two men were to spend the night before tomorrow's festivities.

No sign of a red Beamer convertible.

"We passed several restaurants along the way. I didn't see Buck's car, did you?"

Grace didn't want to admit she hadn't been looking, that she'd still been in the thrall of those kisses. And all that had followed, which had been more than she'd ever dreamed, but not enough. Not nearly enough.

"No, I didn't. Surely if he planned to stop and eat somewhere else he would have let you know. Don't you have a cell phone?"

They were both growing quieter and more and more grim as it occurred to them that something could have happened. There was basically a single narrow highway that led from one end of the island to the other, through all the villages. The side roads led only to small residential areas. There'd be no reason for them to leave the highway.

Unless...

"Look, I'm going to take you back to your place and then I'll check out all the possibilities."

"Such as?"

Pulling into the cracked driveway at Drummer's Court again, he shook his head. "Grace, I don't know. One thing's certain, though." He got out and came around to open her door just as she opened it herself. She stood, and finding herself practically toe-to-toe as he held the door, she leaned forward, closing the slight distance. His arms came around her and they stood wordlessly drawing comfort, seeking—

Seeking something neither of them was ready to define.

"Buck won't take his car on the beach, at least we know that much."

"Should we call the sheriff?"

"And report what? A pair of kids on the eve of their wedding went off somewhere alone together without telling their elders where they were headed?"

"I don't feel like an elder," Grace murmured, her voice muffled against Chandler's tattersall-checked shirt.

"No, you don't," he said as his hands moved over her hips and came around to her breasts.

"You know what I mean," she snapped, but didn't try to move away.

"I know." They had tried calling Buck's cell phone with no success. Obviously there were gaps in the service in this area. Lifting her head, she said, "I'm going inside and call somebody on a real phone."

"Who?"

Flinging her arms out, she exclaimed, "I don't know! This is crazy! At least I can find out if there's been an accident!"

"Buck's a good driver. Fast, but careful."

They were walking toward her unit, his arm around her shoulders.

Grace said, "Maybe he is, but I doubt if every driver on the road is that careful."

She turned on the lights. And then she frowned. Her suitcase was right where she'd left it, but Susie's...

"Grace, I think you'd better read this."

Heart lodged somewhere in her throat, she turned to see Chandler, a scrap of notepaper in his hand. Her first thought was that it was a ransom note. Buck, after all, was a Daye.

And Susie was with him! Snatching the note, she scanned the few lines. Her mouth opened and closed wordlessly. The wedding was off. And then she said softly, "That little *brat!*"

"Make that plural," Chandler said dryly, and cursed for a full minute without once repeating himself.

Having vented his frustration, he told her to pack her bag while he settled with the office. "We've got a perfectly good cottage going to waste. This place smells like fish."

Thinking of the buffet supper for twelve she had commissioned for the next night—it was far too late to cancel, of course—she said, "I hope you like miniature crab cakes and shrimp on a stick."

"That reminds me, I'd better call the preacher."

"And the park people."

"Look, I hate to mention it at a time like this, but I'm hungry. We had lunch in Williamston at a fast-food place, and I still haven't had any dinner. What do you say we check you out of this place, pick up something to eat on the way to the cottage and settle down for some serious unwinding? We'll take care of your crab cakes and shrimp on a stick tomorrow.''

The unwinding had to wait. By the time they reached their cottage they were too hungry to do more than devour the huge seafood sandwiches and French fries. Then Grace, having never been inside a beach cottage before, was ready to explore. Chandler had placed her bag in one of the four bedrooms before disappearing to change into something more suitable for serious unwinding.

Grace was at a slight disadvantage, as her entire wardrobe consisted of the dresses she wore to work, the ones she wore to church, and the rags she wore when she was working on her projects. Other than that, she had whatever she could find on sale at Daye's that fit her and wasn't too tacky. Mostly white jeans and summery tops. Which she hadn't brought because it was only mid-March, after all, and besides, she hadn't planned to be here that long.

Chandler came to the rescue, lending her a pair of jeans and a Carolina Blue sweatshirt, both of which hung from her slender frame.

''We'll go shopping first thing tomorrow,'' he promised, smoothing the soft cotton shirt over her shoulders.

Grace backed away, suddenly wary. Just because she'd let him kiss her and kissed him back—well, a bit more than that, actually—that didn't mean she was going to get involved in anything potentially awkward.

Not to mention painful. She had already let herself be drawn in too deeply. "No, we won't. I'll be going home tomorrow," she corrected.

"Why?"

"Why?" Her arms flew out in a gesture of helplessness. "Well…because, that's why."

"That's not a reason. Look, we need to talk about this thing that's happened to us."

"Nothing's happened to us. Whatever happened, happened to our relatives. We were just—incidental." Her eyes pleaded with him not to argue. Come Monday, she would be back in her cubicle on the ground floor, and he would be up in his executive office, surrounded by his stuffed fish and his do-gooder awards. "And besides, it's over now."

That was when he knocked the wind clean out of her sails, to put it in nautical terms, by telling her that nothing was over. "It's just beginning," he said, holding her with the sheer force of those quicksilver eyes. "Don't you know that, Grace?"

Her heart skipped a beat. She felt as if the room had become a giant vacuum. Instead of explaining himself, he crossed the pine-paneled room, shoved aside the remains of their take-out meal and reached for the champagne he'd left on ice earlier that evening.

"Come on, let's go watch the moon rise," he said, his voice oddly gruff. "It's supposed to be one of the perks of this place—watching the moon rise over the ocean."

And it was. Oh, mercy, it was, Grace told herself later as she stood leaning against the railing, a glass of champagne in hand, with Chandler so close beside her she could hear the quiet, comforting sound of his breathing. As long as she was here, she told herself, she might as well take advantage of the moment. It wouldn't come again, not in her lifetime. She knew about daydreams. She knew about reality. Fortunately, she was far too sensible to mistake the one for the other.

Chapter 7

Between a full moon rising over the Atlantic, sending a glittering path to the shore, and the sweep of the tall striped lighthouse, the very air was luminous. Or maybe, she thought, bemused, luminosity was in the eye of the beholder.

Because the beholder, in this case, was definitely feeling luminous. Feeling young and giddy and incredibly desirable. Tomorrow would come soon enough, champagne or no champagne.

Chandler or no Chandler.

"Here, have some more," he urged, and meek as a lamb, she held out her flute. Within the past hour the air had turned almost balmy, as if a spell had been cast. According to Chandler, it was caused by a shift in the wind, something to do with the Gulf Stream flowing just offshore.

"If the Gulf Stream's been there all along, then why was it so darned cold earlier today?" she asked, taking a sip of the deliciously dry wine.

"Labrador Current comes down from the north. We were under that influence earlier. The two undersea rivers meet right off where we're standing and duke it out. The result's called Diamond Shoals, otherwise known as the Graveyard of the Atlantic."

How on earth could a man look and sound so darned sexy explaining a weather phenomenon?

In spite of the warm evening, she shivered, and he put his arm around her. They were standing on the sunroof, only in this case, it was a moon-roof. Grace felt as if she could fly. It wasn't entirely due to the champagne.

In her slightly befuddled mind, she went over the words of the hastily scribbled note they'd found in the motel room, telling them that Susie and Buck had decided that for once, their elders were right. So they were going to give themselves more time, meanwhile driving up to Duck to join the party. Sorry for any inconvenience.

Inconvenience!

Grace couldn't help it, she laughed. And then she sighed and shook her head. "I still can't believe it—the wedding gown, all that fuss about where the reception was going to be held, and now...this!"

Leaning back against the railing, Chandler pulled
her into his arms, her back against his front. With his
mouth close to her ear, he said, "But isn't this exactly
what we wanted?"

It was definitely what she wanted, only she didn't
think that was what he meant. "For them to wait until
they were old enough to be sure, you mean. Do you
think they'll ever get together?" As long as he was
holding her, she might as well lean her head back
against his shoulder.

"Who knows? At this point, who really cares?
They've served their purpose."

Grace didn't bother to ask what that purpose was.
She knew. She also knew that whatever he wanted
from her it would be short-lived. And it would certainly include sex, because the whole atmosphere practically quivered with it. But he was who he was—a
prominent, successful business owner—and she was
who she was. A fool who had no better sense than to
fall in love with the man she worked for.

Which meant that she would simply have to take
whatever he offered and be satisfied with it.

If it hadn't been for Buck and Susie, they would
have never even met. She'd have gone on working for
him until she retired and he'd have never known she
existed.

If she was smart, she would pack her bag and leave
right now. But she wasn't smart—she'd already
proved that. So if she was going to get involved at all,

she'd darn well better play it for laughs, so that when it ended she could walk away and he would never even suspect she was bleeding inside.

She took another sip of champagne and then she actually began to laugh. Turning in his arms, she buried her face against his warm throat, inhaling the essence of salt air, clean male flesh and his brisk, light cologne.

"What's so funny?"

"Nothing. Everything."

He was aroused. She had that much power, at least. "You know what? For a stuffed shirt, you have a really remarkable vocabulary."

"I do?"

"When we read the note, remember? If Uncle Dockery ever heard you cussing that way, he'd be shocked to the bone."

"Do him good." With moonlight turning his eyes translucent, he frowned at her. "What do you mean, stuffed shirt?"

"Oh, come on, Mr. Daye, everyone knows you're a three-piece-suited pillar of the community."

Feigning hurt feelings, he said, "So? *So?* What do you have against community pillars?"

"Nothing at all," she murmured, standing on tiptoe to nip his chin with her teeth. "They're...delicious."

It was then that he knocked the wind right out of her sails by telling her he wanted to make love to her.

A lot. And for a long time. Like roughly the next fifty years.

"So, um—what do you say?" he finished, sounding oddly uncertain for a certified pillar of the community.

Grace fell back against his arms and stared up at him. Carefully, she set her flute on the railing. Either her brain wasn't working properly or her tongue wasn't connected. She couldn't manage to connect the two.

"You're not saying anything. Don't tell me you're surprised. Even stuffed shirts can fall in love."

In love. Had he actually said the word, or had she only imagined it? *Susie, where are you, hon? Your big sister needs some advice.*

"So anyway," he went on after several awkward moments, "the way I figure it, if you're willing—" He broke off, sounding uncertain. "Grace, I'm not alone in this, am I?"

An uncertain Chandler Daye was more than any woman with a viable hormone in her body could resist. Wrapping her arms around him, Grace willingly handed him her heart. "I'm sort of slow, in case you hadn't noticed. I mean, the feeling's there, all right— oh, my, is it ever! But Chandler, you don't have to— you know— Oh, Lord, I sound like Susie, don't I? With all the 'I means' and the 'you knows.'" And then she started grinning. "Like, I love you, okay? Like, I really do!"

He expelled a great sigh of—she hoped—relief.

With his hands moving over her back to press her closer, it was obvious that any talking that needed to be done had better be done quickly.

So he talked. "Like, I love you, too. Like the kids are never going to let us forget that we took over their wedding."

"Are we going to do that?"

"You betcha. As your boss, I hereby extend an indefinite leave of absence. We'll have time to get a license, change the arrangements to whatever you'd prefer, but right now—" He broke off, closed his eyes and took a deep breath. "Right now, I suggest we get started on the honeymoon."

Which they did. Grace enjoyed her first hot tub experience. Nearly drowned in the process, but then, she'd never been particularly good at underwater sports. Fortunately, she was a quick learner, given enough incentive.

And the incentive was there...oh, my, yes!

The bedrooms were every bit as comfortable as advertised, although the beds in the bunkroom really were too narrow. Especially the top bunk. Giggling helplessly after Chandler accidentally kicked away the ladder, Grace teased him as he eyed the distance to the floor. "Go ahead and jump, I dare you. And here I thought you were such a sportsman."

"Hey, I'm a fisherman, not a pole vaulter."

"Could have fooled me," she said with mock innocence.

He swatted her on the bare behind, dropped to the floor, and scooped her off into his arms. "The next time you get any smart ideas, we lay out a few ground rules before we act on them, agreed?"

"Agreed," she said, meekly containing her mirth—her joy—her love for her wonderful stuffed shirt. "Um…you know that center island in the kitchen? With a blanket thrown over the top—"

"Gra-ace!"

"Okay, okay—just thought I'd mention it."

Outside, the sun was shining. Fishermen on the piers were hauling in big blues. In another room, a *Candleglow* wedding gown that was too short for the bride-to-be hung neglected and forgotten in a closet. In another hour, a wedding feast would be delivered to the cottage aptly named *New Beginnings*.

While inside, two serious adults eased themselves back into a hot tub, discussing the kind of things serious, mature, stripped, stark naked adults sometimes discuss under such circumstances. Such as the way they had both waited to fall in love, almost as if they'd known that one day they would meet and zing! Just like that it would happen.

"Susie and Buck are going to try and take credit for it, you do know that, don't you?" Grace asked, gasping as his hand slid higher on her thigh.

"If they ever do get together, the relationships of our children are going to be so tangled up it will take an act of Congress to untangle them."

"Our children?"

"Theirs and ours."

"Oh," she said softly, as a whole new world opened up before her.

And then nothing else was said for a long, long time.

THE BRIDE'S BIG ADVENTURE
Stella Bagwell

* * *

To all my readers.
Thank you from the bottom of my heart.

Dear Reader,

Each woman has her own idea of the perfect wedding. Some dream of a grand ceremony with a designer gown, long guest list, food, flowers, music, and, last but not least, a dreamy man waiting at the altar. Others, like myself, prefer things more simple. I was married at the minister's parsonage with my high school English teacher as a witness. Which was, I've always thought, rather fitting for a young woman who was destined to become a romance writer!

As for my heroine, Gloria, in "The Bride's Big Adventure," she's expecting to have a large, well-planned wedding with all the trimmings. But what she winds up getting is something far different and far more precious—a man she really loves.

Grand or simple, in the end, I believe that's all a woman really wants at her wedding. A good man, who will always love her. And, if this finds you planning your wedding or wedding anniversary, I hope Gloria and Spencer's journey to marriage will put a smile in your heart.

Love and God Bless,

Stella Bagwell

Chapter 1

Gloria Rhodes raised the tall glass of iced tea to her lips and drank thirstily. The temperature was blazing and dust devils had spun a fine coating of dust on her slender bare arms and long black hair. She needed a meal, a cool bath, a place to lay her head. She needed excitement, passion and adventure. She needed a plan!

Too bad she hadn't been brave enough to order something stronger than tea. A couple of margaritas would've made her forget she was in a coarse little tavern in West Texas instead of her plush home back in San Antonio. The fiancé, the wedding and the furious father she'd left behind would've been little more than a hilarious memory.

Oh well, at least she'd managed to escape. And

driving eighty miles an hour all afternoon had given her some breathing space. But Gloria was smart enough to know it was going to take more than distance to save her from her father's wrath. No doubt about it, Vernon Rhodes would put up a search for his daughter and once he found her, he'd demand that she return and marry the man he'd chosen for her.

Well, she wouldn't do it! She'd wed a stranger before she'd become the wife of a man who viewed her as nothing more than a passionless business venture with her father.

From her seat on a lumpy vinyl cushion, Gloria scanned the long bar running along one end of the room. One man was sitting on a tall stool, nursing a mug of beer. Behind the counter, a middle-aged woman with brassy red hair and a cigarette dangling from her lips was watching a tiny TV screen mounted on a shelf in one corner. Two men were sitting directly in the booth behind Gloria, but so far she'd only heard murmurs from them, which suited her fine. The place was miles away from nowhere and looked like it catered only to rough customers. Not runaway heiresses.

Her father would be horrified to see her drinking out of plastic and reading four-letter words that had been scratched into the tabletop. The image of his outraged expression very nearly made her giggle out loud, but the slightly raised voice behind her suddenly distracted her.

''No, Ike. If I have to sell the bull, then so be it.

I'm already mortgaged to the hilt and the note on him is coming in the next few days. The bank has already warned me they won't defer it again.''

"Maybe another lender—'' That voice seemed to be facing Gloria.

"No lender in his right mind would lend me another dime.''

"Spence, you can't raise quality cattle without Beau,'' his buddy pointed out.

"Go on and say what you mean, Ike. I can't raise quality cattle now that my bank account is drained.''

If it hadn't been for the heavy sarcasm, the one called Spence would have had a delicious voice, Gloria thought. Rich and deep with just a hint of a Texas drawl. It was the kind of voice a woman wanted next to her ear in the dark of night.

The wild thought had her eyes darting to the tea glass in her hand. Had the bartender spiked it without her knowing? She didn't normally have erotic notions waltzing through her head. But then it wasn't her everyday routine to jilt a fiancé either.

Preferring to hear about someone else's miseries rather than agonize about her own, Gloria strained to catch a few more words of the conversation going on behind her.

"Well, Spence, I wish I had the money to loan you,'' the one called Ike said. "I'd give it to you with no interest and no certain time to pay it back, either. You've been the best neighbor and friend I've ever had. Joan and I wouldn't have made it last year if you hadn't helped us.''

There was a long pause, after which the sexy sounding one said, ''Yeah, well, we're both generous hearted, Ike.'' His low chuckle was full of wry amusement. ''We're also both poor ranchers. But what the hell. Better that than rich businessmen.''

Ike laughed along with him, then said, ''It's too bad you don't have a relative with enough money to lend. It would be a shame for you to have to start selling off your stock or land.''

''I'm hoping it won't come to that, Ike.''

She caught the shuffle of boots, then the flare of a match. Soon afterward cigarette smoke spiraled in her direction. Absently, Gloria waved it away, while her mind began to spin. The man behind her needed money and she had plenty of it. Would he be willing to help her?

From the corner of her eye, she could see the man with the cigarette had gotten to his feet. Since the man hankering to hang on to a bull called Beau was still sitting directly behind her that meant Ike was the one with leaving on his mind.

Minutes later, the two friends exchanged goodbyes and Ike had left the tavern. Before Gloria could rationalize the folly of her intentions, she picked up her glass and slid from the booth.

Two steps backward had her standing beside the stranger's table. A man somewhere in his thirties looked up at her with a faintly curious stare. Gloria stared back as she took in deeply tanned features and a pair of eyes shaded by the brim of a black felt hat. At first glance they appeared to be brown, but they could have been hazel. The only thing she was sure about was the squint lines fanning out from the corners and a set of perfectly adorable dimples bracketing his roughly hewn mouth.

"You lost or something, ma'am?"

Gloria could feel his eyes roaming over her, traveling from her mussed black hair to her crumpled linen dress and on to her diamond bracelet. Even in her disheveled state, she understood she looked out of place here in the Horned Toad Saloon.

Clearing her throat, she said, "Not exactly. I was just wondering—" She motioned toward the seat Ike had just vacated. "Do you mind if I sit down?"

One dark brow lifted ever so slightly. The dimples deepened. Gloria got the impression he found her amusing.

"Suit yourself," he said. "But I was about to leave."

His cocky attitude and her own brashness caused a blush to sting her cheeks, but in spite of her embarrassment, she slid into the opposite seat.

Like the table where she'd been sitting, there were names and other crude remarks gouged into the cheap wood. She placed her glass over one particularly foul verb before she dared to look across at him.

"I promise not to take up much of your time. I couldn't help but overhear some of what you were saying to your friend. And I was wondering—" She stopped as her heart began to pound, her mind awhirl with possibilities.

"You want to ask me something?"

Gloria's green eyes widened, then she blurted in a breathless rush. "Will you marry me?"

He responded with a noise somewhere between a snort and a laugh, after which he reached for her glass and sniffed at the brown liquid.

"I don't smell any alcohol. Is there vodka in this?"

Gloria looked properly offended. "Of course not! I didn't come in here to drink!"

Spencer rolled his eyes around the ratty-looking tavern. Drinking was the only thing that took place inside these four walls. That and maybe a few fistfights once in a while. But it was a convenient stop between his and Ike's place. "Well, this sure as hell isn't anywhere to be hunting a husband."

"I didn't come in here for that either. But—"

"Maybe I'd better have Marge call a doctor," he interrupted. "I think you need to go to San Antonio."

Every ounce of blood drained from her cheeks. Her heart fluttered. Surely he didn't know! Her father couldn't have already posted an alert for her whereabouts through the media. He was probably only now coming home from his office.

"Uh—why—uh, do you think I need to go there?"

His frown said she was worse off than he'd first imagined. "For evaluation at the mental hospital, lady."

Obviously intent on leaving, he started to rise. Gloria latched on to to his forearm like a vise grip.

"Please—don't go just yet," she pleaded. "At least hear me out."

Pointedly, his gaze drifted to the small hand clenched around his arm. He'd not been touched by a woman in a long time and never by one wearing diamonds bigger than the chunks of ice in her drink. However, it was the sparkle in her green eyes and not the ones on her wrist that finally sent Spencer sinking back down in the seat.

"If you're really looking for a husband, miss, I think it might do you better to start with someone you're acquainted with. My name is Spencer Tate and as far as I know, I've never seen you in my life."

He was a big man with broad shoulders and a chest to match. Beneath her fingers, the muscles of his forearm felt like bands of iron. The look on his rugged face was more comical than quizzical and she knew she was going to have to talk fast to make him understand she was sober and serious.

She pulled her fingers away from his arm and linked her hands atop the table. "I'm Gloria Rhodes. I'm from San Antonio. At least, I was. But not anymore. Not since this morning. I—" Gloria stopped and licked her bare lips. For the life of her, she couldn't remember a time any man had made her feel so aware of herself. "I left an unpleasant situation back there. One that—I don't ever want to go back to."

Both brows lifted as his eyes continued to survey her face. "A situation with the law?"

"The law! Do I look like a criminal?"

He chuckled. "Maybe white-collar crime. You been doctoring a few accounts?"

She gasped. "Are you insane? I don't even work!"

Sudden dawning lit his eyes, which she could now see were a warm caramel-brown. A mocking grin curled the corners of his lips.

"Oh," he said. "One of those."

Gloria wasn't exactly sure what he meant by "those" but whatever it was had to be an insult. She straightened her shoulders and jutted her chin. "Actually, I do work—I mean, I did. But in a family-owned business. That's not the same."

Grinning smugly, he shook his head. "Naw. Stealing from your family isn't the same at all."

It took supreme effort to keep her from stomping his foot beneath the table. "I haven't stolen anything, mister! I'm—well, I need a husband fast! He would solve all my problems."

Spencer had planned to head home the minute Ike had left the building. He had work piled up back at the ranch and had only stopped here at the Horned Toad to have a beer before he faced the heat and unloading a pickup bed of fencepost and gaucho wire.

But the little dish across from him was the prettiest thing he'd seen in a long time and it wasn't like he got proposals of marriage every day. That was enough to warrant a few more minutes of loafing, he figured.

"Really. And how's that?" he asked, his eyes sparkling with humor.

She tried to glare at him, but found she couldn't. The sexy, teasing look on his face was just too delightful after being engaged to a stuffed shirt for six months.

"Well, if I were married, then my father couldn't make me marry someone else. It would be too late, you see."

"Oh. So the old man is trying to pick you a husband," he said.

Gloria rolled her eyes and groaned. "He's done more than pick. He more or less forced me into an engagement with a business partner of his. Now the wedding is just a week away and I'm—well, I can't marry a deep freeze with nothing but money on his mind!"

Surprise crossed his features, then his look turned to more of a suggestive leer than anything. "Surely a woman like you should be able to...*distract* her fiancé from business."

Laughter erupted from Gloria causing Marge and the other patron to look their way. No doubt she and Hernando were wondering how he'd managed to snare the attention of such a young, upper-class debutante.

He wasn't even wearing clean clothes and had more than two days of rusty brown stubble covering his face. Besides, everybody in Crockett County knew he didn't squire women anymore.

Gloria burst out, "Are you kidding? Paul is one of those men who has to have everything perfect and planned." She grimaced, then waved her hand back and forth in a guilty-like gesture. "I guess that's one of the reasons I allowed Daddy to talk me into this farce of an engagement. I thought having everything settled for me would be easy and best. You know, the ambitious, successful husband, the two kids, the fancy home in the suburbs—no surprises. Paul is only twenty-eight, but he's the sort that's figured right down to the exact penny what he'll be drawing when he retires thirty-five years from now!"

Spencer could see she was getting heated up just talking about the whole thing. Her cheeks were tinged with pink and her eyes were spitting sparks hot enough to set him and the table on fire. At this moment he couldn't picture her married to a deep freeze.

"That couldn't be all bad," he said calmly.

"Bad? It's horrible! Getting him to deviate from his daily schedule is like pulling a tooth without Novocaine. I'm sure if I had been crazy enough to marry him, he would have put our sex life on a schedule, too!"

"That would be a hell of a thing," Spencer agreed.

Her breasts rose and fell as she sucked in an indignant breath then blew it out. "Darned right it would!"

She glanced across the table at him, then blushed as she realized he was studying her intently. The grin on his face exposed startling white teeth against tanned skin. It was the most lazy, sensual expression she'd ever seen on a man.

Gloria cleared her throat and shifted uncomfortably. Sweat had glued her thighs to the vinyl and she felt like she was being treated to a cheap wax job as she ripped her legs from the seat and crossed her knees.

"Well," she said in a somewhat mollified tone. "A woman doesn't want to be considered a job, you know."

"No. Certainly not."

She slanted him another look. "You're laughing at me now."

He pushed the brim of his hat back on his head. Damp, sandy brown curls fell over his forehead. "No. You're entirely right, Ms. Rhodes. In fact, I've never heard anything put so eloquently."

Spencer Tate might not be laughing at her, but he was chuckling, at least. To have a man not take her seriously was a first for Gloria. In fact, no-nonsense men were just about the only kind she'd dealt with in her sheltered life.

"Please don't call me Ms. Rhodes. I'm sick of formality. Call me Glory. My close friends do. And if you're going to be my husband, you can't very well address me as Ms. Rhodes.''

Resting his elbows on the tabletop, he leaned forward. The movement brought his face a scant few inches from hers and her breath quickened as her eyes dropped to the hard chiseled line of his mouth.

''What makes you so sure I'm not already married?'' He drawled the question softly.

Oh, he definitely wasn't married, she thought. The look of a renegade mustang was stamped all over him. Her lips tilted upward in a secretive little smile. ''You're not wearing a ring.''

He shrugged. ''That doesn't mean anything,'' he half taunted.

She sucked in a needy breath and her nostrils were suddenly filled with the male scent of dust and leather and salty sweat. The combination reminded her that this man was a rugged cowboy, not a milksop.

Thanks to her overprotective father, she'd only been exposed to young men with manicured hands and fat bank accounts. But this man's hands were big, the skin tanned and tough as rawhide. As for his bank account, Gloria had already heard it was slim. Funny how that made him even more appealing as a prospective husband.

''No,'' she agreed. ''But when I overheard you talking about the bull and the financing, you didn't once mention a wife or what she might be thinking about the whole matter.''

"Maybe I don't care what she thinks," he suggested cockily.

"There is no *she*," Gloria countered with confidence.

He drained his beer and plunked the mug down next to her tea glass. "Okay, you're right," he admitted, licking the last of the foamy brew from his lips. "I don't have a wife and I'm not in the market for one. So you'd better head on up the road, honey. Bachelors are slim pickins here in Crockett County."

Undaunted, she plowed on. "From what I gather, so is money. We could make each other happy."

His low chuckle was lustful and provocative. Gloria was suddenly imagining herself crushed up against his hard chest, those big hands rough and hot against her naked skin.

Goodness, what was wrong with her? she wondered, while giving herself a good mental slap. She needed help, not an initiation in wild, sweaty sex! But what a thought….

Still chuckling, he said, "We might at that, Glory. For a day or two. But I'm a man who likes my freedom."

"How do you know? You might discover you like having a wife around."

He shook his head. "Already tried it once. That gave me two years of cursing and fit-throwing."

"From her or you?"

His eyes narrowed shrewdly on her face. "Her. I'm

a laid-back kind of guy. It takes a lot to rile me. Except for greedy bankers.''

Gloria smiled at him. ''Well, I don't curse. Not out loud anyway.''

Rubbing one hand over his whiskered jaws, he said, ''I don't mean this as an insult, Glory, but having to sell Beau, my bull, would probably be less painful than taking a wife.''

''But why?'' she shot back at him. ''You're going to have to pay the bank note and with interest. I won't charge you anything.''

The sly twist to his lips said he didn't believe her for one minute. ''Oh, there'd be a charge all right, honey. It might not be in money, but it would cost me something.''

Tossing her long, smooth hair back behind her shoulders, she leaned toward him, her eyes desperate. ''Look. I know this is all a bit unconventional, but think about it,'' she urged. ''I have money—more than you can imagine. I'd be willing to sink a big hunk of it into this ranch of yours if you'd only give me the security of your name. It won't have to be a permanent thing, if that's what's bothering you. I just need to be your wife long enough to make my father see that I mean to live my life in my own way.''

''And how long might that take?''

Gloria shrugged. She wasn't about to scare him off by admitting that she'd been fighting her father's chains unsuccessfully for the past five years.

"Once he takes a look at you—not long," she assured him. "But if you're worried our agreement might get to stretching out too long, we could always set a time limit. Say, something like six months or a year."

Damned if she wasn't making the whole thing sound tempting, Spencer thought. But could he bear having this woman in his house for six months? Better turn that around, Tate, he told himself. Could Glory Rhodes stand living in his house for that length of time? Hell, even her name sounded like something a Hollywood producer had thought up. She'd last on the Rafter T about as long as an ice cube would last on the front porch.

"Whoa, now, honey. You're puttin' the cart before the horse. You don't know anything about me. Where I live or how. For all you know, I could be the sorriest man in Crockett County."

"*Are* you the sorriest?"

The dimples next to his mouth appeared again. "Well, there's only a total of four thousand people in the whole county and since it's three hundred square miles in size, I can't say that I know all of them."

Gloria wasn't discouraged. "Your friend Ike was singing your praises a few minutes ago. I'll take his word for your character."

"I live alone—like a bachelor. No frilly curtains. No rugs. Dust everywhere. The house is more than a hundred years old."

Her eyes widened. "Literally?"

"Yes. My great-grandfather built it in 1900. He had money once. From oil leases. But he squandered it all on women and gambling. The Tates that followed stuck to ranching. Including me."

"Well, a little dust won't bother me. I'm not a hothouse gardenia."

Spencer wasn't so sure. She looked pretty pampered to him. Her silky black hair and creamy smooth skin had obviously been sheltered from the sun. And from the look of her hands, she'd never dipped them into anything harsher than a manicure soak.

To reinforce his suspicions, he reached for her hand and was instantly struck at how soft and fragile it felt curled inside his palm.

"Yeah," he said huskily, "you look real tough. I'll bet you could stay in the saddle all day long."

"I am tough," she countered. "And if need be, I can learn how to rope and brand or whatever it is you cowboys do."

Spencer couldn't help it, he threw back his head and laughed.

"What's so funny?" she asked in an offended voice. "I was serious."

"I know. Sorry. But you're just—" He shook his head and grinned. "It's been a long time since I've thought about anything but cattle and grass and the weather and bills. And I didn't have any idea my stop here at the Horned Toad was going to be so entertaining.''

Gloria grimaced. "I'm not trying to be your entertainment, Mr. Tate! I'm trying to make a deal with you!''

She started to draw her hand back, but he tightened his grip. Better that she understand right now that he wasn't a monk and that just the sight of her pert little breasts pushing against her dress was enough to make him forget he'd sworn off women.

"Call me Spence," he invited, then added, "just how long have you been engaged to Mr. Perfect?''

"*Was* engaged," she corrected. "For six months.''

He whistled under his breath. "That's a good little spell.''

Didn't she know it. "It was easier to go along with the thing than to fight my father.''

Before Spencer realized what he was doing, his fingertip began to trace a pattern of circles on the back of her hand. "So tell me—what made you decide to make this sudden break?''

The feel of his hard, tough hand, the movement of his finger against her skin was making her breathing quick and raspy. Heat was gathering in her neck and face. Hopefully the dim lighting in the place wouldn't let him see she was having some sort of chemical reaction to him.

"Does that really matter?" she asked.

"It does if you expect me to take you seriously.''

Her heart jolted to a stop, then began to thud wildly. She felt like a hunter who suddenly knew she had a slim chance to capture her prey.

Carefully, she said, "Well, believe me, it wasn't an overnight decision. I've been trying to get out of this thing almost from the very start. But you see, I'm my father's only child and since my mother died he's practically smothered me. I'm twenty-three now, but he still has this notion that if he plans out my life I'll be safe and secure and happy. He can't see that he's making me miserable."

"What about the fiancé?"

Gloria snorted. "Paul? He and my father have been business cronies for several years and this marriage would mean quite a hefty merger for Paul. After the wedding Father had promised to make him the VP of his marketing firm plus give him a lump of stock in the company. It all boils down to money and position. Both of which Paul loves."

"Maybe he loves you, too."

Her short laugh was mocking. "Paul doesn't love anyone but himself. He barely has five minutes out of the day for me. I mean, if you'd been engaged for six months to a girl you were madly in love with would she still be a virgin?"

Spencer coughed, then reached for his beer mug before he remembered he'd already drained away the last dregs. "Uh—well, I don't think—if I intended to marry someone, I wouldn't wait around for six months to tie the knot.''

Gloria nodded in fervent agreement. ''Darn right, you wouldn't. So now do you see why I need help? When I marry I want to be deliriously in love. I want passion and romance and a husband that will still find me wildly attractive when I'm eighty.''

Spencer wished he hadn't given up smoking. Right now he needed a cigarette badly. ''Then maybe you'd better wait and find the right man,'' he suggested. ''I doubt like hell I'll make it to eighty.''

She giggled and squeezed his hand and Spencer felt a strange, spontaneous connection.

''You look pretty healthy to me,'' she said. ''Besides, look what you'll get in return. You'll get to keep your bull. I'll see that you get whatever your ranch needs. Horses, tractors, barns—you name it.''

He shook his head with comical disbelief. ''Do you have any idea what those things cost?''

''Five figures at the very least,'' she answered without batting an eyelash. ''That's no problem. I have more money than I'll ever be able to spend.''

She was serious and that scared him. Women like her weren't meant for men like him. Put the two together and it always equaled trouble. But then life would be boring without a few rough bumps to travel over, he reminded himself.

''You shouldn't be telling me things like that, Glory. I could try to take advantage of you.''

"You could," she agreed. "But you're not that type. You have honest eyes."

He chuckled. "My ex-wife didn't think so."

A sly little smile lit Gloria's face. "Then she didn't know you very well, I'd say."

Spencer didn't know what it was about this woman, but she was contagious. There was a freshness about her, a hopefulness that lifted his spirits. Being around her for six months couldn't be all that bad. It might even be nice to have someone to talk to besides the horses and the cows.

"Uh…when were you thinking you needed this new husband?" he asked guardedly.

"As soon as possible! Today!"

Somehow her answer didn't surprise him. The moment she'd sat down across from him, he'd felt a sense of urgency about her.

"Not possible. There's a three day waiting period here in Texas. And you're still a long way from the state line, no matter which direction you decide to drive."

If he'd meant to deter her, he hadn't succeeded. If anything, her eyes were sparkling with sudden excitement. "Forget about driving. We'll fly to Vegas. We can be married by tonight!"

She was backing him to the edge of a cliff. He was going to have to jump or fall. And the way he saw it, either choice was likely to break his neck. "Vegas! Look, Glory, there's no commercial flights in or out of Ozona. And that's the only town around here for miles!''

"Is there an airport there? With smaller planes?"

"Yes, but—"

"Then we'll charter one," she said with a smug smile. "How soon can you be ready?"

"Ready?" he repeated inanely. "I haven't said I'll marry you yet."

Her smile deepened. "But you will. You know you want to."

Long moments passed. She waited while Spencer's common sense fought like hell to whip his impulsive nature.

Finally, he wiped a hand over his face and growled out, "Damn it. All right. You win."

With a tiny squeal of joy, Gloria leaned up and over the table and planted a kiss square on his mouth. "Oh thank you, Spencer Tate! You're an angel. And I promise this is going to be the best investment you've ever made!"

His lips still tingling from the connection with hers, Spencer snatched her up from the booth and guided her quickly toward the door.

From behind the bar, Marge called out, "Going home, Spence?"

"Hell no. I'm going to get married!"

Chapter 2

Outside the Horned Toad, the sunlight was ferocious. Gloria rapidly jammed a pair of sunglasses on her face, but even the cool gray lenses couldn't dim the spectacular sight of Spencer Tate.

Far bigger than what she'd first gauged, she found herself looking up at six foot two of brawny muscle and a face so full of rugged sex appeal she felt like she was committing a lustful sin by just looking at it. "Uh—what now?" she asked. "Are you going with me? Or am I going with you?"

Still holding her arm, he led her over to where her sleek green Jaguar was parked beneath the raggedy shade of a half-dead mesquite tree. "First of all," he said, "neither of us is going anywhere until we get this deal straightened out."

Deal. He was calling their marriage a deal. Well, that was good, she thought. Better than being counterfeit and masking a business arrangement with artificial affection.

Feeling oddly weak in the knees, she said, ''Maybe you'd better tell me what you mean.''

He dropped his hold on her arm and looped his thumbs over the heavy belt at his waist. ''Look, Glory. I know this offer you made me seems simple and genuine to you. But our verbal agreement might not cut it in a court of law. Especially if that daddy of yours tries to make waves. I don't want him, or anyone, thinking I've married you for anything more than what you've offered to give me.''

Gloria had never swooned in her life, but the heat or maybe the sight of this tough cowboy was doing something to her head. To keep from toppling toward him, she leaned most of her weight against the car door.

''What anyone else thinks doesn't matter,'' she said. ''As long as we keep our promises to each other. And I trust you.''

Her guilelessness charmed him in a way he'd not expected it to. ''That's foolish, Glory. As your husband I'd have a legal right to a part of your assets— if I wanted to assert those rights. Then you'd be in a mess.''

A wry smile touched her mouth. ''I'm already in a

mess, Spencer. I'm counting on you to get me out of it."

He folded his big arms across his chest. "I'm not moving a step until we get all this down in writing." He inclined his head toward her shoulder bag. "Do you have something in there you can write on?"

Impatient, Gloria rolled her eyes. "Do we have to do this now? It's blasted hot out here. We'll do it on the plane."

"We'll do it now or there won't be any need for a plane."

From the resolute look in his eyes, she could see he was a man who would stick to his guns. Arguing with him any further would only be a waste of time. Besides, he was probably right, she mused. A written agreement would make everything safer. For the both of them.

"All right," she agreed. "Let's get this over with."

Slipping her bag from her shoulder, she began to dig through the contents. After a moment, she said, "I can't find any sort of paper except extra deposit slips in my checkbook."

"That's too small."

She flashed him a mocking look. "What are you planning on writing, a saga?"

"Bare facts with no small print," he said. "Maybe I'd better look in the truck. I probably have an old feed receipt."

"No, wait," she called as he started to turn away.

"Here's a napkin I took from a dispenser in the Horned Toad. It's heavy enough to write on. Just dictate how you want it to read."

She unfolded the cheap, but sturdy napkin, then spread it out on the hood of her car. Spencer stood just behind her, peering over her left shoulder.

"I'm sure you're better with words than I," he said. After all, she'd smooth-talked him into becoming her husband in less than thirty minutes, Spencer thought wryly. "Just say that six months after the date of our wedding, the marriage will dissolve. And during that time, as your husband, I will only accept gifts and, or, monies that you want to give me. Otherwise, I will have no legal right to any part of your bank accounts, property, etcetera, whether you are alive or dead."

She looked up at him, her expression dreary. "You don't have homicidal tendencies, do you?"

He wanted to smile, but he wouldn't let himself. This was too serious to let her distract him. Though God knew, he could hardly keep his mind or his eyes off her.

"No. But we don't want to take chances. Our flight back from Vegas might go down and kill you."

She chuckled. "And not you? Or did you stop and think you might die in the crash and then I'd be entitled to your estate?"

Her reversal of his reasoning made him laugh outright. "You'd be welcome to it, Glory. But you wouldn't want it."

Bothered that he was already judging her before he got to know her, she asked, "How do you know that?"

His brown eyes slipped slowly over her face, then down her melon-colored dress and on to the dainty leather sandals, exposing painted pink toenails. "You and I live in different worlds, Glory. Our values about things are not the same."

He was more or less accusing her of being a snob and it was on the tip of her tongue to tell him so. But she kept the opinion to herself. It didn't matter what he thought of her, she told herself. The most important thing now was that she didn't give him any reason to change his mind about marrying her.

"We'll see," was all she said, then carefully brought the pen in her hand down to the napkin.

Five minutes later, Spencer was finally satisfied with the hastily written document. He took the pen from her and scrawled his name and the date across the bottom. Once he was finished, she signed directly under him.

"Okay, that's that," she said with relief. "Now what?"

Never bothering with a watch, Spencer glanced around at the slant of the sun. "I'll head on to the ranch. I've got to feed the livestock and pack a bag. You go on to the airport and see what you can do about chartering a plane. I'll meet you there."

She nodded while wondering why her heart was

suddenly beating with wild excitement. It wasn't anything out of the ordinary for her to get on a plane and fly to Vegas or anywhere she wanted, she thought. This time shouldn't be any different. Except that even in her wildest dreams she'd never had a traveling companion like Spencer Tate. Or a husband like him, either.

"Good," she said, folding the napkin, then tucking it away in her bag. "How long do you think you'll be?"

"My ranch is about fifteen miles north of here. Ozona is five miles west on Highway 10. So give me at least an hour."

"I'll be waiting," she promised.

He turned toward his truck, then paused and looked back at her as though he couldn't quite believe the two of them had just become engaged. "If you want to back out, now is the time to do it. Not once we get to Nevada."

Stepping forward, she placed a hand on his arm. "There's no chance of me backing out, Spencer. I'm not a fickle woman."

His chuckles were a mixture of amusement and disbelief. "Is that so? Then what would you call marrying me?"

"Smart."

The word came out of her without any hesitation or consideration, as though she was certain she'd found a hero instead of a poor cowboy. Spencer didn't know whether to feel flattered or worried. But he was dead certain about one thing. It was damn good that this marriage was only going to be temporary. Otherwise, he'd be in big trouble.

"I'll see you in Ozona," he told her, then hurried off to his truck.

With a soft little sigh that she was totally unaware of making, Gloria watched him until he drove out of sight.

An hour and fifteen minutes later, Gloria was standing outside the tiny airport terminal. Her bags were sitting next to her feet. Out on the runway, a pilot was readying a plane for their takeoff.

Spencer Tate had told her to give him an hour and it was only fifteen minutes past. A number of things could have detained him. There wasn't any cause for her to worry. Yet she could feel her insides beginning to twist into knots.

If he didn't show, what would she do? she asked herself. There wasn't much she could do, she thought, except cancel the plane and regroup. She'd have to get back in her car and keep heading west toward her grandmother's, as she'd first intended to do. But she would be swamped with disappointment.

Which didn't make one whit of sense. Spencer Tate wasn't the only man in the world who might help her out of this problem. But her mind had already pictured *him* as her husband. She'd already imagined herself as *his* wife, living on *his* ranch. Another man just wouldn't do.

Nervously she glanced at her wristwatch. One more minute had passed. She tapped her toe against the tarmac. How long would the pilot wait, she wondered. How long could she wait?

"Are you thinking you've been stood up?"

The deep male voice behind her left shoulder was so unexpected, she jumped with a start, then whirled to see Spencer Tate grinning down at her. The whiskers were gone from his face. He was dressed in starched blue jeans, a white shirt and a black hat and boots. A nylon duffel bag was suspended from one big fist.

Gloria was so relieved and happy to see him, she flung herself straight at him and pressed kisses over his face.

Stunned by the affectionate assault, Spencer unwittingly dropped his bag and closed his hands lightly around her waist. By then she'd moved her attention toward his mouth and for a few brief moments, he tasted the warm sweetness of her lips.

"Well," he said, once she'd eased down off her tiptoes and severed the kiss. "If I'd known I was going to get this kind of greeting I would have hurried."

In the heat of kissing him, her cheeks had warmed to a subtle pink. Her eyes sparkled up at him. "I'm so glad you're here! I was beginning to think you'd gone home and forgotten all about me."

If Spencer lived to be the eighty she'd talked about, he couldn't forget her. A man just didn't forget a woman like this one. He wasn't quite sure what to make of her reception. Maybe now that she'd ended her engagement to the deep freeze, she was thawing out and letting her hair down. Or maybe she was simply showing her gratitude that he was going along with her plan. Either way, she was doing a damn good job of making him feel wanted. Even if he was only going to serve as a wall between her and her father.

"We made a deal," he said. "I don't back out on deals. Even when I know I'm going to lose."

She slipped her hand into his as though she'd been doing it for years. Spencer suddenly realized she was one of those persons that instinctively caressed and petted and touched. Dear Lord, the next six months with her was either going to be pure heaven or downright hell.

She said, "Well, you're not going to be the loser this time. I promise you that."

Spencer watched her slip her sunglasses back onto her nose and direct her gaze toward a small, twin engine plane.

"Is the pilot ready?" he asked.

"I think so." She angled her face up to his. "Are you?"

Grinning, he reached down for their bags. "Viva Las Vegas!"

* * *

The small plane took Gloria and Spencer as far as El Paso where they were fortunate enough to find a commercial flight straight to Vegas. The two of them had just enough time to purchase tickets and take a seat before the big jet lifted into the desert sky.

In Vegas, a taxi drove them straight to the strip with its endless string of casinos and connecting hotels. After renting a room in the first one they came to, Gloria took Spencer by the arm and urged him across the huge foyer to a secluded spot behind a group of palms and a tinkling fountain.

"What's wrong?" he asked.

She grimaced. "What makes you think anything is wrong?"

He touched a finger against her forehead. "There's a deep wrinkle right here that I haven't seen before."

Shrugging, she focused on her toes. So far their trip had been much nicer than she'd ever expected. During the long plane ride, Spencer had instinctively seemed to understand she needed to relax and keep their conversation steered toward lighter things like music and movies and food. By the time they'd landed in Nevada, she was surprised at how much the two of them thought alike and how easy it was to be in his company. Now that the time was approaching for them to be married, she didn't want to do anything to break that bond between them.

"There's nothing wrong, except I—" Her eyes lifted back up to his face and she felt her heart give a little jolt. The same way it had when she'd first looked up at him outside the Horned Toad. "Well, I know this whole thing is putting you through a lot that you didn't ask for. I don't want to make matters worse for you by making a big to-do over our wedding. If you'd like, we could just have one of those drive-through ceremonies where you don't even have to get out of the car."

Much to his own surprise, Spencer didn't have to ponder over her suggestion. He didn't like it. Maybe the marriage was only going to last for six months, he thought, but it was still an intimate binding between two people. He wanted the event to be more than just reciting a few words through the open window of a car.

"I don't even get a burger through the drive-through, Glory. I sure as heck don't want a wife that way."

Surprise lifted her brows. "Then what would you like?"

The answer stunned him as he realized he'd like to have what every real engaged couple had when they got married, including the love. But seeing that they'd only met, he knew the love part was out of the question. *Hell, Spence, even six months from now it would be out of the question.* He had to remember that. But for now it wouldn't hurt to dream. Tonight he could let himself believe he was starting over fresh. That he wasn't a man who nearly had been crushed emotionally and financially by a woman.

"You go find yourself a pretty dress," he told her. "I'll go find a wedding chapel, then meet you back in our room in a couple of hours."

Gloria glanced at her wristwatch. By then it would be eight o'clock. But what would it matter? she asked herself as excitement began to surge through her. Vegas was a town that never closed and if Spencer wanted an actual wedding, she certainly didn't want to disappoint him.

"I'll be ready," she told him, then because it didn't feel right to just let him walk away without any sort of gesture of farewell, she raised on tiptoe and kissed his cheek. "Don't get lost."

The sudden flare of his nostrils told her she'd vexed him in some way.

"Maybe you can't tell it by looking," he said, "but I've been to town a time or two, Glory."

Irritation that he'd misunderstood flushed her cheeks with color. "I didn't mean you were a country bumpkin, Spencer." She squared her shoulders, not wanting to admit, even to herself, that she was beginning to feel possessive toward this man. "I just meant... Well, there's lots of distractions in this town. Especially beautiful women. I wouldn't want you to get sidetracked and forget about *us*."

The stiffness went out of his expression and then suddenly he was bestowing her with a glimpse of dimples. "Why, Glory, I didn't realize you were going to be a jealous wife."

Even though she was glad to have his teasing mood back, Gloria shot him a mildly censuring look. "I'll see you in two hours," she told him.

The dress was sexy. That was the only word to describe it, Gloria decided, as she stood twisting one way and then the other in front of a mirrored wall in the hotel room.

Just skimming the top of her knees, the white silk was fitted and draped against her curves in a subtle, yet provocative way. The neckline was scooped low, exposing just enough cleavage to be tantalizing.

It was not a dress she could have worn for Paul, she concluded. No, the heavy Victorian gown back in San Antonio had suited his staid personality perfectly. But thankfully, she'd never have to bear the weight of that dress or a loveless, dreary marriage. Instead, she was wearing a sensual garment for a sexy man and just the idea of it left her feeling liberated and happier than she could ever remember being since her mother had passed away.

Before she'd shopped for the dress, Gloria had spent forty-five minutes in the hotel beauty salon. Now, except for a portion she'd pinned behind her ear with a real gardenia, her glossy smooth hair cascaded to her shoulders.

A sound at the door caught her attention. She

glanced away from the mirror to see Spencer entering the room. His arms were full of white roses.

Spotting her, he stopped in his tracks. The sight she made with her breasts playing peekaboo with white silk and her shiny hair falling against the curve of her cheek was enough to make him stare in awe.

"I'm not late, am I?" he asked, his voice husky.

For some reason, the room around them began to fade and all she could see was his face. "No. I'm— I finished getting ready sooner than I thought. Did you find a chapel?"

Spencer nodded. "Right down the street. The minister will be looking for us in about twenty minutes."

Wide-eyed, Gloria stepped toward him. "You— We're going to be married by a *real* minister?"

A puzzled frown marred his features. "Yes. Why? Are you not a religious person?"

"Uh—yes, I am a spiritual one. That's why... Well, having a minister seems to make it all so real."

With a look of relief, he handed her the roses. "It *is* real, Glory. We're going to be man and wife no matter how you look at it."

Gloria was suddenly trembling and she wasn't exactly sure why. She wanted this marriage. In fact, from the moment she'd sat down and faced Spencer across the booth table, she'd known she wanted this. With him.

"You're right. But—" She lifted her eyes from the creamy white roses and locked gazes with him. "You don't think it might appear mocking? I mean, we're not exactly a couple bound by true love. And God will know.''

His smile gentle, he lifted a big hand to her cheek. ''Glory, I expect He'll know we probably have more tender feelings toward each other than most of the couples who think they're in love but wind up yelling at each other before the ink dries on their marriage license. And I'd like for Him to bless us. Even if it's only for six months.''

Tender feelings. Yes, Gloria thought, latching on to the two words with a bit of relief. That's what she had for this man. That's why she felt all soft and mushy each time she looked at him, each time he touched her. The way he was touching her now.

''Yes, you're right,'' she murmured, then smiled at him. ''The roses are beautiful. I didn't expect you to go to this much trouble.''

Spencer hadn't expected it of himself either. Hell, he wasn't a romantic guy. Never had been. But something about Gloria was pulling things out of him that he hadn't known were there.

''Well, a girl can't get married without flowers,'' he said with a sheepish drawl. ''Or a ring.''

Stunned, she stared at him. ''A ring!'' she blurted. ''Spencer—''

''There's no need for you to get all excited, Glory,'' he interrupted before she could say more. ''It's just a plain band. No diamonds. Nothing sparkling.''

He pulled a small velvet box from his jeans pocket then opened the lid on a wide gold band. To Gloria, its simplicity somehow symbolized a true marriage much more than if he'd exposed a hunk of diamonds. For a moment she was caught off guard by a strange tug of mixed emotions.

"You shouldn't have bothered, Spencer," she murmured.

"You don't like it."

The disappointment in his voice bothered her even more. He was marrying her to help her. Whether he pleased her, shouldn't matter to him. Or to her. But somehow it did.

"I like it very much." Too much, she realized. "I just meant that—well, a ring signifies that—oh, you know."

"That you belong to me," he said. "Well, you will be my wife for six months, Glory."

Was she hearing something sensual in his words or was she simply starting to fantasize about this man? she wondered. Either way, she had to get a grip on herself. This was a business arrangement, not a love match. She didn't really know Spencer Tate. He didn't know her. And in six months they would part ways.

The roses clutched to her breasts quickly lifted upward, then fell as her lungs gulped for extra air. "Uh, yes, I suppose I will be your wife—in the eyes of the law," she added, then looping her arm through his, she urged him toward the door. "We'd better be going or we'll be late getting to the chapel."

As they stepped into the corridor, Spencer paused to look at her. "And I'll be your husband—in the eyes of God," he added.

Why did he have to keep bringing Him into it, Gloria wondered fretfully. Why was he making it all so romantic? To make her feel good or guilty?

"You still have time to back out of this," Spencer went on, totally unaware of the turmoil he was creating inside her. "We could catch a plane back to Texas and forget we'd ever met."

Forget Spencer? That would never be possible, Gloria thought. Not even if she lived to be a hundred.

Gripping the roses and his arm a little tighter, she said, "Let's go. The minister is waiting."

Chapter 3

Five blocks away in a small, quiet chapel filled with
fresh flowers, the two of them exchanged vows. Spencer placed the gold band on her finger and the minister
said a final prayer. Gloria was suddenly so overcome
by it all that her eyes misted over with tears.

She was struggling to blink them away when the
minister informed Spencer he could kiss his new bride.
Expecting a light smack to seal their bargain, she suddenly found herself enfolded in the tight circle of his
arms and her mouth branded with a long, possessive
kiss.

Dazed and sizzled by the unexpected embrace, Gloria signed the marriage license beneath Spencer's sig-
nature. As they departed the chapel, the minister, along

with his wife and daughter, who'd served as witnesses to the ceremony, all wished them congratulations and Godspeed.

Outside, they quickly hailed a cab. In the back seat, Spencer held her hand tightly between the two of his as though they were two happy kids just let loose on a playground. "Where are we going now?" he asked, grinning.

She looked at him, her brows arched into wary question marks. "What do you mean? Aren't we going back to the hotel room?"

To Gloria's dismay a dull flush spread along his strong jawbones and then he chuckled as though her question had surprised, but pleased him.

"Well, I was thinking we ought to have supper and maybe look the town over before we—go back to the room."

Was he thinking she had going back to the hotel room and making love on her mind? Oh dear heaven! Her thoughts must be registering on her face.

"Oh—yes, that sounds good," she agreed, then quickly added, "we haven't eaten anything since we grabbed that hot dog in the airport at El Paso. Let's find a restaurant first."

With a lopsided grin, he somehow managed to tug her even closer. Gloria tried not to dwell on his rock-hard thigh pressed against hers or the breathless feeling she got each time her husband's broad shoulders squared around toward her.

"You're right," he agreed. "We can't hold up without food."

Hold up to what? Gloria wondered wildly. Had they not discussed sleeping arrangements? No, she'd been too busy trying to talk him into marriage and he must have taken it for granted that once they were married, they were married.

She glanced over at his strong face and was struck all over again at his rugged profile, the sexual energy that oozed from every pore, every movement he made. Being a virgin, she didn't know exactly what it felt like to make love to a man, but she intuitively knew that sharing a bed with Spencer would be as unforgettable as the man himself. And he was her husband now, she silently pondered. Why put stipulations on their marriage that she might later live to regret? After all, she was a grown woman now. A wife. She didn't have to live by her father's rigid rules any longer.

With a tingle of excitement, Gloria leaned up in the seat and ordered the driver to take them to a restaurant where they could have champagne and soft music.

"Well, it's not Lone Star beer, but it's good," Spencer teased, as some minutes later, he raised his champagne glass to hers.

After Spencer had somewhat proudly informed the restaurant hostess that the two of them were newlyweds, the older woman had led them to a secluded little balcony overlooking the city. Palms and other tropical plants grew in clever spots around the table, giving Gloria the feeling they were sitting in their own little private jungle. To their left was the panoramic view of the desert sky, which was now a soft black and dusted with starlight.

"I'll signal the waiter that brought us the champagne," she told him earnestly. "He might actually be able to find you some Texas beer."

Spencer laughed. "Glory, I'm not *that* redneck. Besides, champagne is the drink to celebrate a wedding. We'll be back in Texas soon enough."

Gloria lifted the fluted glass to her lips and wrinkled her nose with pleasure as she sipped the fizzing bubbles. "What are your friends going to think when they find out you've married?" she asked.

"Most of my friends think I'm half-crazy, but I figure this is one time they'll all be floored. I never planned to marry again after what Lori put me through."

During the plane trip, their conversation had never steered toward the private sides of their lives. As if they were both reluctant to uncover too much about the other one. But now Gloria felt exuberant. Curiosity about her new husband was growing in leaps and bounds.

"I overheard some of what you said about your exwife in the Horned Toad," she admitted. "I take it the divorce was costly for you."

He grimaced and shifted in his chair. "The divorce

was her idea. And like a fool, I thought she'd be fair about the whole thing. I didn't see any need to hire a lawyer to protect my interests. But she got a jim-dandy. One that specialized in cleaning out ignorant ex-spouses.''

Gloria studied his face and wondered just how much emotional damage the woman had caused him. She didn't like to think about him being hurt or to picture him without his easy smile or the sparkle in his eyes.

"So that's how you got into financial trouble?" she asked.

He nodded soberly. "Before the mess with Lori, I was at least going forward instead of backward.''

"You've never considered working at anything else?''

She watched his big hand close around the fragile champagne glass. He was a man bred for the outdoors, as his sons would be. What sort of woman would eventually marry him for real and give him children? Gloria wondered. But her mind instantly shied away from the question. Right now Spencer was her husband and she didn't particularly like to imagine him in the arms of another woman.

"I've never wanted to be anything but a rancher. And I'm smart enough to know I'd be unhappy doing anything else.'' He sipped the champagne, then leveled a frank look at her. "I might as well admit that's the only reason I let you talk me into this. I want to hang on to the Rafter T. In a bad way.''

Gloria wasn't surprised by his admission. She understood the ranch was more to him than just land to raise cattle and horses. It was a legacy that had begun with his great-grandfather. And suddenly, for the first time in her young life, she felt needed and happy that she was doing something important and meaningful.

Impulsively, she reached across the table and covered his hand with hers. "And I'm going to make sure that you do get to hang on to your ranch," she promised.

The heat from her touch warmed him far more than the desert breeze wafting across the table. Spencer leaned forward and scanned the dark green eyes gazing back at him.

"I don't know why," he murmured. "You're not getting much out of this bargain."

Dainty dimples dented her cheeks as the corners of her lips tilted upward. "You have no idea what a fate you've saved me from," she said.

"I'm curious to know why you waited until today to leave San Antonio. Something must have triggered you off."

She sighed. "The closer the wedding got, the more suffocated I began to feel. But I kept trying to tell myself that a daughter should honor her father, not fight him. Then yesterday, I got a letter from my maternal grandmother who lives in Phoenix. Granny said she was sorry, but she wouldn't be attending the wedding. She knew it was a hatched-up business deal of

Vernon's—that's my father—and she wasn't keen to see her granddaughter ruin her life.''

Spencer digested her words as he watched the breeze play with her black hair. The flower behind her ear gave her an exotic look. He could still smell the sweet scent that had filled his nostrils when he'd kissed her in the chapel.

He said, "So yesterday was the first you knew about your grandmother's disapproval?''

Gloria shook her head. "No. She'd more or less told me flat out that she didn't like Paul. And how could I argue that point? I hardly liked the man myself.''

"I don't understand. If you already knew your grandmother disapproved, then what difference did her letter make?''

For the first time since he'd met her, Spencer saw sadness cloud her eyes.

"Because the letter wasn't exactly written by my grandmother. It had been written years ago—by my own mother. In it, she was pouring her heart out to Granny, telling her how miserable she was being married to a man she didn't love. And how much she resented her father for forcing her into such a cold business arrangement.'' Gloria paused and for a moment her eyes grew distant, woeful. "I—I hadn't known that's the way it had been between my parents. I don't believe Granny wanted me to know. That's why she waited so long before sending me the letter.

I guess she was hoping I'd come to my senses before I had to be shown the hard truth.''

Spencer pulled his hand from beneath hers, then wrapped her fingers in his. "I guess every child needs and wants to think that their parents love each other. But it's not always that way."

Grateful for the comfort of his touch, she smiled at him and nodded. "After I read the letter I was heartsick. But it made me see that if I walked down the aisle and married Paul it was going to be history repeating itself. Actually, I thank God that Granny was wise enough to see this and do something to stop me."

"I expect this marriage of ours is going to come as a shock to your friends and family," he said.

Gloria's giggle quickly erased the somber moment. "Oh my, yes! I've never done a rash or impulsive thing in my life. Father made sure of that. And if they could see you—well, I have a sneaking suspicion that Granny is going to adore you. But Father will be in shock."

He shot her a puzzled frown. "What do you mean 'see' me? Do I look funny or something?"

She giggled again and squeezed his fingers in a reassuring way. "No. Of course not. You're just—" With smiling lips and shining eyes, she carefully studied his chiseled features. "You're just nothing like Paul."

"I'm relieved to hear that. I wouldn't exactly appreciate being described as a deep freeze."

Gloria was still laughing when the waiter arrived with their food and for the next forty-five minutes they enjoyed several courses that concluded with a rich, chocolate concoction. By the time they left the restaurant she was stuffed and the champagne had left her warm and relaxed.

As they stepped into an elevator, she held on to Spencer's arm while telling herself she needed the support because she was giddy. But if she was really being honest with herself, she would admit that she was holding on to him because it felt wonderful. Her father had never been a physically affectionate man and Paul had been even worse, brushing her hands away as though she was contaminating him. But Spencer seemed to like being close and connected to her.

"Would you like to go down to the casino floors? You might want to try your luck at a table game or slot machine," she suggested to him.

Since no one else was on the elevator, he took his time to answer before pushing the button to direct them downward. "I'm not much of a gambler. I don't even buy lottery tickets. I've never been a lucky person anyway."

"Maybe your luck is changing," she murmured.

He looked down at her upturned face and at the sight of her bare lips felt something stir deep inside him. Although this woman had so far had a rich, pampered life, she was not a snob. He liked that about her. That and the way she smiled at him. The way she tilted her head and listened intently to what he had to say. She respected him as a person. Him. A cowhand from Crockett County.

"What makes you think that?"

She smiled and he groaned inside at how young and brand-new she made him feel.

"Because you found a way to keep your ranch. And just think about it, Spencer, just what were the odds of us finding each other like we did?"

Leaning toward the control panel on the wall, he jabbed a finger at the bottom-floor button. If they didn't get out of this damn elevator fast he was going to forget why they married and start concentrating on the fact that this was his wedding night and his beautiful wife was clinging to him like a ripe peach.

"The odds would be too minuscule to calculate," he told her.

"That's right! So don't you see how lucky the two of us are?"

As the elevator began a quick descent, Spencer dared to look at her once more. The excitement he found on her face was very contagious and he suddenly found himself laughing.

"Maybe you'd better decide that when you get a look at the ranch tomorrow."

On the bottom floor they had a choice of turning toward the jingle of slot machines, the sound of a live band, or an exit door. Not brave enough to head back to their hotel yet, Spencer guided Gloria toward the music.

"Do you want to dance?" he asked her as they wound their way through a maze of tables.

"Do you know how?" she countered.

He shot her a comical frown. "Any respectable Texan knows how to dance. Especially the two-step."

With a hold on her hand, he led her past the band and a small dance floor, through a glass door, then onto a huge outdoor terrace, where a few couples were dancing under the stars.

As he drew her into the circle of his arms, Gloria didn't want to admit to him that her social life had been so restricted she could count the very few times she'd danced with a man.

"Spencer, I'm not exactly good at this," she warned. "I'll step on your toes."

He took her left hand and placed it on his shoulder, then enfolded her right one in his big palm. "I'm wearing boots," he said with a grin. "I'll never feel it."

But she was feeling him. Every hard inch of him, she thought, as the front of her body made contact with his. Fighting the urge to wilt like a scorched sunflower, she said, "You don't understand, Spencer, I'm not a respectable Texan. I mean I am respectable. But I don't know how to dance well."

He looked down at her miserable expression. "Oh honey, don't go getting all fretful on me. This isn't a test. It's our wedding night. We're supposed to be having fun.''

"Fun?" She let out a little disbelieving laugh as she carefully matched her steps to his. "I didn't know fun was going to be a part of our bargain."

With slow, smooth steps, he guided her across the terrace. "I hope so," he said. "I can't speak for you, but it's been a long while since I've had much to laugh about."

Laughter. Fun. Gloria suddenly realized those were two things that rarely entered her daily life. She was only twenty-three but somehow she'd allowed herself to be led into a life more suitable to the geriatric crowd.

Tilting her head back, she looked up at him. "I've got to confess, Spence. I don't know much about going out on the town and having a good time."

He frowned. "You don't expect me to believe that, do you? You're young and beautiful. I bet there's always been plenty of young guys around to fill your social calendar."

She grimaced. "Not really. Did you ever try to ask a girl for a date with her father standing behind her shoulder?"

He looked amused. "Can't say that I have."

With a roll of her eyes, she said, "Well, believe me, most of them didn't try. The ones that did were forced to go through rigorous questioning. To make sure they were suitable, of course."

"I thought that's the way all daddies were supposed to be toward their daughters?"

"Oh, I'm not talking high school, Spence. I'm talking about being twenty-one and in college!"

His brows lifted. "Surely you made it clear that you didn't appreciate his interference?"

The image his question conjured up made Gloria laugh. "Of course. But somehow he'd always twist things around to make it look like he was only protecting me—out of love." She snorted. "I've never been able to make him understand that loving someone doesn't mean smothering or controlling them."

He glanced down at her. She was from a family of money. From the time she was a baby, she'd no doubt had anything and everything given to her. But that wouldn't mean too much if it meant trading in your freedom. "Hmm. Then I guess you haven't had much of a chance to go out and drink Lone Star beer or dance to Bob Wills music."

"Oh heaven forbid! My getting to go to a dance meant watching the ballet from the balcony section."

The arm around her waist tugged her a mite closer. Gloria's rising body heat went up another degree as her breasts flattened against his chest.

"Hmmm," he said, "somehow I'm getting the picture that I wouldn't fit into your father's choice of a son-in-law."

He was so opposite of what Vernon Rhodes expected her to marry that she laughed long and hard, then once her laughter died enough that she could talk, she finally managed to say, "I don't think you meet any of the requirements. Thank goodness! I like you just as you are."

She could have said I love you and it wouldn't have meant nearly as much to Spencer. Because he would've known the declaration wasn't true. But it was possible that she *liked* him. And somehow that was even better than love. He'd married one woman who'd said she *loved* him, but later he'd realized that Lori hadn't liked him as a friend, or a companion and he'd wound up lonely in their marriage because of it.

"Really. You like me?" he asked.

The faint disbelief in his voice surprised her. Her first impression of him at the Horned Toad was that he was a confident man. Especially when it came to dealing with women. "Yes, I do."

He let out a sigh that she could only decipher as pleasure. The sound thrilled her.

"Then I'm glad we got married, Glory. I'm glad I can help you get out from under your daddy's thumb. You're a grown woman and I'll do whatever I can to make him see that."

The music stopped, then started again to a slower beat. Gloria rested her head on his shoulder and closed her eyes. Being this close to him filled her with an odd mixture of comfort and excitement and as they moved slowly around the terrace, she had to keep reminding herself that her feet were really on the floor.

"I'm glad we got married, too, Spence," she whispered. "Very glad."

His wife was a virgin. All during the taxi ride back to the hotel, Spencer kept repeating the fact, reminding himself that, even though they'd exchanged wedding vows, she wasn't really his for the taking. But now as he watched her kick off her high heels and fall back on the king-size mattress with a pleasurable sigh, her innocence was the last thing on his mind.

"What a day!" she exclaimed.

What a night, Spencer thought. He'd gotten married to a beautiful, young heiress. Downed a bottle of expensive champagne and danced for hours. Back on the Rafter T, his wildest dreams hadn't even come close to this.

From his seat in a wing backed chair, he studied the slow rise and fall of her breasts beneath the folds of white silk. He doubted she had any idea of the sort of effect her body had on him. In her innocence, she probably didn't know that when a man had a female form draped all over him, he was bound to get itchy.

Damn it, he silently cursed, taking her dancing had been a bad idea. But when they'd left the restaurant, he'd believed dancing would be a hell of a lot safer than being confined with her in this cozy, plush room. Especially after the marriage ceremony had left him feeling just a little more than possessive toward his new wife.

Now he wished he'd followed her suggestion to play the slots. Losing a few dollars wouldn't have been nearly as bad as the ache he was experiencing now.

"I'm sure you're tired," he said. "I am."

Like a flash, she flipped over onto her side. With her head propped on one hand, she looked at him anxiously. "Oh, I hope I haven't worn you out."

He kept his groan to himself. "I'm not *that* much older than you, Glory."

An impish smile curved her lips. "Well, when you woke up this morning I don't expect you were planning to fly all the way to Las Vegas and get married."

The shift of her body had caused the neckline of her dress to slip sideways. From his angle he could see a dainty strip of lace covering the tip of one very full breast. Even if he'd been threatened at gunpoint, he couldn't have looked elsewhere.

"Uh—no," he replied. "I didn't exactly have that plan penciled in on my agenda. A trip to the feed store in Ozona for some post and wire was going to be my excitement for this week."

She laughed deeply. Then with a sigh, she smiled at him. "Oh Spencer, is being married to you always going to be this fun? I didn't know I could laugh like this. Or feel like this."

The bliss on her face made something swell in his chest, but he did his best to ignore it. "It's the champagne. When we get back to the ranch, I'd better hide my beer. I don't think you could handle it.''

Another laugh slipped past her lips. ''I only had two little glasses and that was hours ago. But you're right in the fact that I'm drunk—but not on alcohol. I'm drunk on freedom and the excitement of starting a new life with you.''

Was he imagining the permanent ring to her words, he asked himself. ''Six months isn't a lifetime, Glory.''

His reminder didn't appear to dim her mood. She continued to smile at him. ''No. But it's much longer than six days or six weeks.''

Yeah, he thought. Twenty-four weeks. Or one hundred sixty-eight days. He'd already mentally calculated their time together. How was he ever going to live through it without making love to her?

Spencer was searching for an answer to that question when his mind suddenly jerked to a sudden halt. Just wait a darn minute, he thought. He hadn't made a promise to keep his hands off her. In fact, the only promise he'd made was to stay married for six months. If he wanted to make love to his wife, he didn't see anything stopping him.

Except that she was a virgin, he quickly reminded himself. She was saving herself for her *real* husband. She wasn't going to waste herself on a pretense. He couldn't let it happen. Not and live with his conscience afterward.

Like a cornered house cat, he jumped from the chair, sidled around the bed, then stood with his back to her as he looked out the French doors leading to a private balcony.

"You're not thinking about jumping, are you?"

Her teasing voice broke into his frustrated thoughts. "Jumping?" he repeated blankly.

"Off the balcony," she clarified.

"Oh. No," he said absently, then glanced over his shoulder at her. "I was thinking we need to call down to room service and have them bring up a portable bed."

She sat up abruptly and he swallowed as the white silk rode high on her thighs.

"But why?" she asked, frowning prettily.

Yeah, she was way too innocent for the likes of him, Spencer decided. "There's only one bed and no couch. I'm not too keen on sleeping on the floor."

The frown on her face vanished as she slid from the bed and walked over to where he stood. Spencer felt every muscle in his body clench as her fingers curled softly against his forearm.

"There's no need for that, Spencer. We're adults and we're married. Doesn't that mean we can sleep together in the same bed?"

Back in Texas it did.

"You're willing to share this bed with me?"

She laughed as though his question was both charming and totally unnecessary. "I'm going to be sharing part of my inheritance with you, Spence. Sharing a bed with you will be easy."

Easy, he silently repeated. For her, maybe.

Chapter 4

Her husband didn't have plans to make love to her. Ever. If she'd had any questions about it back in Las Vegas, she'd had them answered now.

"I realize it probably looks pretty rough compared to what you're used to," Spencer was saying, "but after you get the dust cleaned off, it ought to be comfortable. I don't guess anybody has slept on that bed since my little sister, Shelley, got married and left for Louisiana."

Less than an hour ago the two of them had landed at the Ozona airport, then driven straight here to the Rafter T. After giving Gloria a brief trip around the dry, mostly barren ranch yard, he'd brought her inside to show her the house. Eventually they'd gotten as far as his bedroom, where he'd only allowed her to have little more than a cursory glance before he'd led her across the hall to a room he had intentions of becoming hers.

Gloria lifted a doubtful gaze from the bed to him. "I'm sure it would be comfortable, Spence. But I don't understand why you think I'd want to sleep on it. I'd rather be sleeping with you."

He looked like a man who'd just been whammed in the midsection with the backside of a shovel. Several moments passed before he could cough, much less talk. "Uh—Glory, maybe—"

She made a palms-up gesture. "I'm being forward. You don't have to tell me that. But like I told you last night. We *are* married. And the more I think about it, the more I'm convinced this whole thing will go much better if we behave like man and wife."

He stared at her as a quick release of breath fairly whistled past his teeth. So far today his new wife had continued to surprise him. He'd expected her to hate the ranch at first sight. Before they'd gotten within ten miles of the Rafter T, he'd already braced himself for a fit and a flat-out refusal to live in such a run-down, godforsaken hole. Instead, she'd found everything *interesting* and *charming*. Ideas and plans to make improvements on the place had been rolling out of her with youthful excitement for the past hour. Now here she was wanting to take their union a step further. A mighty step further.

"Glory, you don't know what you're saying."

Gloria knew exactly what she was saying. Last night in Vegas as she'd lain on one side of that king-size mattress and he on the other, she'd realized that being close to him, feeling the warmth and security of his body was far nicer than trying to keep her distance. Maybe she was asking for trouble, but she'd already been brave enough to burn bridges behind her. Now she had to be brave enough to go after what she wanted. And it wasn't separate beds.

"I do know what I'm saying. And—"

With his hand on her wrist, Spencer yanked her out of the bedroom.

Gasping, Gloria tried to dig in her heels and stop their forward motion down the hallway. "What are you doing?"

"Taking you to the kitchen! You need something to drink. You must be dehydrated and talking out of your head. Stuff like that happens to people who aren't used to this heat."

"I've *lived* in Texas all my life, Spencer. I'm used to the heat."

"But not the dry kind like out here in West Texas."

At one end of a planked table made of varnished pine, he pulled out a chair and pushed her into it. Dishes and various pots and pans that should have been washed a week ago graced the table and littered the cabinet counters. Funny how the mess only made the old house seem even homier to Gloria.

Spencer grabbed a long-necked beer from the refrigerator, twisted off the cap, then thrust it at her. Just to appease him, she took a few sips then added the bottle to the rest of the clutter on the table.

"Spencer, what's wrong with me?" she pleaded anxiously. "Until I know, I can't do anything to fix it."

The misery on her face coupled with the glaze of moisture in her eyes had him groaning contritely. "Oh, honey, now don't worry. There's nothing wrong with you." He took a seat on the chair next to hers, then leaned forward and tightened a hold on both her hands. "You're just worn-out, Glory. These past couple of days have been too much for you. You'll be all right after you get caught up on your rest."

She wailed with frustration. "I don't mean—I'm not sick! I meant what is wrong with *me,* Spence, that you don't find me...desirable."

Understanding flickered across his face, followed by awkwardness. Slowly he removed his hat and raked a hand over his sandy brown hair. She could see he was thinking long and hard about his next words.

"Glory, there's nothing wrong with you. Why, you're just about the prettiest thing I've ever seen."

Her face brightened. "You really think so?"

The uncertainty in her voice amazed him. From the moment she'd stood by his table in the Horned Toad, he'd sized her up as a woman who was used to twisting men around her little finger and keeping them there for as long as she wished. Since then he'd been shocked to find out she was a virgin. Not only that, she didn't realize she had enough natural assets to knock a man sideways. That deep freeze she'd called a fiancé must have left her believing she was lacking. The jerk.

He smiled gently. "Sure I do."

Gloria reached out and gripped her fingers around his. "Then why are you trying to put me in another room? Was last night that horrible? Do I snore?"

Last night had been a combination of heaven and hell for Spencer. He'd lain awake for ages, inhaling her scent, listening to the slightest movement of her body sliding against the sheets. Then after he'd somehow managed to fall asleep, he'd unconsciously rolled toward the tempting heat of her soft body, only to wake up later and find their legs tangled and her cheek pressed against the middle of his chest. It was a miracle she'd survived with her virginity intact and him with any sense at all.

"Last night wasn't horrible. But—" He swallowed as he ran his thumbs over the backs of her hands. "I don't think the two of us being that close is a good thing."

Being close to Spencer was the best thing she'd ever experienced. She had to convey that to him somehow.

Leaning forward, she brought her lips close to his and whispered, "Why?"

A helpless groan slipped past his throat. "Because

a man can't sleep with a woman like you and not make love to her.''

"Make love.'' She repeated the words blissfully. "That sounds nice, Spence. Very nice. Why don't we try it?''

"Glor—''

Her name was smothered as she suddenly planted her lips over his and proceeded to kiss him with all her limited experience.

Spencer was an honorable man, but he wasn't made of iron. The taste of her lips sent electric heat sizzling right through him. Every sensible thought in his head was suddenly fried dead. Getting her closer was the only thing his brain cells could focus on.

With his hands on her shoulders, he eased the both of them to their feet, then deepened the kiss by coaxing her lips open and slipping his tongue inside.

Like a flower pushing itself toward the sun, she went up on tiptoes and wrapped her arms tightly around his neck. The movement pressed the tips of her breasts against his chest and brought the intimate juncture of her hips on a level with his. Fire flared in Spencer's loins and made his hands urgent, his mouth even hungrier. From the back of her waist, his hands took a downward path until they reached the plump curve of her bottom. Once his palms were cupping her warm flesh, he yanked her tight against the growing ache in his jeans.

Gloria's head reeled with the scent of him, the taste

of him. Her body burned. The need to have his skin next to hers made her want to tear off his clothes. Her mind was on a one-way journey and making love to her husband was the only destination.

It was the agony for air that finally forced Spencer to break the connection of their lips. Yet all he could manage was to lift them enough to breathe and whisper raggedly, "You're only saying these things because all of this is new to you, Glory."

"No!" She practically whimpered the word.

"You're only reacting to a male body. Not me."

"I've not been *that* overprotected, Spencer. I've had a male body next to mine, including the man I was engaged to. None of them made me feel like this—like you do."

She sounded certain and that scared him. "Look, Glory, this thing with us will end in six months. When that time comes I don't want to think—well, I don't want to be the man who ruins you before you find that real husband you want. You know—the one that will still curl your toes when you're eighty."

Six months and this would all end! The reminder was like a hard slap to Gloria. Dazed, it dawned on her that she'd been so enchanted by her new husband in this past twenty-four hours, she'd allowed herself to forget their bargain.

Slowly, her eyes focused on his and in that moment she realized she was seeing him and their marriage in a different light. It was impossible to envision her future without him. She didn't *want* to envision it without him! When or how that had happened, she didn't know. But she was smart enough to understand Spencer Tate wasn't ready to hear her self-revelation. Right now this business with the beds was the first thing she had to tackle.

Smiling now, she tightened her fingers ever so slightly against the back of his neck. "It's nice to know there's still a man around with a gallant streak, Spence. But we're no longer living in the Victorian age or even the nineteen hundreds. A woman isn't ruined just because she loses her virginity. Besides, if she can't lose it to her husband, who can she lose it to?"

Her hands slipped from his neck and flattened against the middle of his chest. The light touch of her fingers was enough to knock the wind from him. Desperation hoarsened his voice. "I'm not your husband. I mean—not really."

Gloria's brows lifted. "You made a point of getting a real minister to marry us. *You* said in the eyes of God you would be my husband, remember? And husbands and wives do sleep in the same bed, Spence."

He groaned at her reminder, plus the fact that he didn't want to turn loose of her pert little bottom. Or anything else. "You're not playing fair, Glory. But I can see it'll be safer to quit arguing with you. Okay, we'll *sleep* in the same bed. But that's all I'm going to promise you.''

If he'd just handed her a million dollars he couldn't have put a more glorious smile on her face. Making a woman happy was heady stuff to a man, he suddenly realized. He could get addicted to having her look at him like he was Mr. Wonderful. If he was lucky, the six months would pass before his wife realized she was married to nothing more than a poor cowboy. But he wouldn't hold his breath. Lori had figured him out in six weeks.

Two days later Gloria stood in the center of the kitchen and smiled at the sight. Everything was clean and sparkling. The faded linoleum, the old white cabinets, the cookstove and refrigerator had all been scrubbed. Instead of hidden by dust-rotted curtains, the row of windows by the table were now bare, the glass panes washed free of layers of grimy film. Now she could look out and watch the windmill whirring in the wind and the cattle milling about the water tank.

On the table were a steaming bowl of spaghetti and meatballs, hot garlic bread, tossed salad and a pitcher of iced tea. Next to Spencer's plate was a long white envelope, a surprise she'd been saving for him since she'd returned from town this morning.

A sound at the back door told her she'd timed the meal just right. Turning, she watched Spencer enter the kitchen. Dust covered him from head to toe and spurs jingled as he moved toward her. The sight of him never failed to thrill her and she thought how lucky she was to have found this man that made her heart beat fast. She thanked God that she'd had enough courage to leave San Antonio. Otherwise, she might have lived her whole life without ever knowing what it was like to be in love. And she was in love. Totally, overwhelmingly in love with her husband.

"My goodness, this doesn't look like the same room!" he exclaimed as he pulled a battered straw hat from his head.

Yesterday, she'd heard a similar exclamation from him after she'd tackled the living room, bedrooms and bathroom. Back in San Antonio, in her former life as she now thought of it, she'd always been interested in domestic things and had picked up special tricks of keeping a house clean by jumping in and lending the servants a hand. But she'd never imagined that house-cleaning could give a person such a sense of accomplishment. Nor had she dreamt that an old ranch house with unlevel floors and ancient fixtures could give her so much pride.

"I hope that means you approve," she said, smiling at the awe on his face.

"I'd be crazy not to," he said, then his attention was taken up by the meal on the table. So far since they'd returned to the Rafter T, he'd done all the cooking. "Where did this come from?" he asked, walking over for a closer look.

The wonder in his voice made Gloria laugh. "From me."

He shot her a wide-eyed stare. "You cook? You know how?"

Placing a finger against her lips, she made a shushing noise. "Yes, but don't tell anyone. My father's not supposed to know."

A comical frown marred his features. "Why not?"

Gloria laughed good-naturedly. She could afford to now that she was out from under Vernon Rhodes's thumb. "Are you kidding? Not *his* daughter. Cooking is too menial. It's just something the servants are supposed to do. But I've always been interested in cooking and learned a lot about it without my father ever finding out that I was spending time in the kitchen. In fact, that's what I really wanted to do with myself after I got out of high school. Go to culinary school and become a chef. I even dreamed of having a little restaurant of my own. Not too big. Just a cozy place that made people feel good. But Vernon was outraged by the idea. I *had* to get a degree in business administration. He wouldn't be around forever, he'd argued, and someone had to take over the business."

Spencer shook his head. Obviously she was nothing like her father and it amazed him that she'd kept any sort of spirit under such a crush of pressure. "I've never known anybody that rich."

She wrinkled her nose with distaste. "Being rich doesn't have anything to do with it, Spence. I had rich friends while I was growing up but they lived differently—more normal is what I guess I'm trying to say. My father is... Well, snob is not the right way to describe him because he does care about people less fortunate than him. But he's always had this idea that his daughter is too special to live and do things like common folks. Believe me, it gets so wearing. I tried to move out several times, but..."

Spencer rubbed his palm against the back of her arm. "But he played on your soft heart and convinced you that he needed you, right?"

She nodded glumly. "Over and over," she admitted. A smile chased away the shadows on her face as she glanced up at him. "But that's in the past. Our dinner is getting cold. Hurry and wash. I've got a surprise for you!"

He left the room. After a few short minutes, he returned, his hair slightly damp, the dust and spurs gone. Once they were seated at the table, she snatched up his plate.

"I'll fill this for you while you look at that," she said, inclining her head toward the white envelope.

As Spencer eased open the loosely sealed flap, he

cast her a wary smile. "Is this a thank-you note for not making you sleep in the spare bedroom?"

Gloria laughed. He might not have made love to her yet, but he was already sleeping much closer. And this morning she'd woke to find him standing beside the bed with a freshly brewed cup of coffee for her. While she'd drank it, he'd sat down on the edge of the mattress and talked to her. As though spending time with her was more important to him than anything. As though he really cared about what she had to say. If she hadn't already fallen in love with him, she would have tumbled right then.

"It's a note. But not that kind," she said, watching him as he unfolded the official document. As he read, emotions streaked across his face, but they were tangled and impossible for her read.

"This is— You paid off the note on the bull!"

"Yes," she said happily. "I made you a promise, remember. And I do keep them, Spencer."

He lifted his gaze from the banking papers to her happy face. "When did you do this?"

"This morning. When I drove into Ozona for groceries. I didn't see any point in putting it off. You only had a few days left before the payoff was due anyway."

That much was true, Spencer thought wryly. But why did he have this bittersweet taste in his mouth? he asked himself. Holding on to Beau had been an obsessive worry to him for the past three months. Certain that, in the end, he'd have to sell the bull, Spencer had all but given up hope. Now Beau was truly his, free and clear to roam the Rafter T. Yet this great, generous thing Gloria had done for him was a bold reminder that their marriage was only an arrangement. And though he didn't know exactly why, he had to admit that the reality saddened him like nothing had in a long, long time.

"I don't know what to say, Gloria. Except—thank you," he said lowly. "And that sounds mighty lame."

She continued to smile at him. "You don't have to say anything, Spencer. Thank you is more than enough. I started to pay off the remainder of the notes you had at the bank, but I was in a hurry to get my groceries out of the hot car and I knew it would take the clerk some time to get all the paperwork completed. I'll go back tomorrow or the next day and take care of it," she promised.

"No!" he blurted, then seeing the puzzled look on her face, he quickly added, "I mean, there's no hurry. We'll talk about all of that later. Let's eat."

Gloria placed the filled plate in front of him, then helped herself to the food. Once she began to eat, she carefully studied his downcast face. "Spence, aren't you happy? You don't have to worry about your bull now."

He glanced up to see she was clearly perplexed. "Sure, I'm happy. What man wouldn't be?"

"You don't really seem like you're happy," she said.

She sounded faintly hurt, which made Spencer feel even worse. Since they'd come home to the Rafter T, she'd worked very hard to make the place more comfortable for him. Everything she did, it seemed she did for him. He didn't want her to be the only one to do any giving in this arrangement. But what did he possibly have that a rich woman like Gloria would want or need? he thought wryly.

With a sheepish grin, he leaned across the corner of the table and kissed the soft curve of her cheek. "I'm sorry, Glory. I'm just a coarse cowboy. I haven't had much practice in saying thank-you to a beautiful lady. I guess—well, I don't guess I've had much just given to me over the years. I don't know how to act."

To his surprise tears sprang to her eyes and she reached up and touched his face with tender fingers. "I don't need a special thank-you, Spencer. Just a sign to know you're pleased."

Something deep inside him softened and melted. He'd never felt so weak and helpless.

Knowing he was drifting toward trouble, he eased back in his chair and away from her tempting face. "Well, I'm pleased, Glory. You can rest assured on that."

He began to tackle his food with earnest. Across the table, Gloria said, "Is it true what you said a moment ago? About not being given anything?"

He shrugged. "Pretty much. But don't get me wrong, Glory. I wasn't complaining, just explaining. You see, a man likes to get for himself. He doesn't want things given to him." He darted her a grin to soften his words. "Unless it's given in friendship or love."

Now why the hell had he added that? he wondered.

She smiled back at him. "What about this ranch? I'd taken it for granted that your father had given it to you. Hasn't it been handed down through his side of the family?"

"It was given to my father by my grandfather. But I bought it."

"Bought it?"

Nodding, he said, "My dad needed money and was going to sell the place. I wasn't living here at the time. The two of us never did get along and I moved out of here after I graduated from high school. He never wanted to ranch and when it appeared that he didn't have any prospect to lease the mineral rights to any oil companies, he put the ranch on the real estate market."

Gloria looked appalled. "But didn't he care that he was selling your inheritance? After all, it was given to him."

Spencer shrugged again. He'd long ago accepted the fact that his father cared about as much for him as he had Spencer's mother and sister. And that had been precious little. "Yeah, but Walt Tate isn't a sentimental or responsible man, Glory. He could care less if he leaves me or my sister a dime when he dies. But then, I doubt either one of us would take it. Seeing he didn't bother to take care of us while we were growing up."

"Do your parents live close?"

He shook his head. "They've been divorced for years now. Mom remarried and lives in Montana. The last I heard, Dad was somewhere around Dallas, probably spending three-fourths of his time in a bar and the rest doing the least amount of manual labor that he can to survive."

Amazed by his whole story, she said, "So you paid him for what should have rightly went to you in the first place."

"I saw the whole thing as a business deal, Glory. I got what I wanted. And this way Walt can never lay any claim to the place."

"And what about your sister? Was she never interested in owning a part of the ranch?"

"No. Shelley hated this place." He looked up at her, his expression naked with candor. "I expected you would, too."

With an understanding smile, she reached over and curled her fingers over his forearm. "I don't have any bad memories of this place as, I expect, your sister does. That makes the difference, Spence. You ought to know by now that it's not where or what a person lives in that makes it special. It's who lives there with you."

At twenty-three, he'd not expected her to be so wise. And because she was rich, he'd not expected her to view life in such a simplified way. What a surprise she continued to be, he thought. And, oh heaven, what a temptation.

"Have you been able to get in contact with your father today?"

She shook her head with grim disgust. "No. I'm still only getting the answering machine or the servants. And I don't want to leave any sort of message. I want to talk to him directly when I give him our news."

Our news. She said that like the two of them were really married. And Spencer was beginning to suspect she believed that they actually were a man and wife planning to spend the rest of their lives together. The idea was far more scary to him than the notion of losing this ranch.

"You could call him at work and get it over with," Spencer suggested.

She lowered her gaze to her plate. "No. I don't want to discuss something so personal with him while he's at work. I've had to do that ever since—well, even as a child my father was always at work when I needed him. He can wait on me now.''

"Are you afraid of what he might do?'' Spencer prodded. He didn't want to think Gloria was worried or upset. He didn't want to think that even here on the Rafter T her life was being shadowed by her domineering father. "I won't let him hurt you, Glory.''

She reached for his hand and clung to it tightly. "Just don't let him take me away from here—from you, Spence.''

He frowned at the desperate edge in her voice. "He can't take you away, Glory. You're my wife now.''

A long breath slipped out of her and she gave him a wobbly smile. "You really mean that?''

"Yes. I mean it.'' And God help him, Spencer prayed.

Chapter 5

The next morning Gloria finally decided to leave the ranch's number with one of her father's maids, along with a message for him to call his daughter. By late that afternoon the telephone rang.

"Where the hell are you, young lady?"

The abrupt greeting was just like Vernon Rhodes, Gloria thought. Straight to the point, he would always be a businessman first, a father second.

Drawing in a bracing breath, she said, "West Texas. On my husband's ranch."

The line went silent. Obviously, she'd knocked his feet out from under him. The notion stiffened her spine with renewed confidence.

"What, pray tell me, does that mean? Your husband?'' he asked in low measured tones, then before she could have possibly answered, he bellowed in her ear, ''Your fiancé is back here in San Antonio! Wondering what to do with all these wedding gifts!''

Gloria squared her shoulders. ''Tell him to return them. I'll write my personal apologies to everyone who sent gifts.''

That was not the answer he'd been expecting her to say and the line went silent for another long stretch.

''Gloria, if you think this is amusing, it isn't working. I am damn furious with you! You've made our family the laughingstock of San Antonio! And just when I was trying to land the most important merger of my life! Besides that, the office is crawling with auditors. If not for them, I would have already been out combing the countryside for you!''

Deliberately ignoring the last part, she said, ''Funny, but I haven't thought of us Rhodeses as a family in years. Not since Mother died.''

''Don't you speak of your mother at a time like this!'' he roared once again. ''Alice is probably turning over in her grave right now because of you!''

The letter she'd received from her Granny was suddenly in the forefront of Gloria's thoughts and she wondered if Vernon had ever realized how much Alice had resented their marriage, how miserable she had been as his wife? It would serve Vernon Rhodes right for her to question him about the past. To tell him that she knew how he'd gotten to be Alice's husband in the first place. But she couldn't be that mean. Even at a time like this.

"No, Father, I think you're wrong. I think from where Mother is sitting up in heaven, she's cheering loud and long for me."

He huffed out an angry breath, then tried a different approach. "When are you coming home?"

"I'm married, Father. I'm *not* coming home. At least not anytime soon and then it will only be for a short visit."

"Like hell, you're married! I don't believe it! You're making all this up just because you don't like Paul. Well, let me tell you, young lady, you'll never find another man to equal him. And if you have any sense at all, you'll get yourself back here and try to apologize to him. I'm sure if you show him how truly wrong and sorry you were for running off, he'll take you back."

"God forbid," she muttered lowly.

"What?"

"I said Paul is nothing but a spoiled kid. And even if I was still single, I wouldn't take him back on a silver platter. He was your choice, not mine!"

"You're behaving childishly! And—"

"I'm a grown woman, Father. It's time you realized that I'm not one of your business assets!"

More silence, then in a gentler, somewhat wheedling tone, he said, "This isn't like you to talk to me this way, Gloria. What has gotten into you?"

She sighed and tears stung her eyes. Not from guilt on her part. No, she was saddened by the realization that Vernon Rhodes would never know what it was really like to love someone other than himself. "I want to live my own life, Father. In my own way. And I'm very happy now. Please be happy for me."

"If you think I'm going to just let you ruin your life out there in some wasteland, you're crazy! I'm coming after you. Now give me the address!" he demanded.

"Come as soon or whenever you want," she invited as coolly as she could manage, "but rest assured that Spencer won't let you take me anywhere."

Vernon cursed. "I don't know why you're trying to lay such a cock-and-bull story on me. It's only been a few days since you told me you didn't want to be married, period."

That much was true, Gloria thought. She hadn't wanted to get married. Not until she'd found the right man for her. She'd not expected to stumble miraculously onto him in a beer tavern.

"Not to a man you chose for me," she retorted. "I wanted to do my own choosing. And I have."

He snorted. "What did you do? *Pay* some man to marry you?"

His sarcastic question bit deep into her heart. Maybe in black-and-white she had paid Spencer to marry her. But she wanted to believe he would have helped her anyway. No matter about saving his bull. He was that kind of man. "Spencer doesn't—"

"Every man is out for money, Gloria. You'd be a little fool to believe otherwise."

You ought to know, she wanted to fling back at him. But she couldn't let her father taint her with cynicism. She couldn't let his remarks fill her with doubts about Spencer.

"I'll take my chances with Spence. And since you believe your daughter is so capable of lying, I'll send you a copy of the marriage license!"

"Gloria, this won't—"

The jingle of Spencer's spurs suddenly caught her attention and she turned just in time to see him entering the living room. With frantic desperation, she slapped a hand over the receiver.

"It's my father," she explained. "He doesn't believe I'm married. Will you speak to him long enough to tell him?"

"Gladly," Spencer said, then taking the receiver from her hand, he quickly spoke. "Mr. Rhodes, this is Spencer Tate, your daughter's new husband. She said you were having a little trouble believing her. I'm sorry to hear that. You ought to know Glory doesn't lie."

Spencer could hear a male voice spluttering on the other end, then demanding haughtily, "Who the hell is this?"

"Since I've already told you, maybe you'd better

write it down. Spencer Tate. I own the Rafter T here in Crockett County. If you want to visit your daughter in a kindly fashion, you're welcome here on the ranch. Otherwise, I'd appreciate it if you wouldn't call and upset her anymore."

"Why, you impertinent cowhand! I don't know what you're up to, but I can promise you this—you'll never get a penny of my daughter's money!"

Dear God, the man had a beautiful, loving daughter, but his first concern was money. In a way he was no better than Walt. The realization made him sick.

"That's jake with me," Spencer all but snarled. "Now if you'll excuse us, Mr. Rhodes, we've got more important things to attend to."

Wide-eyed, she watched Spencer deliberately drop the phone back on its hook.

"What was he saying? What did you mean 'That's jake with me'?"

She was pale and trembling. Spencer took her into his arms and pressed her cheek against his chest. As he stroked the back of her hair, he said, "Oh, that's just old cowboy slang. It means whatever you say or do is all right with me."

She reared her head back far enough to look up at him. Fear glazed her eyes. "What's he planning to do? Tell me, Spence!"

Vernon's insinuation was partly true, he thought sickly. He'd married Gloria to save Beau. "I'm not really sure. But whatever it is, let's not worry about it, honey.''

"But he—"

Placing a hand beneath her chin, he finished for her, "Isn't here. So let's not borrow trouble."

His strong touch calmed her and she blinked away her tears. "I knew that talking with Father about this wasn't going to be pleasant. But like an idiot I'd been hoping that my leaving might have opened his eyes and made him see my side of things." She shook her head with regret. "I should have known he isn't capable of changing."

"You can't make him change, Glory. He'd have to do that on his own."

She bit down on her lip as worry creased her forehead. "He won't let this drop, Spence. Now that he knows where I am, he'll come after me."

"Let him come! What's he going to do, physically drag you into his car?" He shook his head. "That would only happen over my dead body, Glory. So quit fretting."

Groaning, she pressed her cheek against his. "Oh, Spencer, I don't want Father to ever come between us. Promise me he won't." She tilted her face up to his. "Promise me!"

With her warm curves pressed against his body and the tender light in her eyes shining up at him, he was afraid she could probably make him promise her anything.

Grinning down at the point where her breasts were flattened against his chest, he said, ''He'd have to be awfully thin to get between us right now, don't you think?''

She laughed. And then because he made her feel so good, she rose up on tiptoe and pressed a kiss to his lips.

Combustion was instant and for long moments, Spencer treated her lips to a series of broken kisses. Each of them from a different angle and each of them growing deeper by degrees.

Eventually, Gloria could no longer remain on her tiptoes. Even as she strained to hold on to their kiss, all her weight collapsed against him.

His hands firmly planted against her back, Spencer steadied her. Then lifting his head, he said in a ragged voice, ''I think as nice as this is I've got work to do and—''

She interrupted with a husky plea. ''But Spencer—''

His body was already aching to make love to her. One more minute like this and he'd have her in the bedroom. He'd forget all about their six-month agreement. And her damned virginity!

Before she could make any more appeals to his manhood, he eased her out of his arms. ''I have something to show you down at the barn that I need your help with.'' With his hands on her shoulders, he turned her toward the hallway, then gave her bottom a swat.

''Go put on some jeans and I'll meet you out on the porch.''

The huge barn and adjoining shed row were set back some thirty-five yards behind the house. One mesquite tree shaded a corner of the run-down building, while a lone cottonwood stood over the working pens. Hot south wind sent dust swirling around Spencer and Gloria as the two of them made their way across the barren ranch yard.

Off to their left, five horses, each of a different color, hung their heads over a corral fence and whinnied for attention.

Enthralled with the animals, Gloria said, ''They want us to pet them, Spencer. Don't we have time?''

He chuckled. ''They want us to *feed* them,'' he corrected, then glanced down at her. ''Sweet Glory, this is a different world to you, isn't it?''

Totally different, she thought. And she never wanted to leave it.

With her arm already looped companionably through his, she squeezed a tighter hold on him. ''I'm not totally ignorant about a ranch,'' she informed him proudly. ''I know about horses, Spence.''

He cast her a skeptical glance. ''Really? You haven't told me this.''

This time she did the chuckling. ''There's a lot I haven't told you—yet,'' she teased.

''Okay. So what do you know about horses?''

"Well, not a whole lot. But I do know how to ride."

Her statement was enough to stop Spencer in his tracks. "You know how to ride?"

Nodding, she said, "I thought I'd told you."

"You told me you wanted to go to a dude ranch when you were a kid but your father wouldn't allow it."

She grimaced. "He used the argument that horses were wild, temperamental creatures and that I'd fall or be bucked off and break a bone, or even worse, my neck. He put all sorts of wrong ideas in my head to scare me off the idea."

"So how did you manage to learn how to ride?"

An impish grin tilted her soft lips. "The same way I learned how to cook. Without him ever knowing about it. Fortunately, I had a friend whose family owned several horses. I learned through her."

"Glory Tate," he said with teasing admonition, "I'm beginning to find out my wife is a bad girl."

"Why don't you let me show you just how bad," she countered, loving the sound of her new name on his lips.

The sexy gleam in her eye was as hot as the wind on his face. Quickly taking her by the hand, he yanked her toward the barn. "Come on," he ordered, "before you really get yourself in trouble."

Inside the dim interior of the barn, Gloria noticed the building was in need of a new roof. In several places, afternoon sunlight slanted down through ragged holes. Much of the space that should have been used for sheltering livestock was taken up by a large tractor and several farm-type implements. The ranch needed another barn, she mentally planned. A bigger one made with heavier corrugated iron that could endure hail and wind.

At the back, Spence led her toward a small wooden stall. Gloria gasped with delight when she spotted a new baby calf.

"Oh, how adorable!" she exclaimed.

As she went down on her knees to pet the dark red calf, Spencer said, "I don't know about adorable, but she's very hungry. The mother has mastitis. I'm treating her, but until the infection in her udder is gone, she can't feed her baby."

Concerned now, Gloria glanced up at him. "But how is the calf going to eat? It's too little for hay and such, isn't it?"

"Yep, milk is the only thing the little heifer can handle right now. That's where you come in."

"Me! What can I do?"

"Hand feed her with a bottle. It's a job that takes a lot of time and patience. Two things I'm short on. Do you think you can handle it?"

"Of course," she said, already cuddling the calf next to the warmth of her body. "Just show me what to do."

Just because I'm a rancher's wife doesn't mean I have to handle livestock or clean out stalls. The memory of Lori's opinionated words suddenly came to him out of nowhere and pointed out to him just how opposite Gloria was to his ex-wife.

"What are you smiling at?"

Her question penetrated his thoughts. With a slight shake of his head he brought himself back to the present. "The two of you. After a few days of feedings, she's gonna think you're her mother. She'll be following you around like a puppy."

"Then she'll be my little girl," Gloria assured him. "May I name her?"

"You can do more than name her. I'm giving her to you." It wasn't the same as a full-grown, purebred Santa Gertrudis bull, Spencer thought, but at least he was giving her something in return.

She looked at him in total surprise. "Oh! My very own cow! I'm a real ranch woman now!" she said with a thrilled laugh. "What can I call her?"

"How about Vegas? After the town we were married in."

For answer, Gloria rose to her feet and planted a kiss on his cheek. The affectionate display brought a sheepish grin to his face. "What was that for?" he asked.

"For giving Vegas her name and me a home."

An invisible hand suddenly squeezed his heart. "Don't make me into a hero, Glory. You could have bought a home for yourself. In any place you wanted it to be."

Her gaze connected with his. "You can't *buy* a home, Spence. Just like you can't buy real love."

Was she saying she'd found something here with him that was worth more to her than wealth? *Don't be stupid, Spence.* Yes, maybe the next six months of living here would be fine for her, a pleasant novelty in a way. But to ask her to stay longer would be asking for trouble.

He heaved out a long breath, then turned away from the stall. "I'll go get a bottle," he told her.

Gloria's hand caught his arm before he was able to walk completely away. Pausing, he looked back at her.

"Did I say something wrong, Spence?"

"No."

He was *doing* something wrong, he thought. He was falling in love with his wife.

Chapter 6

A week later, Spencer saddled two of the horses and they rode out to check on the cattle. It was the first time she'd been any distance from the ranch house, and in spite of the scorching heat, she was enjoying the feel of the blue roan beneath her and the chance to see more of the Rafter T.

"There's the cattle," Spencer said, pointing to a spot about two hundred yards ahead of them. "Let's ride in slow, or they'll spook."

She nodded while keeping a firm grip on the roan's reins. "Is Beau with them? I'm anxious to see him. The way your friend Ike talked about him, he's a wonder bull."

Yesterday, Gloria had met their neighbors, Ike and

Joan. She didn't have any idea if Ike remembered her from the Horned Toad Saloon. But she soon decided it didn't matter. The couple treated her and Spencer as if they were newlyweds who'd fallen instantly and deliriously in love, not two people who'd made a marriage barter.

Gloria had taken an instant liking to Joan. The plain, hardworking woman had been especially kind and welcoming to her. Already the two of them had made a date to have lunch together and plan a birthday party for Ike.

Astride his own black mount, Spencer chuckled. "Ike knows a good bull when he sees one. Beau's been the most expensive investment I've made on the ranch and I suppose it's been a gamble. But the cows are throwing off the first of his calves now and I haven't lost one yet. He's going to make the Rafter T a better ranch, Glory."

The pride in his voice swelled her heart with gladness. As she looked from her handsome husband to the sage-dotted plains and the ball of fiery sun painting the western horizon, she felt sure she had truly come home.

She smiled at him with certainty. "I'm sure he will."

The words had hardly left her mouth when they rode upon the big red Santa-Gertrudis lying listlessly in the flimsy shade of a ragged mesquite tree.

"What's wrong, Spencer? Is he sick?"

They pulled their horses to a stop and Spencer quickly dismounted. "I thought he was just resting in the shade, but—" He moved closer and the bull eyed him with dull, feverish eyes. "Something is wrong."

Filled with concern, Gloria threw her leg over the saddle horn and jumped to the ground. "How can you tell? Maybe he's just hot."

She stood back a few steps as Spencer moved to inspect the bull.

"No. The corners of his eyes are matted with infection. And his nose is dry. He's dehydrated."

"Maybe the windmill quit working and the water tank went dry," she suggested, hoping against hope that he was wrong and the bull was only thirsty.

"No. Look at the cows. They're all fine and full of grass and water."

"How long has it been since you saw him last?"

"I'm not exactly sure. A few days ago. The range is big. You might have to ride two or three miles before you find the herd," he explained. "I don't check on them every day. Not any rancher does."

"Is he— Will he be okay?" She held her breath as she waited for his answer.

After a quick look at Beau's legs and hooves, he ran a hand over the bull's neck, then moved on to inspect his mouth and gums. "I don't know. He looks bad. A lot of weight has already fallen off of him. I doubt he's eaten or drank anything in a day or two."

"Oh, Spencer! What are you going to do?" she asked fearfully.

"Ride back to the house and call the vet."

"Will he come all the way out here?"

"Yes. If he's not tied up elsewhere. Otherwise, I'll bring back medicine and doctor him myself." He glanced at her. "I'm going to ride hard. Can you stay here with Beau?"

Gloria didn't hesitate. "Of course."

He snatched up his horse's reins and vaulted into the saddle. "Don't worry, Beau's not mean. Even when he's well, he's a pet. But to be on the safe side don't get too close to him. And if you see any rattle-snakes, just get out of their way. They won't bother you if you don't bother them."

She nodded to convey that she understood.

He quickly untied a canteen of water and tossed it down to her. "I'll be back as soon as I can," he said, then spurred the horse into a gallop.

Nearly two hours passed before Gloria spotted Spencer's dust trail moving at a fast gait across the far-off range. As he drew closer, she could see through the waning twilight that he'd changed the black for a sorrel. Saddlebags and a pack roll were tied behind his saddle. Foamy sweat lathered the horse's shoulders and heaving flanks. The fact that Spencer had pushed the horse in such heat told Gloria he considered the condition of the bull as grave.

She jumped from her seat on a rock and joined him as he removed the horse's saddle.

"Thank God you're back," she said. "I've been so worried about Beau. And you."

"Has he moved or tried to stand?" Spencer asked abruptly.

"He's moved his head up and down. But only a little."

He handed the horse's reins to her. "Will you cool him off while I tend to Beau?"

"What about the vet? Isn't he coming?"

"No," he said grimly. "He's up in the north corner of the county dealing with an emergency. He sent instructions to me over a cell phone. I've got to inject him with an antibiotic and some more medications. Then it's a wait and see thing."

"Couldn't we take him to another vet?" she asked.

"Even if there was another vet around that I trusted, he's too sick to walk into a stock trailer. I'd have to rope him and have the horse drag him in the trailer. Beau's in such a weakened state now, the trauma might kill him."

Gloria didn't ask more. Instead she began to walk the tired horse around in a large circle.

A few hours later darkness was truly upon them. After Spencer had doctored the bull, he urged Gloria to ride back to the ranch house where she would be more comfortable while he stayed here with Beau. She'd flatly refused.

Eventually, Spencer had given in to her wishes and picketed the horses with a lariat from his saddle, then went about setting up a crude camp near the ailing bull. Now the two of them were sitting on a sleeping bag, eating packaged cheese, crackers and meat sticks and drinking coffee that he'd boiled in a can over a small fire.

The coals from the dying fire illuminated a scant circle around them. In the faint orange glow Gloria could see Spencer's features were stern. Since he'd returned from the ranch, he'd spoken very little. Gloria knew he was consumed with worry and she'd tried not to make a pest of herself by chattering or asking questions. Yet she longed to comfort him, to let him know that Beau meant as much to her as he did to Spencer.

"I've been praying that he'll get better, Spencer. I believe he will."

He glanced at her, then reached for her hand. "You shouldn't be out here, Glory. This is no place for a woman like you."

"A woman like me?" She grimaced. "Don't tell me I'm too soft, or pretty, or rich to camp out on the range with my husband. I can do anything you need for me to do."

He gave her a wry grin. "I'm beginning to believe you."

She wrapped her fingers around his and squeezed. "How long will it be before you can tell whether he's getting better or worse?"

Spencer glanced over at the bull. So far he hadn't attempted to move or get up and that was a bad sign. "Another hour or two maybe. I'm not sure." He looked back at her. "Why don't you lie down here on the sleeping bag and try to rest. I'll wake you if there's any change."

If it would make him happy to see her resting she would be glad to do it.

"All right. But please wake me if you need me."

After finishing the last of her crackers, she stretched out on the sleeping blanket that Spencer had unzipped and folded out in order to make it larger.

Laying her head a few inches from his thigh, she closed her eyes, even though she knew it would be impossible to sleep. Not because the ground was hard beneath her. No, she was so tired the earth felt like a welcome cradle to her body. But her mind was wide-awake, churning with doubts and fears. None of which she had voiced to her husband.

Her husband. How was he going to feel if something happened to Beau? she wondered sickly. He'd pinned all his hopes and dreams on the bull. He'd risked all his money on him as a last-ditch effort to make the Rafter T productive. The only reason Spencer had married her in the first place was to save that bull. And in his own way, the big brawny animal was a symbol of their marriage. If he died, she feared their marriage would die, too.

Squeezing her eyes tightly shut, she buried her face

into her forearm and tried not to give in to the tears burning her throat.

Back under the mesquite, Spencer injected Beau with another dose of medication, then rubbed the rangy animal between the ears. The bull blinked his eyes, but made no other movement or showed any interest toward the shallow bowl of water sitting nearby.

Behind Spencer the fire crackled lowly and in the far distance coyotes yipped at the half-moon hanging over the silver sage. Cooler air had moved in with the night and above their heads the wide Texas sky was strung with stars. It had been a long time since he'd spent a night out on the range and he wished this time with Gloria would have been under different circumstances.

His eyes focused on her still form. The past few days he'd been letting himself think and dream. About her. About the ranch. And about their marriage. Beau played a big part in his thinking. The calves he sired would be worth much more than the mixed breeds he'd been raising before. Once the steers were grown, the profit they made would eventually get the ranch out of the red and back to making money. But if Beau died it would change everything. Even if he wanted to, Spencer couldn't ask Gloria to stay hooked to a losing cause.

Spencer's dismal thoughts were suddenly interrupted by a low groan. His head jerked back to the bull.

"What is it, boy?" he whispered as he stroked a dampened cloth over Beau's long red face.

The bull groaned again, louder this time. Then to Spencer's great surprise, the animal pushed his nose toward the bowl and began to drink.

"Glory!" he shouted. "Gloria! Wake up! Come look!"

She was on her feet instantly, stumbling across the rough ground until she was on her knees beside Spencer.

"He's drinking!" she cried. "Does this mean he's better?"

"Oh yes! He's better. Get the canteen. I think he'll drink more."

By the time Gloria returned, Beau had slurped up all the water in the bowl and wanted more. Laughter bubbled out of her as she emptied the canteen for the thirsty bull.

"That's the way, Beau! You're going to feel better now, boy. Keep drinking," Spencer encouraged the animal.

Slowly the bull took in all the water, then after a few moments he drew his legs beneath him and with a weak snort pushed his huge body to a standing position.

Relief and joy rushed through Spencer with such magnitude that he actually felt weak. He wanted to shout, but his throat suddenly had such a hard lump in it, he couldn't make a sound.

Beside him, tears of happiness filled Gloria's eyes and rolled onto her cheeks. "Thank God, Spencer. Our bull is going to get well."

Her voice was full of the very emotions he was feeling and as his gaze locked with hers, he felt a sense of connection that he'd never felt with anyone in his life. Their hopes, prayers, and thoughts had been one and the same.

"Oh, Glory," he whispered rawly, "come here."

Drawing her into the circle of his arm, he pulled the bandanna from his neck and awkwardly dabbed at her tears.

"Beau's on the mend. You shouldn't be crying now," he softly scolded.

She gave him a wobbly smile. "I know but I was so afraid." With a desperate little cry, she flung her arms around his neck and gripped tightly. "Hold me, Spencer!"

With his emotions already ragged, there was no way he could gather any resistance to fight the desire suddenly exploding inside him. Her warm body was like a refuge after a violent storm. He couldn't let go. Not now.

Tugging her head away from his chest, he covered her lips with a hot, needy kiss that instantly sapped the strength from her legs and forced her to grip the front of his shirt to stay upright.

"Glory. Oh, sweet Glory," he murmured softly as he pressed kisses across her face and neck. By the time his seductive nuzzle reached the sensitive point behind her ear, Gloria was delirious with desire. Groaning with need, her hands began to explore the breadth of his shoulders and chest, then pushed eagerly beneath the tails of his shirt to touch his hot flesh.

"Wait," he commanded softly, then scooped her up in his arms and carried her to the makeshift bed spread near the low fire.

Once they were lying together on the thick sleeping bag, he tossed his hat out of the way, then reached for her again. Crushed in the circle of his arms, she whispered his name and showered kisses over his cheeks and lips and whisker-rough jawline.

"This isn't the place for this," he said thickly. "But I want you, honey. And I think you want me. Tell me right now if I'm wrong."

Something in her heart burst and showers of joy radiated to every point of her body. "This is all I want, Spence," she whispered fervently. "You and me. With the stars as our ceiling and Rafter T soil as our bed. This is the best and biggest adventure I could ask for."

Even if Spencer had wanted to argue, he couldn't. Not at this point. For the past two weeks his body had hungered for her, now his heart was hungering, too. The combination was too strong to fight.

His hands shaking, he tugged off her boots, then

began to peel away her clothes. At the same time Gloria was touching him, kissing him wherever her hands and lips could make contact with his shifting body. By the time he had her fully undressed, her skin was hot with desire. The night air did little to cool her as he moved away to deal with his own clothing.

Being naked in the wide open spaces was a new and erotic experience for Gloria. But then so was being naked in front of a man. Yet strangely she felt no embarrassment as Spencer turned back to her and his brown gaze slipped over the dips and swells of her body now bathed in the orange glow of the dying embers. Instead, she felt a sense of freedom and a rush of feminine pleasure at the longing she saw in his eyes.

Leaning over her, he pushed his fingers into her tangled black hair. "I've never seen anything more beautiful than you are at this moment," he murmured.

The thick hoarseness of his voice touched her even more than the words he spoke. Love filled her heart until it was overflowing, bursting through her like a golden river. A cry of longing slipped from her lips as she reached up and tugged him down to her.

"Oh Spencer, make love to me," she begged against his mouth. "Make me yours!"

Her plea sent hot shivers rippling through him and he struggled to keep his arousal under control as his hands cupped her full breasts and his legs pinned hers to the blanket. She was a virgin. He had to go slow.

Yet he wasn't even close to being inside her and he was already about to explode.

"Oh, honey. Sweet Glory, I don't want to hurt you," he whispered roughly.

Her fingers skittered over his bare chest. "The only way you could hurt me is to turn away, Spence."

She smiled then. That glorious, inviting smile that she gave to only him and suddenly all his doubts melted away. Nothing mattered but the moment and the fact that they wanted each other.

The next few minutes he spent adoring her body, preparing her for the shock of being connected to his. By the time he finally did enter her, Gloria hardly noticed the pain. White-hot desire swiftly enfolded her, gripped her with a ferocious hunger all its own. In a matter of seconds the two of them were bathed in sweat and panting with the urgent need to race to the end of their wild, reckless journey.

Riding the desperate thrust of his hips, Gloria gripped his shoulders and reveled in the delicious pleasure. Then all too quickly it seemed, she felt a part of herself leaving her and floating upward to him. Above them, the stars suddenly seemed to pour down from the night sky and explode right in the center of her being. Against her throat, Spencer's groan was guttural and as primitive as the distant call of a coyote.

Long moments later, she lifted her hand to his head and weakly pushed her fingers into his damp hair. "Did I do it properly, darling?"

Spencer tilted his head back just enough to look at her bemused face and suddenly he was laughing so hard that both their bodies shook from it.

"Oh my sweet, little wife. There wasn't a proper thing about it."

Too drained to laugh along with him, she smiled sweetly. "Maybe I should have used another word. Like *right*. Was it?"

He closed his eyes and pressed his lips to her cheek. "If you'd done anything more right, I'd be dead now."

When daylight came, Beau was still on his feet and was even attempting to graze. Spencer gave him another dose of antibiotic and then the two of them saddled up and rode slowly back to the ranch.

Once she'd showered and dressed in clean jeans and a loose cotton blouse, Gloria prepared them a hearty breakfast of sausage, eggs and pancakes. Afterward, they finished the last of the coffee in a swing on the front porch, then Spencer headed to the barn to attend to his daily morning chores.

Gloria went back inside to the kitchen, where she cleared away the breakfast mess while she happily hummed to herself. She still wasn't sure what last night had meant to Spencer or to their marriage. So far she'd avoided any serious discussion with her husband about their lovemaking. Beau's illness and recovery was still uppermost on his mind. She'd decided it would be better for her to broach the subject when she had his undivided attention. Like tonight, she thought dreamily. In bed.

By midafternoon, Spencer fired up the tractor and hauled a bale of alfalfa and more water out to Beau, just in case the animal still wasn't strong enough to make it to the watering tank. Thankfully, he'd found the bull had already returned to his herd of cows and was rapidly recovering.

Eager to share the news with Gloria, he hurried back to the ranch and into the house. When he entered the kitchen and found it empty, he frowned with surprise. After two weeks of being married to the woman, he'd learned it was her favorite room of the house and if she wasn't helping him down at the barn, he could find her there most any time of the day.

"Glory?" he called happily. "Where are you?"

When she didn't answer immediately, he headed down the hallway. "Glory?"

"In here, Spence."

Directed by her muffled voice, he turned into the living room, then halted in his tracks. She was sitting on the edge of the couch. A white envelope was on her lap and a single sheet of white paper was clutched in her left hand. Tears were streaming down her face while her shoulders shook with racking sobs.

Shaken by the sight, he rushed to her. "Gloria? Honey, what's wrong? What's happened?"

Wretched, she handed the paper up to him. "It's Father. I told you he would do something. I just didn't realize that he—'' She broke off as another sob forced her to swallow and struggle to gain her composure. "I didn't know he would go this far," she said strickenly.

He didn't have to read all the paragraphs to get the content of the message. Vernon Rhodes had taken away all of Gloria's money. She was now penniless because she'd married Spencer. Numbing shock was quickly replaced by anger and guilt.

He looked at his wife's tear-stained face and felt a sinking weight drop to the bottom of his heart. He'd never experienced anything like he'd shared with Gloria last night. And afterward, he'd let himself believe, to hope that their marriage could be a true, lasting one. He'd finally had to admit to himself that he loved this woman. Loved her more than anything. But now a life with her would be impossible. Vernon Rhodes had made sure of that.

Feeling as though he was on a roller coaster of highs and lows, he sank onto the cushion next to her. "How could he do this?" he asked flatly.

Her eyes full of despair, she lifted her gaze to his. "He's a selfish, vindictive man. That's how," she choked out.

"No. I mean, can he legally take your money? You are an adult."

She sighed.

"The bulk of my money is in a trust fund. Which he has control of until I'm twenty-five." She snatched the letter from Spencer's hand, crumpled it viciously, then tossed it on the floor. "Well, he can just do whatever he wants to with the damn money. I don't care!"

"You know that isn't true," he gently scolded.

She bent her head, then jammed her fist against her eyes as they filled up once again with hot tears. "No—it's not entirely true," she said in a low, gritty voice. "I wanted that money for you! For the ranch! There's so many things I wanted to give you—and now he's taken all that away!"

Spencer had never felt so torn or humble in his life. She made it sound as though she loved him. But he couldn't let himself think of that now. It was too late.

"Glory, I'm not concerned about this for me. I don't want any of the money. Not for myself. But I can't—I won't let our marriage ruin your life."

Her head jerked up and she stared at him fearfully. "What do you mean ruin my life? What are you trying to say?"

Not wanting to add to Vernon's hurt and betrayal, he tried to choose his words carefully. "Just that—well, if it means losing everything you have, we'll have to—to dissolve our marriage. Surely your father will relent if you leave me and go back home."

Stunned, she gasped loudly. "I can't believe what I'm hearing! I thought I meant something to you!"

He reached for her hands and held them tightly when she tried to draw back. "You do—you mean everything to me. That's why I can't let you sacrifice your fortune for me!"

Suddenly, as Gloria studied the misery on his face, she understood and her heart melted in spite of everything. "Oh, Spencer," she said softly. "Don't you understand that you're worth more than any fortune to me?"

Not wanting to let anything she might say sidetrack him, he shook his head. "No. You're not thinking, Glory. At least, you're not thinking about on down the road—weeks and months from now. Right now I'm a poor cowboy. And even though I don't always expect to be poor, I'll never have the money you do—"

"I don't have it," she abruptly reminded him.

"Yeah, because of me! Glory, do you know how guilty that makes me feel? There's even been a few times since we married that I've secretly wished you were poor like me. So that we could be man and wife on equal terms, so that I might have some sort of chance to be your real husband. Now my wish has come true and—"

Shaking her head, she pulled her hands from his and flung her arms around his neck. "Stop it! Stop it! Just say you love me."

He buried his face in the soft curve of her neck. "I do love you, Glory. More than I thought it possible to love anyone or anything."

Her fingers gripped his hard shoulders. "And I love you, my darling. If you think this matter of money is going to change my mind, you're wrong."

Lifting his head, he gazed into her eyes. "You don't

understand, Glory. I'll never be able to give you all the things you deserve. All the things you've been accustomed to having.''

Once again, she shook her head. "It's you who don't understand, Spencer. Yes, I've grown up in luxury. I've had nice *things* all my life. But do you think those things made me happy? Do you think I'm so shallow that *things* are all I want out of life?''

''No. I don't think you're shallow or a snob. I don't even think you're spoiled. But damn it, just having me wouldn't be enough.''

Before she could respond, he pulled away from her and rose to his feet. Gloria watched him walk to the other side of the room, where he stared out the window as if the whole world was just beyond the glass pane.

After a moment, she went to stand in front of him, then crossing her arms against her breast, she tapped her toe defiantly. "Spencer Tate, you don't have to have money to give me what I want!''

Wry skepticism twisted his features as he turned to look at her. "My mother lived here. But after a while it wasn't enough for her. She left my dad and her kids.''

"She left because she wasn't happy with your father. It wasn't about this place and you know it.''

His conviction wavered but only for a moment, then he said, "Lori tried living here, too. Once we were married, it didn't take her long to get her fill of the place. She wanted me to leave here—to take her to some city where there were more opportunities. But I couldn't do that. And she accused me of being selfish.'' He swallowed as his gaze continued to adore her face. "I guess I was selfish, Glory. But a man has to be true to himself or he's not worth anything to anyone. Living in a city just wouldn't be me. Working inside four walls would ruin me.''

Gloria stepped forward and placed her hand on his forearm. "Don't you think I already understand all that? I know what kind of man you are.'' She moved closer as her hand began to slide back and forth against the hard muscle and bone of his arm. "From the moment I met you, I admired you for your honesty. Because you are a man who doesn't pretend to be something other than what you are. I think my heart started falling in love with you—even before I was aware—because it knew you would never be capable of being like my father or Paul.''

He drew in a deep breath, then slowly released it as he struggled to reason out all that she was saying. "No. I couldn't be like them. My wants are too simple for that, Glory.''

The front of her body pressed against his as she rested her palms in the middle of his chest. "So are mine, Spence.''

He frowned down at her. "What about being a chef? Owning your own restaurant? You couldn't do that here! If I asked you to stay here on the Rafter T with me, I would be just like your father. Maybe in a different way, but the end results would be the same. I'd be taking everything you ever wanted away from you. Just because I was selfish, just because—because I wanted you here with me.''

The broken anguish in his voice told her everything she needed to know. Her heart was so full it was spilling over as she smiled up at him. ''Who says I can't be a chef? Ozona could always use another little restaurant—someday. After I have our babies and get them up to a self-sufficient age.''

''Babies?'' he repeated blankly.

''Yes, babies. That's what I've been trying to tell you, Spence. All I want is your love. Your children. If I have that, I know we can make this place go. We can make it a good hearty ranch—a home for us. I don't have money now. Neither do you. But that just makes us like regular folks. Maybe I was disappointed when I first opened the letter, but that was because I wanted to give you things—to spoil you—because you're the man I love. But now—'' She broke off as a provocative smile tilted her lips. ''I realize there's plenty of other ways to spoil you rotten.''

His expression suddenly grew wondrous. ''Babies,'' he repeated softly. ''I never imagined I'd find a woman who'd want to stick around long enough to want a family with me.''

''Well, you have now,'' she said saucily, then before he could kiss her, she quickly moved away from him and headed out of the room.

"Where are you going?" he called as hurried to catch up to her.

"The bedroom."

Amused and surprised, he followed her down the hallway and into the bedroom. "You want to start on the babies now?" he asked.

With her back to him, she pulled out a dresser drawer and began to rifle through the contents. "First things first," she answered.

"What are you hunting?" he asked as he came up behind her and fitted his hips to her pert little behind.

"This." She turned and held up the paper napkin the two of them had signed outside the Horned Toad Saloon.

The satisfied gleam in her eye had him asking, "What do you aim to do with that?"

Gloria proceeded to tear the napkin into tiny shreds and toss the debris into a nearby wastebasket. "Put it where it belongs," she said smugly.

Chuckling, he slipped his arms around her waist. "All right, honey. You've convinced me. If we go down now, we go down together."

She lifted her face up to his. "Now you're talking my language, cowboy." Moving her lips next to his, she whispered, "Can Beau do without you for a while?"

"Beau is going to be just fine now," he assured her as his hands quickly went to work on the buttons between her breasts. "And so are we."

* * *

Nearly a month later, Spencer walked straight into Vernon Rhodes's plush office and tossed his dusty Stetson onto the shocked man's desk.

"I think we need to talk."

"What is the meaning of this?" Vernon sputtered as he reached for the phone on his desk. "How did you get past my secretary? Who are you?"

A cool smile spread across Spencer's face as he stared down at the thin, graying businessman. "I walked past. And you might as well put the phone back down 'cause there's no chance in hell she'll come to your rescue. I gave her a fifteen-minute break."

Slowly, Vernon eased back in his chair as his gaze measured the vast height and breadth of the man standing before him. "Well," he said finally, "you must be Spencer Tate."

"That's right. Your daughter's husband."

Not waiting to be invited, Spencer sank into the leather chair facing the older man's desk. Across from him, Vernon's lips thinned to a flat line of disapproval. "I suppose you're here for money."

Vernon's comment didn't really surprise Spencer, but it did disappoint him. These past weeks since he and Gloria had married, he'd been hoping and praying the old man would have a change of heart and approach his daughter with open, loving arms. But so far it hadn't happened.

"This may come as a shock to you, Mr. Rhodes,

but not all people are motivated by money. I didn't have any before I married Gloria. And I don't have much more now. But that's a matter that my wife and I had rather solve ourselves. I'm here for an entirely different reason.''

The older man arched a skeptical brow at Spencer. "I don't believe you," he said flatly, then leaning forward, he asked, "Does Gloria know you're here?"

Spencer shook his head. "She thinks I'm attending a horse sale with a friend.''

A smug look settled over Vernon's narrow face. "So you lied to her and snuck off. That doesn't surprise me. Not from a man who would take advantage of a young woman the way you did!''

Throughout the long drive to San Antonio, Spencer had told himself he couldn't allow Vernon Rhodes to anger him. Not if he expected to make any headway with the old man. But right at this moment it was costing him dearly to keep from grabbing him by the shirtfront and shaking the devil right out of him.

"No, you have this whole thing backward, Mr. Rhodes. You're the one who's been taking advantage of Gloria. Not just these past few months, but for years. You've used a father's love as a whip to bend her to your will. And then when she does find enough courage to break away from your chains, you decide to punish her by taking away her trust fund and your—''

"See!" Vernon bellowed as he aimed an accusing

finger at Spencer. "I knew this little visit was all about the money. You're here because *you* want it! I'll not—"

Suddenly Spencer was on his feet, his hands planted on the oak desk as he leaned toward Vernon Rhodes. "I'm here because I love my wife and I want her to be happy. She gave up a lot to marry me and, frankly, I don't feel good about it. Yes, the money is a part of it. Any man worth a grain of salt would feel guilty about making his wife lose her financial nest egg. But that's still not the important thing here. She's lost her father and, though she's trying to hide it from me, I know it's breaking her heart."

Vernon stared at him for long moments, then his shoulders sagged as though every ounce of air had left his body.

"I—I never meant to hurt her," he said, his low voice full of remorse. "I was only trying to make her see things my way."

Spencer picked up his Stetson and curled both hands around the rolled brim. "Gloria is a grown woman. She's wise enough to know she has to choose her own way in life. But she'd be a lot happier if she had your blessing. And so would I."

Vernon glanced away from him then, as though he was ashamed to look his son-in-law in the eye. "You really aren't here for the money, are you? You don't want it and from the looks of things, Gloria had much rather have you."

A wry smile twisted Spencer's lips. "Do what you feel is right about the money, Mr. Rhodes. All I'm asking is that you let Gloria know you love her. That's all she really needs to make her totally happy."

Vernon looked at him with doubt. "Maybe it's too late," he mumbled. "I've made such a mess of things that my daughter might not ever forgive me."

Spencer slapped his hat back on his head, then offered his hand to Gloria's father. "All you have to do, Mr. Rhodes, is show up on the Rafter T and I'll make sure she thinks it was all your idea."

Vernon rose and gripped Spencer's hand with silent gratitude.

Two days later, the smell of mesquite smoke and sizzling beef filled the evening air beneath the huge cottonwood.

Spencer shut the lid on the barbecue grill and turned to face the crowd of three who were sitting in lawn chairs and impatiently waiting for their supper.

"Spence, you know I just like the hide and hair knocked off my steak. If you burn those ribeyes, you're gonna lose a buddy," Ike warned.

Spencer chuckled. "Just a few more minutes. And while we wait we can finish cranking the ice-cream freezer."

"Why not," Ike grumbled good-naturedly as he pushed himself out of the lawn chair. "I always like to work on an empty stomach."

"It doesn't look that empty to me," Joan teased her husband.

"Well, it is," he said, pretending to be insulted. "I'll bet you two gals can hear it growling all the way over there."

"I don't hear a thing," Gloria spoke up.

He waved a dismissive hand at the women, then went to join Spencer, who was adding chipped ice to the old wooden freezer.

Gloria looked across at her new friend. "I'm so glad you and Ike could come over this evening. After Granny came for a three-day visit, Spencer discovered he likes having company."

Joan glanced thoughtfully at the two men. "Spencer is a changed man now that you two have married," she told Gloria. "He'd been so hurt in the past that I didn't hold out much hope of him ever being happy." She looked at Gloria. "I mean, Spencer is a laid-back guy and he always seemed happy enough on the outside, but I knew on the inside he was lonely. I'm glad you came along and changed all of that for him. You're just what he needed."

Gloria smiled at her. "And he's just what I needed, too. I guess the two of us meeting at the Horned Toad was the best thing that could have ever happened."

Joan chuckled with disbelief. "Some things just can't be explained. Like that old place producing a lovematch like yours." She cast her a regretful glance. "I'm just sorry your father isn't happy for you. I'm sure it would make you and Spencer feel better if you had his blessing.''

Gloria shrugged and tried not to let the idea dampen her happy spirits. After she'd gotten his message about taking her money away, she'd called him once and assured him that his actions had done nothing to change her mind. She was married to Spencer and she intended to stay that way, with or without her trust fund. Since then she'd not heard from her father. His desertion hurt. But she was determined not to dwell on the loss of her father and let it overshadow her new life with Spencer.

Gloria sighed with regret. ''Other than Spencer and Granny, he's the only close relative I have. But unless he has a change of heart, it's probably best that he's not mixing in our lives. Spencer is an easygoing guy, but he can get riled,'' she said, thinking back to the anger she'd seen on his face just before he slammed the phone down in Vernon's ear. ''Still, it would be wonderful not to be totally shut out of his life.''

Joan started to reply when both women were suddenly distracted by the sound of a car and the two of them turned to watch a dark sedan slow, then turn down the short lane leading to the Rafter T.

''Are you expecting someone?'' Joan asked.

Gloria frowned. ''No. And that car doesn't look like it belongs to anyone around here.'' Rising from the chair, she called to her husband. ''Spence, we've got company and—'' Suddenly she recognized the person stepping from the car and her words halted, her hand flew to her chest. "Oh my Lord—it's my father!"

"Maybe we'd better go," Joan spoke up worriedly.

"Yeah," Ike added. "Ya'll probably need to be alone."

"No!"

"Absolutely not!"

Spencer and Gloria both shouted the protests in near unison.

"Just watch the steaks, Ike. We'll be back shortly," Spencer said, then taking Gloria by the elbow, he walked with her to meet his father-in-law.

Moments later, Gloria and Spencer stopped a few steps away from where Vernon Rhodes stood beside his car. Immediately, she was struck by the weary lines on his face, the stoop to his shoulders and most of all, the stark empty look in his blue eyes.

At one time not so long ago, this man had been a formidable force to her. Now, she realized with a sense of great relief that he no longer intimidated her. She truly was a grown-up woman. A wife. And though Vernon was her father, he was still just a man.

"Hello, Father. I wasn't expecting to see you all the way out here," she greeted.

He stepped forward, his gaze turning pointedly to the massive cowboy standing close at her side.

"I had a little prodding from someone that opened my eyes." His gaze slipped to his daughter. "I know

I should have called first. But I decided I didn't want to wait any longer to see you.''

"I'm glad,'' she said and meant it.

Clearly dismayed by her welcome, the older man cleared his throat and started again. ''After I realized you weren't going to come back to San Antonio I decided it was time to come out and find out why. Now I can see for myself. You didn't just get yourself a husband. You married a man.''

He extended his hand toward Spencer. ''I'm your father-in-law, Vernon,'' he introduced himself. ''I hope we can be friends.''

Admiring the man for not revealing their little meeting two days ago, Spencer reached out and enclosed the man's hand in a tight grip. ''I'd like that. And I know your daughter would, too.''

Vernon looked at Gloria. ''Is he right? Are you willing to forgive me for all the pain I've caused you?''

His question brought a hot lump to Gloria's throat. ''Oh, Father, do you really mean that?''

Regret filled his face. ''I've been a hardheaded old man, Gloria. I think all these years I've just clung to you so hard because I didn't want to lose you. The way I lost Alice. And then after you left, I realized I'd lost you anyway. It opens a man's eyes to be alone, honey. I made mistakes with Alice. And I turned around and made them with you. Now I've had to face the fact that my wealth meant nothing without you.''

Happiness radiated through her as she realized she'd

made the right choice. Marrying Spencer had given her the home and love she'd always wanted and now her father was making their family complete. Her eyes full of tears, she stepped forward and embraced him tightly. "You haven't lost me, Father. We'll all be a family now. The way a family should be."

Vernon hugged his daughter close for long, long moments, then stepped back and looked around him with keen interest.

"So this is the Rafter T. I've never been on a working ranch before," he admitted. "But I've heard it said that Texas was first made from cattle hide and bone."

Spencer clapped him on the shoulder as if he was a cowhand just in off the range. "We're having a little barbecue with some friends. Come on and join us while the steaks are hot."

Gloria stared in amazement at the pleased look on her father's face.

"That sounds good to me, son."

Epilogue

Two years later, on a hot summer evening, Gloria was doing her best not to scream as labor pains wracked her body.

Glancing desperately upward at the nurse who was kindly sponging her forehead with cool water, she asked, "Do you know if my husband has been located yet?"

"I'm not sure—"

At that moment the delivery door burst open and a man dressed in scrubs hurried toward them.

"Spencer!" Gloria wailed. "Oh thank goodness you're finally here!"

He reached for Gloria's hands just as another pain began to strike her. She gripped his fingers and panted heavily.

He was frantic, crushed by the sight of his wife in such agony. "Dear God, Glory, are you all right? The baby—"

"Is nearly here," an RN finished his sentence. "It's time to get the doctor in here. And time for you to stay out of the way, Mr. Tate."

"Out of the way? Hellfire, I haven't been here two minutes!"

"That's not my fault," the nurse quipped with disapproval.

"Oh—ooooh," Gloria moaned and Spencer looked from the tart nurse down at his wife's sweat-drenched face.

"Glory, I'm never putting you through this again. I don't care how much you beg me!"

The nurses in the room all looked at him with amusement. Between the gripping pains and pants for breaths, Gloria tried to laugh. "Oh, Spence! Having a baby is…natural. As natural…as making one."

Spencer didn't see anything natural about the torturous agony his wife was in and he pleaded with her to accept any of the painkilling drugs the doctor had prescribed for her. But she refused, determined to have a totally natural birth. Thankfully, the delivery was short and a few minutes after the doctor arrived on the scene, their son appeared, squalling at the top of his lungs.

Later, after Gloria and the baby were cleaned and settled in a private room, Spencer leaned over his wife's bed and gently kissed her.

"I don't deserve you," he whispered thickly.

"You're much too good for me. But I'm gonna keep you anyway."

She smiled with drowsy bliss. "What about our son, you think you'll keep him, too?"

Spencer carefully lifted the baby from the crook of his mother's arm and settled the now sleeping boy against his broad chest. "James Theodore Tate. J.T. His great-grandfather would be proud of his namesake. He's a handsome little squirt," he said proudly as he gazed down at the tiny features that were amazingly like his own.

"He's not little," Gloria corrected. "He weighs eight pounds!"

Grinning broadly, he reached down with one hand and gently stroked strands of damp hair off her forehead. "He's perfect, honey. You couldn't have made him any more perfect."

Her eyes were shining with love as she took in the sight of their son cradled safely in his daddy's arm. "You had a hand in it too, you know," she reminded him. "And now that things have quieted down, I'd like to know where you've been. I thought J.T. was going to be born before you ever got here!"

His expression turned apologetic. "I'm sorry, Glory. I found Vegas out in the pasture trying to have her calf. Since it's her first, she was having a hard time and needed my help. When I finally finished with her and got back to the house, I found your note pinned to the refrigerator door. Believe me, I broke all kinds of traffic laws trying to get here."

Gloria was suddenly laughing. "My little Vegas had her calf? Today? I can't believe it. The both of us giving birth for the first time on the same day!"

He tried his best to look disgusted. "What did you two do, get together and plan this? I spent two hours out there with that cow of yours and was half-afraid I was going to lose her and the calf before it was all over with. And then I come home and find your father had driven you to the hospital! Thank God, he decided to stay with us this month until the baby was born. Otherwise you would have been alone!"

"Yes, it's been great having Father around. He's like a different man now," she agreed, then her look of pleasure suddenly changed to one of concern. "Oh, Spencer, is Vegas okay? And the calf?"

"They're both fine now," he reassured her. "The calf is a beauty. He looks just like Beau."

Her face brightened. "Then let's not sell him as a steer," she pleaded. "Let's keep him on the Rafter T for a second bull."

"Hell, Glory. How is a man supposed to make any money keeping every calf on the place?"

She laughed because she knew he was teasing and she knew that he loved her and their son more than the Rafter T, more than any money. And he always would.

"Oh, Spencer, we don't really need the money."

She was right, he thought. Vernon had given Gloria's trust fund back to her two years ago when he'd first come to visit the ranch. Besides that, Beau's offspring were beginning to bring in a profit. A fact that filled Spencer with a feeling of great accomplishment. The Rafter T was going to be a legacy he could proudly hand down to his son.

"All right," he agreed with a show of reluctance. "But little Beau Jr. is going to be the last male calf we keep on the ranch. I'm not keeping another one, Glory. I don't care how much you beg me."

Smiling to herself, Gloria decided she would remind him about that when their second child was born.

"Thank you, honey," she said sweetly. "That's jake with me."

The term of agreement brought his head up from little J.T. and as their eyes met, they both began to laugh.

And they got ready for the rest of their life—their *adventure* together.

*   *   *   *   *

Stella Bagwell's emotional storytelling skills
are highlighted in her next
Special Edition title
WHITE DOVE'S PROMISE,
the first of the new
COLTONS: THE COMANCHES *miniseries.*
Don't miss it this July!

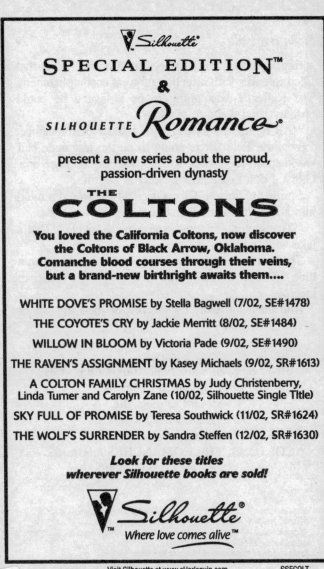

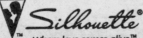

Three bold, irresistible men.
Three brand-new romances by today's top authors...
Summer never seemed hotter!

Sheiks
of Summer

*Available in August
at your favorite
retail outlet!*

"The Sheik's Virgin" by Susan Mallery

He was the brazen stranger who chaperoned innocent, beautiful
Phoebe Carson around his native land. But what would Phoebe do when
she discovered her suitor was none other than Prince Nasri Mazin—
and he had seduction on his mind?

"Sheikh of Ice" by Alexandra Sellers

She came in search of adventure—and discovered passion in the arms
of tall, dark and handsome Hadi al Hajar. But once Kate Drummond
succumbed to Hadi's powerful touch, would she succeed in
taming his hard heart?

"Kismet" by Fiona Brand

A star-crossed love affair and a stormy night combined to bring
Laine Abernathy into Sheik Xavier Kalil Al Jahir's world. Now, as she
took cover in her rugged rescuer's home, Lily wondered if it was her
destiny to fall in love with the mesmerizing sheik....

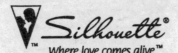

Silhouette®

Where love comes alive™

Visit Silhouette at www.eHarlequin.com

PSSOS